Sunset Val

Flies Again

Her continuing adventures in her own words
as told to

R.M. St.Martin, esq.

The Adventures of Sunset Val

Sunset Val, *or,*
The Pirate Queen of the Seven Skies

Sunset Val Flies Again, *or,*
The Battle Over Libertia

Sunset Val's Hat Trick, *or,*
The Triumvirate of Terror

Published by:

Weird & Wondrous Books
33A Broadview
Pointe Claire, QC
H9R 3Z1
http://www.weirdandwondrousbooks.com

ISBN 978-0-9866531-2-4

This is a work of fiction. Names, characters, places and incidents either are the product of the author's imagination or are used fictitiously. Any resemblance to actual events or persons, living or dead, is entirely coincidental.

ACKNOWLEDGEMENTS

It's often said that no author works in a vacuum. (For one thing, it's incredibly difficult to breathe in there. Personally I wouldn't even fit in our vacuum. But I digress.) There are countless individuals for whose aid I am grateful, and to list them all here would prove prohibitively long. Suffice to say I count myself extremely lucky to have friends who offer so much support, encouragement, and assistance. I will, however, point out the efforts of the following people, all of whom have helped in some significant way: Neil, Pasley, Taras, HRH, Samantha, Regan, Violette, Berny, Sierra, Paula, Kim, Tony, Hayley, my parents, my in-laws, and my beautiful, incredible wife, Kristie.

I absolutely have to point out the specific efforts of two of my staunchest supporters – Karine Charlebois, whose art continues to surpass itself and my every expectation; and Ron Chevrier, who continues to provide inspiration and comedic gold.

I dedicate this novel to the staff, volunteers and especially the attendees of Toronto's Polaris convention, who in no small way are the reason Sunset Val exists.

Terraneus Incognitus
Terraneus Incognitus
The Thousand Tribes
Norsica
Russankya
Zhou
Neppon
Eire
Ys Anglia
Europa
Levantia
Hindystan
Atlan
Saud
Afric
Amazonia
Merimasy
Lemuris
Australy
A Map of Ayrth
Terraneus Incognitus

But First, A Perilous Prologue

The island of Ys lies in the Atlan Sea, west of Europa and north-east of Atlan, making it a perfect stopover for travellers making the journey from one continent to the other. Gentle sea breezes keep its climate mild year-round. It is an island of rolling hills, lush vegetation, and beautiful beaches. Ysian wine is known through the Atlan Empire for its excellence. Mount Ys, the sole mountain at the island's interior, itself a former volcano, provides a scenic vista for tourist and native alike.

Generally speaking, Ysians are stereotyped as calm, peaceful and happy. Surrounded by such natural beauty, it's no wonder. They live in a near-tropical paradise. Sunny warm summers fade gradually into rainy mild winters. With very little industry spewing factory filth into the sky, the air retains its freshness, even in the heart of the largest city on the island, also called Ys.

The city of Ys is a wonder of modernity, with aerioport towers reaching toward the heavens to accommodate the hundreds of ships that swirl and dance through the air high above, manoeuvring for a better berth, finding their way out and away again, ferrying passengers from ship to ship, ship to port, or ship to land. Every size and model of airship flits, floats, or flies across the sky. Huge lumbering passenger vessels. Sleek darting corsairs. Ornithopters and dirigibles and balloons. Even Atlan Aerial Forces, warships bristling with weapons: great troop-carrying Groupers, ornithopter-laden Devil-fish, swift-striking Barracudas, occasionally a Great White Dreadnought, the terror of the seven skies. All are afforded a wide berth by the other vessels. None of the pirate captains would risk drawing attention to themselves, risk angering an Imperial captain, risk being boarded and searched. No, the captains of the other vessels much prefer aerial anonymity. Everyone has things they'd rather kept hidden from prying Imperial eyes.

For you see, in addition to being a tropical paradise best known for its wine, Ys, both the city and the island, are also well known for being a place of low adherence to Imperial legality. Put simply, it is a haven for pirates and smugglers.

Perhaps alone in all such locations, Ys knows none of the wild lawless revelry of the stereotypical pirate haunt. No drunken brawls spilling from taverns into the streets, no duels in back alleys, no raucous visits to the pleasure houses. No, the Minister of Ys knows well that lawless revelry leads to more generalized lawlessness, and that's the sort of thing that attracts attention. Attracting attention is precisely the opposite of what Ys is all about. So the pirates and smugglers who meet to trade and scheme in the hotels and bars and pubs of Ys know well to keep their heads down, keep their carousing to a respectable level, and above all, to keep from attracting Imperial attention.

The seat of government in the city of Ys is the Imperial Ministry, precisely the sort of building designed to attract attention, or perhaps more accurately, to impose attention. Its façade was built a thousand years previous, entirely of gleaming white marble. It towers over the lesser buildings that flank it; indeed, by Atlan decree no building within five hundred yards may be built even close to its impressive, looming thirteen stories. Impressive for the time of its construction of course; Atlan architectss long ago surmounted the limitations of mere mechanical physics, creating masterworks of engineering that challenge the heavens themselves. Thus the aerioports that dot the city of Ys.

Still, the Ministry manages to tower over the aerioports as well, set atop one of the foothills of Mount Ys, looking down upon the entire city. A person gazing from the uppermost windows would see the city sprawling out before them, all the way to the sea; would see cook fires from thousands of homes sending streamers of black smoke into the sky, where they twirl about in the eddies and airflows of airships; would see airships in the dozens and scores and even hundreds.

One such person sits in the uppermost chambers, but his gaze is not fixed upon the cook-fire smoke, nor the dancing airships, nor even the far distant sea. No, this person's gaze turns away from the beautiful panorama, and lies instead fixed upon the people seated before him.

Minister Maximilian Crow is skeletally, cadaverously thin. His cheekbones stretch paper-thin skin almost to the breaking point, hollowing out cheeks that are nevertheless a healthy tan. Dark eyes glitter in his face, onyx and obsidian and jet. A prominent nose centres and dominates the face, but it is the eyes, those deep dark eyes, that hold his visitors' attention. Fierce intellect, ruthless ambition, and dangerous, jungle cunning vie for supremacy there, and it is a supremacy that flashes back and forth. Some have said that to gaze too long into the Minister's eyes is to invite madness.

He dresses in the finest suits from the most sought-after tailors of Albion, all uniformly black. His cravat is likewise black. Indeed the only hint of colour on his person are the ruby ring of office on his right hand, and the streaks of grey at the temples of his otherwise jet-black hair, cropped short against the dictates of fashion.

When the Minister speaks, it is through thin, almost invisible lips, his mouth a bloodless gash beneath his so-prominent nose. Long, crooked teeth hide behind those thin lips, teeth browned from the chewing of tobacco, the Minister's only vice.

"Tell me again," the Minister says slowly, his Atlan unaccented, his voice nasal but deep with authority and power. Power earned, and power taken.

The man seated across the mahogany desk from the Minister is likewise black-haired but his solitary blue eye glitters not with madness but with hate. His voice is low and rough. "Her name is Sunset Val."

The Minister leans back in his leather chair, steepling long, bony fingers before his face.

"She is dangerous," the one-eyed man's companion says sharply. The Minister's gaze flits to her briefly. An attractive woman, despite the scar sneering her face. One sleeve of her immaculate jacket is pinned up, where her arm ends in a stump, just above the elbow. Fierce intelligence shines in her face, but fear hides behind her eyes. He dismisses her with less than a heartbeat's inspection.

"She led the slaves in revolt?" the Minister asks the one-eyed man. Tyr Ebonfury, his name; his companion, Dr. Minati Enerva. The third, clearly younger member of Ebonfury's party stands behind the elder two, obviously desiring to speak, restraining herself only with difficulty.

Tyr nods, though this is the sixth time he has explained what happened to the Carrion and its former captain, the Minister's brother. "Took the ship. Led us a merry chase over Afric. Finally caught up to her, only..."

The Minister smiles in an approximation of sympathy. So difficult for this fearsome warrior to admit he'd been duped and defeated by a mere slip of a girl. The Minister catalogues Ebonfury's pride away, for future study and potential use. "She tricked you," the Minister finishes for him.

"Yes."

Finally the younger companion dares to speak. The impatience of youth makes fools of all children, although she is a woman grown. Curly blonde hair and an athletically slim figure. "Give us the letters of marque and we'll kill her for you!"

The Minister ignores Ebonfury's frustration with her, and the Doctor's blatant disgust. "And you are?"

"Artemis Hawkmoon, your honour," the younger woman says. "Sunset Val killed my twin sister."

"Indeed? My sympathies. How unfortunate for you."

She blushes at the unexpected direction his uncharacteristically sympathetic words have taken. With a shake of her head, she retreats to repetition. "Give us the letters. Let us kill her."

The Minister glances at the papers lying unsigned on his uncluttered mahogany desk. Letters of marque give a pirate free reign to plunder and pillage with governmental authority. Free from the threat of persecution, marqued pirates are a scourge of the skies... and a benefit to their benefactor.

The Minister looks up at the petitioning pirates. "No."

Ebonfury's shoulders sag in defeat; Dr. Enerva glares daggers at young Hawkmoon. The youngest would-be pirate rallies herself to mount an appeal.

As she is about to speak, the Minister reaches for a pen and quickly scrawls his name at the bottom of the letters. Sliding them across to the disbelieving and confused Ebonfury, Minister Crow says simply:

"Bring her to me."

Chapter One

Evening the Odds

I never did figure out how to pronounce Libertia, but then, no one else did, either. I heard everything from 'Liberty-ah' to 'Lie-beer-sha' and all the variants between, with most Europans settling closer to 'Liberty-ah' and most Merinasy using 'Lie-beer-sha'. It seemed to fit with the general atmosphere of freedom in the city. Freedom from laws, freedom from slavery, freedom from Atlan tyranny.

Which wasn't to say there weren't any rules. Basic things like no stealing, no killing unless in self-defence, those sort of rules. Now, I know. They say rules were made to be broken, but in Libertia, if you were caught breaking the rules, it was the gallows, if the crowd didn't string you up first. But otherwise, 'do whatever you like' was the attitude of the citizens, and that suited the crew of The Furies just fine.

My name is Valerie Victoria Ventura, but everyone here called me Sunset Val. Captain Sunset Val, of our good ship The Furies. My crew were all liberated slaves. Well, almost slaves. We'd all been captured and very nearly sold into slavery before I led a revolt and overthrew our pirate captors.

But you probably know that already, so why don't I skip ahead to the good parts?

Sailing the skies over Afric to get to Libertia (and I usually pronounced it Liberty-ah) had taken us nearly a month, zigzagging across the continent to avoid pursuit. We'd encountered two slaver ships and one Atlan warship on patrol. The slavers we'd attacked, boarded, and liberated the slaves, adding whoever wanted to join us to our crew. The warship we'd outrun. Once we were over the strait between Afric and Merinasy, they'd turned about and headed back inland.

So The Furies had more crew than we knew what to do with. My first mate, Serena Heartlace, a vampyri swordmistress of the ninth order, was somewhere out there in the warm tropical night, trying to find the women who wanted to leave a place to live and work that wasn't one of the countless pleasure houses Libertia had to offer. Supposedly the women who worked Libertia's houses of pleasure-for-a-price all did so of their own free will. I had no intention of ever setting foot inside one, so I'd never find out if it were true or not. Still, it wouldn't surprise me if it were. A lot of women, including a lot of my crew, freed of the strict rules of behaviour of Atlan society, had pretty much gone to town, partying as hard as they could. Drinking, smoking and sleeping around were apparently everything that had been denied them, growing up under the thumb of Atlan morality and Atlan laws. Not that men had any of the same rules applied to them. The Atlan Empire was incredibly sexist that way.

So my girls were out, partying it up, and had been for the last two weeks. I'd enjoyed some of the freedoms Libertia offered, but nothing would get me to try smoking, thank you very much, and my first hangover permanently scarred me for life over the dubious merits of getting drunk ever again. As for boys, well...

I'm the captain of an airship, a liberator of slaves, and I turn into an utter spaz around boys. Well, that is, boys I might like, or boys who might like me. A babbling idiot would be more coherent and keep it cooler than I do. I don't know why. It's a curse. Also, a bit of a blessing. Since I am such a spaz around boys, I tend to find other things to do than subject myself to further embarrassment and ridicule. Like being captain.

And right at that moment, being captain meant winning at cards.

I'd never been very good at poker, but my brother Tommy, back home? He's amazing at it. He's always on some poker site or another, winning virtual money that he uses to get into bigger and better games.

Oh yeah. For those of you just tuning in, I'm not from this world, Ayrth. I'm a visitor from another world called Earth, brought here by a mad scientist, Dr. Montgomery Sweetwater. If I ever find him again, I won't know whether to beat his head in or thank him.

Because back home, I'm just another high school student living at home with too many siblings and almost no friends. Here, I'm captain of my own airship, with good friends but no family. Mixed blessings, both ways. There are days when I really, really want to go home. And there are days when I absolutely love it here and never want to go back.

So anyway, poker. They had a similar game here called six-card. Two cards face up, two cards in the pot for everyone to use, two cards in your hand. But Tommy showed me playing poker (or six-card) isn't about the cards in your hand. It's about what your opponent *thinks* you have in your hand. Basically, it's all about psyching the other guy out.

I put down my evens spread. Two through to twelve, all evens. A good hand. Hell, a great hand. I grinned at my opponents.

The Hispanian grimaced, swore in Hispanian, and threw down his cards in disgust. The lizard animan stared at me for a long time, his chameleon face giving nothing away. Then his eyes darted off in two different directions. He folded his hand and stepped away from the table without a word.

My final opponent licked her lips, staring at her two cards. She had a pair of eights showing. Another pair in her hand might force a draw. This is where it gets confusing (because playing poker without face cards but with an entire suit of special cards like in a tarot deck isn't confusing enough). Unlike poker, in six-card, you can have a hand that ties with another player's hand, and then that goes to a draw. Simple cut, and the best hand of your seven cards wins. If she folded, I'd win the pot. She barely had any cash left, anyway. She was sweating, but in the tropical Libertian warmth and all those layers of clothes she was wearing, that's not saying much. My read on the situation was that she thought she had a good enough hand to beat me square, but then I produced all evens, and she could only tie that. She could force the draw, but there's no way my hand would suffer, while the chance of her getting a better hand was very small.

She put down her cards, face up. A pair of tens, plus the third ten in the pot on the table. We were tied. Not a smart move on her part, because the only way she could beat me and win the pot was if she drew the last ten.

"Looks like a draw," I said.

"Sure an' it does," she answered in Eire-accented Atlan, reaching for her glass. She was drinking gin and lemonade. Everyone in the tropics drank gin. I thought pirates all drank rum, but apparently in Merinasy, gin was the drink of choice. It was supposed to keep away the mosquitoes, which kept away the malaria. Personally I don't like the stuff, but I guess it was better than dying from malaria. I drank it in a ten parts lemonade, one part gin ratio, but my final opponent preferred hers more like two-to-one.

I watched her sip from her glass. Pale skinned, with a light spattering of freckles across her cheeks. Bright blue eyes with long dark lashes.

We'd met once before, so I knew her raven-dark hair was quite long, though just then she wore it in an elaborate bun piled high on her head, pinned in place with an itty-bitty top hat that had more to do with Gallian fashion than any kind of protection from the sun or the elements. Elegant hands, a doctor's hands. Slender without being skinny. Taller than me, but then, find me someone who isn't. I may be only five-foot-two-and-a-quarter, but I make up for it by being big on personality. Handy, in a pirate captain. But enough about me.

She had pair of spectacles, the kind that pinch onto your nose, hung on a silver chain around her neck, though I hadn't seen her wear them. Dressed in a dark blue puffy-sleeved waist coat and matching ankle-length skirt, with a cream cotton shirt buttoned to the throat and a black silk choker with an ivory cameo of a unicorn.

Doctor Regan Westmore finished her drink and wiped sticky condensation from her upper lip. Everything hinged on the next cut of the cards.

We each drew a card. I drew first, since she had forced the tie and the draw. She glanced down at her card; I did likewise. I'd drawn The Gear.

Ayrth's playing cards didn't have any face cards. No Kings or Queens to remind the world that once Atlan hadn't ruled everything. No Jacks or Aces. Just numbers, in four suits – the round yellow suns, the black crescent moons, the blue six-pointed stars, and the red equal-armed crosses. Then there was the fifth suit, the Mechanisms. All simple mechanical objects, like what I'd just drawn, The Gear. The Lever would have been better, because then the Doctor and I would have been forced to trade hands. The Gear was useless on its own.

Except in an all-evens spread.

The Gear, being useless without any other Mechanism card, effectively counted as a zero, the only zero in the entire deck. As such, it could be added to an all-evens spread, without counting as a card. Except that it obviously was a card, making my hand of six a hand of seven. This was a very rare way to win, calling Evening The Odds, since my all-evens spread now had an odd number of cards. Personally I thought it should have been named Odding The Evens, since that's what it, y'know, actually did, and all, but I didn't invent the game, so whatever. Point was, as one of the rarest hands in the deck, it was nearly impossible to beat.

To give the Doctor her due, her face barely registered any kind of reaction to her card. But when she shoved all her chips into the pot, and declared "All in," I knew what card she'd pulled. Or rather, what card she hadn't.

"You're bluffing," I said, shoving my (much larger) pile of chips into the pot, too. She didn't have enough chips to match my call and raise.

"Am I?" she asked, showing no kind of emotion in her face.

"What's more, you can't match my raise."

She smirked a cheeky half-smile. "Sure, an' could be ye're bluffing, now." Her Eire accent thickened when the game was hot, I'd noticed. "I've money aplenty to cover the pot."

My turn to smile cheekily. "Where is it, then?"

"On the off chance ye win the game, we'll head to me bankers."

"No good, Doc," I said, shaking my head. "Cash on the table or you forfeit."

She lost her cheekiness, face going flat, serious. "Double or nothin', then."

"I don't understand."

"Ye win, I'll double what's in the pot. I win, ye pay me nought but the pot in front o' us."

"No, I understand what double or nothing means, but if you can't cover what's already here..."

"I'm good fer it, I tell ye."

She had to be bluffing. There were maybe two hands better than mine in the entire game, and she didn't have any of those cards. Unless she'd drawn The Lever, in which case she'd get my hand. But she couldn't know what card I'd drawn, so she didn't know I had a winning hand, so she might not want to Lever my hand.

"That's a lot of money," I said, pretending to think it over. "Double the pot would be..." I did a quick estimate. "What, half a year's salary to a doctor such as yourself?"

She glanced at the pot, greed shining in her eyes, and some of that cheekiness settled back on her features. "At least."

"Well, turns out my ship's in need of a doctor," I grinned.

"Is that right, then? Well, ye win this hand I'll do ye one better. A year of me services," she offered with casual magnanimity, downing the last of her gin-and-lemonade.

Did she have The Lever? Did she know I had the Gear?

See? Cards is all psyching the other guy out. And Doc Westmore here had done a pretty good job of it. Or else I had done a good job on myself.

She couldn't have The Lever. She couldn't know I had The Gear. She had to be bluffing. She had to be.

I stood up suddenly, startling her. The Hispanian backed away from the table, chair scraping on the wooden floor, hand lowering to rest near the six-gun he wore at his hip. Around us, the crowd quieted, but didn't overtly watch for fear of attracting my potentially lethal attention.

I leaned across the table, hand outstretched. "Shake on it."

The Doc let out a nervous laugh.

I put on my bitchiest bitch face, a look I borrowed from my sister, Melanie. "Welch on this, and you'll regret it." As a pirate captain, I had a certain reputation for ruthlessness I needed to uphold.

She swallowed hard and took my hand, pumped it twice with obvious reluctance, then loosened her grip. I held onto her slackened hand for a moment past comfortable, then let go and sat back down. The Hispanian sighed with obvious relief.

Doc Westmore licked her lips and glanced back at her last card. Some of that cheeky, smug certainty returned to her face.

"I accept your terms," I said to the Doc, turning over The Gear.

The smug certainty of her victory disappeared, shattering into astonished disbelief. The blood drained from her face. She flipped the last ten over. "But..."

She hadn't been bluffing after all. She honestly thought she had the better hand. Oh well.

"I'll send my girls to fetch your things, noon tomorrow," I said, scraping the pot toward me with both hands.

Doc Westmore looked at me, still shocked. She shook her head, as though she weren't quite sure what was happening. "Ye can't be serious!"

"My ship needs a doctor, and you just wagered a year's service," I replied, feigning confusion. "And lost. In front of a witness." I nodded my head toward the Hispanian, who didn't appreciate being drawn into this drama.

"Ye can't hold me to that!"

Back came my bitch face. "You're welching on this?"

She leaned away from me, as far back as the chair would allow. "No. No, I... That is..."

"It's settled then. Noon tomorrow. Where are you staying?"

The words stumbled through her shock. "The Pig and Whistle..."

"Good!" I smiled at her. "Relax Doc, it won't be nearly as bad as you think."

She stood suddenly. "If ye'll excuse me, I... I've things need seein' to." Then she turned and left without waiting for a reply.

"Sure thing, Doc," I called after her. I caught Tring's eye. She'd been watching us from a darkened corner, calming sipping tea. I glanced after the departing doctor. Tring nodded and followed her out into the night. As the leader of my Open Hands, my bodyguards who'd sworn never to use a weapon, Tring spent a lot of time following me around. For once, she did as I wordlessly asked, and followed the doctor instead. As Tring left, Domina entered the saloon.

I stifled a sigh. Ever since her cousin Viola had died during action aboard The Furies, Domina had made herself my personal assistant. I hadn't asked her to, but she'd latched on and wouldn't be distracted from her duties, no matter how enticing the offer. I'd had to start giving her orders like "Go and lay in that hammock for an hour, test it out for me," just to get her to relax a bit. Of course, at the end of the hour, she'd reported that the hammock was quite sturdy and comfortable, and that I would very likely enjoy it.

"Captain, she's ready," Domina said, dark eyes shining with pride, taking the chips I'd scooped into my bowler hat without a word from me. I poured the chips into her arms.

"Take care of this, would you?" I asked her, leaving my winnings with her. I planted my bowler at a suitably jaunty angle and headed for the door. "I've got to see her."

Chapter Two

Assassination Station

I hurried out into the warm tropical night, a couple of my girls rushing to catch up. I couldn't go anywhere in Libertia without a couple of the girls following me, usually armed to the teeth. Except Tring's Open Hands. They never carried anything. Somehow that seemed to get us more respect.

I flagged down a passing rickshaw and the three of us climbed in. "The aerioport," I ordered. The horse animan grunted a reply, his thickly muscled legs pulling us forward.

Libertia was truly a city that never slept. People crowded Market Street, even though the sun had set hours ago. Shops were open at all hours here, eager to eke whatever trade they could from the crews that sought to spend their shares of whatever booty they'd taken. Pawn shops plied a brisk trade, no matter what time of day. Hawkers tried to get our attention, waving their wares above their heads, calling to us as we hurried past. Electric lights glowed bright yellow-white next to flickering orange torchlight and steady blue-white gas lamps, brightening the tropical night into a semblance of day. In the marketplace, at least.

We turned off Market Street and rode uphill and inland toward the aerioport, a series of towers at the outskirts of the city. Freed from the blinding glare of the market, we could at last see the moon, huge and full, sinking toward the sea behind us, a million jewels of dancing light in the waves.

I rested my head on the seat's back, excited but tired. I hadn't intended to win Dr. Westmore's services. I just wanted to get a sense of her character. She seemed okay. Hopefully she was a better doctor than she was a card player.

Anyhow, she was the last of the crew we needed to get back into the open skies. I'd been amazed at the list of skilled crew we needed to keep The Furies flying. Amazed, and somewhat impressed that we'd been able to keep her going without those experts for as long as we had.

Since arriving in Libertia, two consecutive days hadn't passed without me interviewing someone or another for a slot on The Furies. First of all, we'd needed a proper navigator. Molly had done an okay enough job of it that we'd been able to find our way to Libertia, but it hadn't been easy for her. The sight and sound of her mechanical hand clenching and unclenching in nervous frustration as she picked through the maps in our map room hadn't exactly inspired confidence. So we'd found a navigator. Molly, I think, had mostly been relieved to have someone else take over that slot.

Then we needed an aeriologist, someone who understood the gas mixture in the balloons that kept us flying. After we'd found one, we'd needed an engineer's assistant, someone who could help Gigi keep the ship running. And a carpenter. And a rigger. And a sailmaker. And a bosun, whatever that meant. And so on, and so on. All specialists in fields that couldn't just be figured out by a bunch of ex-slaves. When I thought about it, it was a minor miracle we hadn't crashed and burned up in a giant yellow-green fireball. So, yeah, I don't think about it too much.

What made matters worse was, by unanimous vote, we'd decided to keep the crew all-women. So instead of trying to find any available navigator, that navigator had to be female. The prevailing argument, led by Miss Merryweather, was that in addition to it being improper for some of our younger crew to be alone with a unrelated crewman, men tended to overly complicate things. The real reason I'd voted for it was that, with the way some of our girls were carrying on in Libertia, where the men were plentiful and plenty willing, imagine how vicious it would get with five or six of my girls all going after the same lonely single guy on our ship? He'd have his pick, and the rest would be all angry gossip behind that 'lucky' girl's back. I didn't want that kind of distraction aboard my ship.

Plus, it wouldn't do for the captain to get all spazzy around a crewman. If the hypothetical male crewman had been the least bit cute or charming, how was I supposed to give him orders? No, best to avoid the possibility altogether.

Where was I? Oh yeah. Getting back to The Furies by horse-animan-drawn rickshaw. I wasn't nuts about riding in a rickshaw, but carriages were way expensive, and beyond that we had two choices – walk, or ride on an elephant bird. I'd ridden the giant, ostrich-like birds before. They were at least twice my height and had a tendency to ignore an inexperienced rider's attempts to steer, which was how I wound up in a pig sty that one time I'd tried it. No thanks. As for walking, well, it was late, I was tired, so whatever. Rickshaw.

His hooves clattered against the cobblestone streets, louder now that it was so quiet compared to Market Street. The rickshaw's hard wooden wheels didn't make for the smoothest of rides, either. But somehow Suzanna, on my left, was lulled to sleep by the rattle. Dalmar, on my right, watched the streets and alleys for any sign of attack. The long brick warehouses and storage companies we passed didn't make for the greatest scenery. Too excited to try to strike up a conversation, I silently willed the driver to run faster.

Up ahead, the aerioport loomed against the night sky, a hundred pinpricks of yellow light spilling out into the night, blotting out the white stars. Above us, dozens of airships floated, docked serenely in the berthing stations all around the tower. I didn't look for The Furies there. I knew she'd be where I left her, in the Repair Hangar.

I nudged Suzanna awake when we arrived. Dalmar paid the animan and we headed for the main gates into the aerioport compound.

Out of nowhere, a huge figure lurched toward us, cloaked despite the night's warmth. My first thought was he was just some drunk, looking for a place to pass out. But the flash of metal in his hand as he lunged made his deadly intent clear.

I ducked under the first swing of his knife as Suzanna shoved me hard, sending me off-balance to tumble into the gutter. Dalmar had already gotten around our attacker by the time I got back to my feet. Suzanna made a grab for his knife hand and got a huge fist in the side of her head. She went down on the cobblestones, unconscious.

He moved so fast it was a miracle we weren't already dead. I drew my sword, hoping to hold him at bay while Dalmar got herself into position. She had a dagger in each hand, one of my best knife fighters. This guy was toast, now that he'd wasted the element of surprise.

My eyes had finally adjusted to the lamplight from the aerioport's gate, and I saw our attacker's scarred face. A patchwork! Sewn together from the pieces of many, for lack of a better word, donors. Part of his face was from an Afric donor; the rest seemed Europan.

I lunged forward and he parried my blade so hard he nearly knocked it out of my hand. Fast like a viper and strong like an ox are not exactly my favourite combination of attributes in people trying to kill me. I prefer my assassins slow, lazy and stupid, but they're pretty hard to find.

Dalmar jumped him from behind but he spun around and slashed her forearms. She grunted in pain and stepped back, blood spilling dark against her darker skin. I lunged again, but he turned to face me. So fast! It seemed impossible, but then, I'd learned very quickly that the things I considered impossible were pretty common on Ayrth.

Something distracted him, made him turn his head just as I lunged a third time. He dodged out of the way, and I only scored a slight scratch on his arm. He snarled and jumped. Not at me, his target, but straight over my head, landing on the rooftop of the warehouse across the street. He paused only to look back, point his knife at me, and then he disappeared into the night.

The sound of hard boot heels pounding against cobblestones made me turn, just in time to see Serena at my side, breathing hard, sword drawn.

"Who vas it? Are you hurt?" she asked, angry.

I turned back to scan the rooftop again. "No idea. Some patchwork. I'm fine, but Suzanna took a nasty hit."

Serena's nostrils flared angrily and she swore in Vampyr, her native tongue. "Get to the ship. I vill see vhat I can find of your attacker."

I didn't ask how she'd known I had been attacked. We had a kind of psychic link to each other, the side effect of my having willingly given her my blood to drink. The spike of adrenaline in my system had been enough to warn her of my danger, and she'd come running.

She sheathed her sword and headed off after the attacker. She climbed the wall of the warehouse so fast, anyone who didn't know her would have sworn she'd run straight up it.

Serena had changed, once she'd found a vampyri supplier. Regular feeding kept her sharp, strong, focussed in a way that I hadn't seen previously.

No, she wasn't chomping on the crew, or on any unfortunates who happened to be walking around the aerioport. We had an entire shelf of five-gallon metal containers in our cold storage aboard The Furies.

Inside the containers were Serena's life savings. Seems in the Vampyri homeland, blood banks are the only banks, and cold cash isn't just an expression. An economy that uses a pint of blood as its basic unit of currency had to invent refrigeration pretty quickly, and on this world, the Vampyri had done just that, hundreds of years ago.

I felt her along our psychic link, eager for the hunt, the scent of blood a homing signal in her nostrils. I tried to block it out, focussing on getting Dalmar's slashed forearms bandaged with strips torn from our shirts. Then she and I carried Suzanna to The Furies.

Chapter Three

Winged Warrior Women

I left the girls with Angel and Mary, our two nurses who'd taken over our limited surgeon's room. Both were Anglic, trained in Albion, and these sort of injuries had become pretty much routine to them in their brief careers as former slaves turned pirates, so I knew Dalmar and Suzanna were in good hands. I made sure they were okay – Suzanna still hadn't woken up, and the side of her face had begun to swell and purple with bruises – and left the ship.

The Furies floated six feet above the cement floor of the Repair Hangar, an immense building built low to the ground, behind the docking towers of the aerioport. The clatter of hammers and the grind of wrenches and the hiss of welding torches mingled with the shouts of men and women, echoing off the corrugated tin roof three hundred feet above us. Even this late at night, crews worked to fix their ships. When you paid by the hour for a berth in the Hangar, you worked that much quicker to get back out into the skies. The Hangar could house twice as many damaged ships as it currently held, but still managed to feel cramped and crowded compared to the glory of the open sky.

We were doing okay for money. At least, that's what Mrs. Shorty, our quartermaster – quartermistress? – insisted. That's not her real name, of course. Elegiac Throckwaddle's a bit of a mouthful, though, and the nickname stuck once I accidentally let it slip. Anyhow, Mrs. Shorty told me over and over that the haul of booty we'd taken from Captain Caliper's ship alone was enough to keep us in the Repair Hangar for three months, if we had a mind, and we'd taken two other ships since then. Not that it would take Gigi three months to get everything fixed, but it was good to know we had enough money for a while.

By the soft glow of gaslamps, the harsh glare of electric lights and the flare of welding torches, I studied my ship. She was beautiful, I had to admit. One hundred twenty feet long by thirty wide, seven decks tall, suspended by a netting of ropes and cables under a rigid sausage balloon with a cruciform tail fin. We'd just had the entire balloon painted black and gold to match the ship's hull. Completely against tradition, everyone had said, but I'd insisted. I thought it looked bad ass.

I spotted my Chief Engineer at the bow of the ship, directing a crane boom from a wood-and-brass podium reached by a metal-rung ladder. I walked over.

"Zut!" Gigi swore. Her furry ginger hands flew over the controls, and the crane boom swung back.

From the boom hung an enormous figure, completely enshrouded in a canvas tarp. The figure wasn't especially well balanced, it seemed, and it teetered on the chains that held it aloft.

I climbed the ladder and took a spot next to Gigi on the podium. "I want to see her."

Gigi's focus remained on the dangling figure as it neared the bow of the ship. "And you will Captain, I promise, if I can ever get her to ZUT!"

"Gigi?" I turned to face her. "Gigi. Seriously. Just calm down."

She looked at me with those huge green cat's eyes, narrowed just then in frustration. If her ears had been flattened too, I wouldn't have gotten anywhere near her. "I could have built a crane that would be much easier to operate faster than use this ancient piece of..." The rest was lost in feline rowrling.

"I know. I know you could. You're just that good. But for right now, could you please just take a breath and, you know, not break the one thing I spent almost all my share of our booty on?"

Gigi giggled, eyes widening as her frustration dissipated. She nodded and turned back to the podium. The controls looked needlessly complicated, almost as though they'd been designed for someone with three hands. I stepped closer and grabbed the third control.

"Not too far," Gigi directed me. "She is a fickle one, that control. Not enough, and she gives you nothing. But just the tiniest bit too much, and ZUT!"

"Sorry!"

"No, that was me. Okay. One last time."

This time, I barely moved the control at all. The shrouded figure slammed into place with a crash of metal on wood.

Gigi winced. "Well, she should be alright. She is made of metal."

"Metal over oak," I said. "How do we unwrap her?"

"Oh, but that is easy!"

She pushed a lever on the control podium and electricity, naked raw bright white, ran up the crane boom and down the chains. I didn't know how long I would live on Ayrth, but I doubted I would ever get used to their casual use of bare electricity. As far as I was concerned, electricity should be kept hidden inside wires and cables, or at least caged behind non-conductive glass.

It was pretty to watch, though.

The electrical command had its effect, and activated something somewhere inside the canvas shroud, because it unwrapped itself from the figure, falling free to land on the cement floor in front of us.

"Wow," I said. Gigi just grinned.

The formerly-enshrouded figure was twenty feet tall, with a wingspan about the same. Armoured in a style somewhere between Joan of Arc and Xena – solid brass breastplate (and I do mean breast, those things were bigger than my head!) with a skirt of brass strips, brass wrist-guards around her forearms and brass shin-guards encasing her calves. No helmet; blood red ringlets curled away from a face that would have been beautiful if it weren't contorted into a snarl of rage and vengeance and well, fury. Arms outstretched overhead held a huge sword, longer than I was tall, again of solid brass, which would eventually be fixed to the forward yardarm that jutted from the bow of the ship. Her 'skin' had been painted pale Caucasian, her eyes a brilliant glittering green. The brass wings that erupted from her shoulders spread out in a V shape behind her, and would run along the hull. Coincidentally, she would be placed just outside where my bed rested inside my quarters. I'd be sleeping between those wings.

I turned to grin at Gigi but she had already gotten back to work, directing her girls to begin fixing the figurehead to the ship. I needed to share the moment with someone and I looked around, trying to catch the eye of one of my girls. That's when I noticed the control podium had been surrounded by Tring's Open Hands. None of them were looking at me. They were watching the hangar, on the lookout for any threat.

A small Hindystani girl approached the control podium, eyes on me. "A word, my captain?"

A couple of years younger than me, and a couple of inches shorter,

Padmini had taken a kind of ship's runner position, carrying messages back and forth. I couldn't wait until Gigi finished installing the intercom system we'd bought. Until then, Padmini did the job well enough.

"Yes, Padmini?" I asked as I descended the ladder.

"Your presence is required aboard ship, my captain."

"By who?" I didn't fail to notice that as I moved toward the gangplank that led up into the Flight Deck, the Open Hands took up positions all around me. I guess news of the attack had already spread, and Tring's second-in-command, Mei, tended to be the more cautious of the two, if that were possible. Tring took her bodyguarding really seriously.

"Our esteemed aeriologist, my captain," Padmini answered.

I repressed the urge to sigh. Aeriologists were in charge of keeping the gas in our balloon stabilized, pressurized, and whateverized. Basically, whatever it took to keep us from blowing up. The one we'd hired had already made herself enough of a … well, let's just call her a presence (instead of a nuisance) aboard ship that I had more than once wondered if she was worth it.

"Where is she?" I asked Padmini.

"In the balloon, my captain."

"Okay." I yawned. It was nearly dawn. "Better I should see her now?"

Padmini just shrugged and gave a little smile that said, *I don't tell the captain what to do, I just run messages.*

I nodded. "Okay. Oh, go tell Angel and Mary we found a doctor? She'll be here at noon. And tell Adina to make sure the doctor's quarters are good and cleaned. Thanks, Padmini."

"Pleasure, my captain."

Yeah, 'pleasure' was exactly what it was not going to be. I climbed the stairwell from the Flight Deck, where our ornithopters, Booty Hold, and cold storage were, through the maze of catwalks, steam pipes, ladders, water tanks, and stairwells that was our Operations Deck, up the spiral stairwell past the Gun Deck and the Crew Deck, and finally up the private stair at the bow of the ship into my quarters. Through the thick wooden walls I could hear screwdrivers boring the screw mountings into the wood that would hold our new figurehead in place. I tossed my jacket and hat on the chair and pulled my tangled red curls into a ponytail.

I took a moment to appreciate my own room, my own space. Back home, I'd shared a room half this size with my sister. Here, it was all mine. Despite the grind of the drills and the pounding of the mallets outside, this was my sanctuary.

I didn't have much by way of personal effects, and Domina kept my room ship-shape and tidy. Sometimes a little too tidy. Still, it was nice not having to do my own laundry.

I knew I couldn't delay the inevitable any longer, so I rolled up my sleeves and headed topside.

My room had doors that exited onto the Main Deck, the exposed area between the ship and the balloon. I noticed some girls were waiting outside my door. Not Open Hands, this time. Hilda, our cook's daughter, big and brawny and blonde, was deep in conversation with our new Cannoneer, Inga Bludsdotter, who was even bigger, brawnier and blonder. But where Hilda was all soft rolling hills and warm smiles, Inga was harsh fjords and icy glares.

"Captain," Hilda smiled at me. Inga just nodded, once, a sharp jerk of her head in my direction.

"Ladies," I said as I passed by, heading for the rigging.

I took a deep breath and started climbing. I wasn't the best in the rigging – we had girls who could zip through the ropes like monkeys – but I was okay. What made me pause, ironically, was being so close to land. Eight hundred feet up, I could climb the rigging sure-footed enough. But with the ground only eighty feet away, I wanted to hurl. And it wouldn't do to have the ship's captain throw up every time she had to climb the rigging.

I reached the rigid outer hull of the balloon and opened the hatch. The outer sheath may have been rubberised linen, but it was stretched over a framework of thin metal ribs and braces. There was a crawlspace about three feet high between the outer sheath and the inner balloon.

I thought, when I first took over the ship, that the balloon was also a rubberised cloth of some kind, like silk. I'd been wrong. I'd learned a lot the last couple of months. The interior gas cells were actually made of something far more disgusting – bull's intestines. Auroch, to be precise. They were a kind of giant Eire ox, and aeriologists had long ago perfected the stretching, tanning, and sealing process that turned a thick rubbery tube into long flat strips of material ideal for containing the gas mixture that floated the boats.

"Hello?" I called out. The balloon was nearly one hundred and fifty feet long, and I had to travel on my hands and knees, or bent over nearly double. Hands and knees was the more comfortable but slower way to go. I had no intention of travelling further than I had to, and heading off in the wrong direction wouldn't have helped me any.

"Oi!" answered a high-pitched voice. "That you, Cap'n?"

"Yes, Moonchance, it's me." Who else would it be?

You know, being told that Gigi had seen a unicorn once in a zoo somewhere, or even spotting that pride? flock? of sphinxes as we sailed the Afric skies hadn't nearly prepared me for the shocking reality of seeing a pixie up close.

Moonchance O'Malley flew at me, landing inches from my face. She was about the size of a Barbie doll, with huge glittering dragonfly wings jutting out her back, and that's pretty much where her similarities to dolls and Disney characters ended. She looked pretty much like a miniature human, though her dark brown eyes were slightly large for her face and her ears were definitely pointed. Her mostly light brown hair was cropped in uneven tufts that she usually kept trapped under an aviator's cap and itty-bitty brass goggles. The cap, she'd informed me, was genuine rat leather. She wore an oil-stained short-sleeved shirt that revealed her tattooed arms and knee-length shorts held up with suspenders. Her lower legs were bare and tattooed as well, and leather work boots completed the outfit.

"I arsks you fer sailmakers and what d'you gives me? Seamstresses!" she yelled, punctuating nearly every word with a gesture.

It had taken me nearly a week to understand a word she said. She sort of reminded me of watching those old black and white movies with no sound, where everyone looked like they were moving just a little too fast, too jerky. And she spoke so quickly, with a thick Albion Anglic accent, that I'd had her repeat pretty much every word out of her mouth during that first week. We hadn't exactly started off on the right foot.

"Seamstresses! I arsks you!" she continued, arms waving wildly. "What good'll seamstresses be to us in a storm, eh?"

I settled back, sitting on my calves. "You wanted sailmakers. Sailmakers sew holes shut. Seamstresses sew holes shut. I'm not seeing the problem here."

She fixed me a know-it-all glare, crossing her arms in a huff. "Know all about sailmaking, do you? Whyncha do it for us then?"

"Because I'm the captain, not the chief sailmaker," I sighed. It wasn't the first time we'd had this argument. "I'm not about to hire on a whole new crew. Look at it this way, at least now you'll be able to teach the girls I've given you the way you want things done, instead of dealing with a bunch of sailmakers who want to do things their own way."

She sniffed at that, unwilling to concede the point but unable to argue against it, either. But she rallied quick enough. "Look, Cap'n, I ain't arsking you to 'ire on a new crew. I knows just the people what could solves both our problems. A sailmaker and a rigger whats looking for a berth. That's a fair bit, innit?"

She'd set me up for this, I could tell. Oh well. "Who are they?"

Moonchance put two fingers to her lips and gave a surprisingly loud whistle.

Two more pixies zipped toward us, landing behind Moonchance.

"This 'ere's Apple Addams, rigger, and Wren McKenzie, sailmaker," she said, jerking a thumb at each. Apple had a round face with a pert nose spattered with freckles, short curly red hair, and a broad smile. Wren had long dark hair and a serious look to her dark eyes. Both were dressed similar to Moonchance, and both were covered in tattoos.

"You're both looking for work, then?" I asked.

"S'right."

"Too right we are."

I yawned, covering my mouth with the back of my hand. "Alright then. Moonchance stands for you. You're hired. Now if you'll excuse me, I'm going to bed."

I left the pixies celebrating their new employment and climbed down the rigging, hoping I wouldn't regret what I'd just done.

Chapter Four

The Doc at the Dock

You'd think that with all the hustle and bustle in the Repair Hangar so late at night, or more accurately so early in the morning, that it would be impossible to get any sleep during the day, and you'd be right. Except for the fact that when I'd gotten all the stokers protective ear covers, I'd snagged a set for myself. So my sleep was blissfully quiet, for the six or so hours I was permitted to sleep. Not enough, but it would have to do. I'd catch a siesta during the afternoon heat, like the rest of the island.

Domina woke me, and from the angle and amount of the light streaming in the windows, I could see it was around midday. She started talking before I took off my ear covers, something she could never seem to catch on to. I made her repeat herself as I slipped off the ear covers and got out of bed.

"The new doctor's arrived, Captain."

"You woke me for that? Has Adina gotten her quarters squared away?"

"Yes, Captain. Her girls finished up just after breakfast."

At the mention of breakfast my stomach rumbled. I went to use the bathroom, which was what I called the screened-off corner of my room where the chamber pot was. I swear, some things about Ayrth were so backwardly weird. They had robots, but no radio. Airships, but no parachutes. They could sew pieces of different people together and bring them to life, but indoor plumbing was rare.

When I was done, I handed Domina my nightgown. I'd learned the hard way that just tossing it on the bed while she stood there frustrated her. She was determined to do her job and my insisting I didn't need a yeoman just made her miserable. So, I let her dress me. Fresh cream linen shirt, burgundy corset over top, a knee-length tan skirt today instead of slacks.

Then Domina helped me with my tangled curls.

"So OW! What's the problem with the new doctor?"

"She's brought rather a surprising amount of luggage, for one." Domina worked the brush through a particularly tough knot of hair. I winced. "And she'd refusing to haul her own weight."

Pirate tradition insisted that a member of the crew could only bring aboard as much stuff as they could carry, a tradition my girls had embraced fully – though one or two of them complained that they'd be limited to only two or three outfits. Others had pointed out that when they were slaves, they'd only had one outfit, a brownish grey potato-sack dress that itched and chafed, so maybe some perspective was in order.

As with everything aboard an airship, it was a question of weight. The balloon could only lift so much tonnage, and the more personal effects our crew carried aboard, the less booty we could haul.

I checked out the damage we'd done to my hair in a silver hand mirror. Not bad. Good enough, anyway. "Okay, I'll talk to her. Where's Tring?"

"Watching her like a hawk, Captain."

Which meant she'd tried to run out on her debt. "Okay. Did Serena come back last night?"

"She's safely in her quarters."

"Good," I said, grabbing my bowler and stuffing it onto my head. "Let's see about this luggage."

Domina followed after me as I slid down the stairwell by the rail, both of us laughing like kids. Then back down through the ship's decks, through the hustle and bustle of the daily tasks that needed doing. Miss Merryweather had sort of taken on the job of figuring out what needed doing and organizing work crews to get things done, which I'm told is the bosun's job, and she had done it amazingly, too. With her in charge, there were so many things that just got done, without me worrying about it. In some cases, without me even knowing about it. Which was fine by me, it left me clear to keep an eye on the bigger picture. Like making sure we had all the right crew, and what we were going to do next.

Now, when I say hustle and bustle, it wasn't exactly a crowd of chaos and chores. Most of the crew were sleeping off their revelries from the night before. Some of them weren't even aboard ship, having opted to spend their share of the booty on lodgings in town, where they didn't have to share a bedroom with five other women. But we had enough crew, and enough chores needing doing, that we could run two shifts. The daytime shift just had to be quiet to accommodate the night shift's sleeping.

Domina and I stopped by the crew's mess on the way down to the Flight Deck to pick up something to eat. There were fresh cinnamon buns waiting, so I grabbed a couple and finished them both before we got to the launch bay at the centre of the Flight Deck. I sauntered down the gangplank to find Dr. Westmore sitting on a steamer trunk, in front of a mountain of steamer trunks.

Dressed in a simple black dress with a black top hat to match, a parasol perched on one shoulder despite being in the shade, she looked absolutely miserable. Tring stood nearby, arms crossed and scowling. I went over to her, first.

"Any trouble?" I asked.

"Nothing but, Captain," the leader of the Open Hands replied. "She tried to escape the terms of her position just before dawn. When confronted, she barricaded herself within her quarters. After I demonstrated to her the error of her thinking, she insisted on packing everything she owned. Then getting it here, and now this. She is far more trouble than she is worth, if you ask me."

Aboard ship, we didn't exactly speak perfect Atlan, or Anglic, or any other language. It was more a hodge-podge mish-mash of every language we knew, Anglic and Atlan, Gallic and Bavard, Levant and Hindystani and Zhou. So Tring basically said all that, but not in any way the doctor would have understood, much less take offence over.

"Right. Thanks for the warning. Get yourself something to eat and then sleep. We'll be leaving before the end of the week and we'll need to round up the rest of the crew."

Tring bowed her head and left with one last scowl for the doctor.

"Dr. Westmore," I said in my best Anglic. It's almost exactly like English, just a matter of my accent being unheard of on all of Ayrth. I smiled at her. "What's up, Doc?"

Of course, she didn't get the joke, but it amused me, at least. She glared at me. "I've been keelhauled, that's all. Stolen from me rightful home. Press-ganged into service aboard a pirate vessel. Sure, an' no good'll come o' this. Mark my words, Captain Val, no good at all."

"Have you been drinking?" I asked.

"If only I had!" she pulled a handkerchief from her sleeve and wiped a tear from her eye. "Then p'raps me terrible fate would be bearable. But no!"

"So what's all the luggage?" I asked, refusing to be drawn into her drama.

"Medicine. Equipment." She hopped off the trunk and looked around the Repair Hangar. "Who knows when we'll be in a civilized port again, or if we'll all be blown to bits? Farewell, civilization!"

"Oh, cut it out already," I said. "It's not that bad. We have running water and everything. You absolutely need all this junk?"

"Absolutely."

I rolled up my sleeves. "Fine. I'll help you get this aboard."

"Help me? But. I mean." She sputtered a bit when she saw I was absolutely serious, picking up a couple of bags and hauling them up the gangplank. "Why not order the crew to do it for us?!"

"Because half the crew are asleep, and the others have more important things to do than haul your baggage," I explained. "At the moment, I've nothing pressing to do, so I'm making myself useful. You might consider doing the same."

Looking suitably chastised, she folded up her parasol and took her little black doctor bag aboard ship. When she looked around for some place to put it on the flight deck, I took it and her parasol from her and put them down. Then I grabbed her by the arm and led her back down the gangplank.

Together we managed to get her luggage aboard ship. Four trunks, six cases, three hat boxes, a small locked box that I wanted to ask about but didn't, and her doctor's bag.

"Leave these here for now," I said. "I'll get some of the girls to move them later."

"But? I thought ye said!"

"I know what I said. I was making a point, Doc. Everybody works, aboard this ship. And everybody follows my orders. I know you think that you were cheated somehow, having to serve aboard The Furies for the next year, but the simple truth of the matter is your own greed got you into this mess, and it's up to you to figure out if you're going to make the best of it, or if you're going to make yourself miserable."

I have to admit, I impressed myself with that little speech. I didn't know where it came from, but if it worked, who cared?

She didn't have anything to say after that, so I said, "Come on, I'll show you our surgeon's quarters, and your personal quarters."

She sniffed a little, squared her shoulders and answered. "Very well."

Chapter Five

Dealing With Women Ain't Easy, but Men are Impossible

I led her up the stairs, through the maze of catwalks and steam pipes of the Operations Deck, up a ladder to the Gun Deck, and then things got less confusing. The Gun Deck was basically a huge open room with a low ceiling and cannons lining either side, twenty in total. Not a lot of guns, supposedly, but enough for a pirate ship our size to threaten our prey into surrender. They hadn't been fired since I'd taken command, but our new Cannoneer Inga informed me they were in pretty good condition. Pretty good wasn't good enough for her, though, so she'd set a crew of women to cleaning and oiling the cannons, and organizing the armoury.

We threaded our way through the gang of women on duty and climbed the staircase to the Crew Deck. The doctor remained silent, and I wasn't inclined to play tour guide. I figured it would calm her a little if she saw her room first, so I led her there and opened the door for her.

The room wasn't much, a small bed built into the wall, next to a closet for her clothes and personal effects. The bed also had drawers underneath and shelves above for more storage. There was a small folding desk opposite the bed, and a chair. It was one of our best rooms. Plenty of storage, privacy, and even a porthole.

"Ye must be jokin'," Dr. Westmore said.

I turned to look at her. Her face was white with horror, one hand clutching at the collar of her dress.

"Is there a problem?"

"There're prison cells bigger than this, this closet! I'll have t'step outside t'change me mind!"

"It's not that bad, Doc," I said, stepping inside. I spun in place, arms wide, to show her how much room she had. It might have worked, if I hadn't kicked the chair in the process, throwing myself off balance. I landed on the bed.

"Nice soft newly stuffed mattress, too," I compensated.

"Oh, do us a favour," she answered sarcastically.

I got off the bed. She still hadn't entered the room, opting to stay in the doorway. "Let's show you the surgeon's quarters then."

Luckily it wasn't far, just down the main corridor that ran the length of the Crew Deck. Between the surgeon's quarters and the doctor's new room was a storage locker that held all our medical supplies. I told her about it, but she didn't seem interested in examining the contents, so I led her to the surgeon's quarters.

Inside there were three women. Suzanna lay on the operating table, still unconscious. Angel Clearly, tall and willowy, and Mary Pence, short and round, stood nearby, fussing over Suzanna.

"Ladies, this is Dr. Westmore," I introduced when they looked up at us.

"Doctor."

"Doctor."

Surprising me, the Doc went straight to Suzanna. "What's all this, then?"

"We believe her skull is fractured, Doctor," Angel explained.

"Ye believe?" the Doc asked. She very carefully felt Suzanna's bruised face. "Jaw's dislocated too. Bring me that light."

Mary grabbed the nearest lamp and brought it to her. Angel moved to stand next to a tray of instruments. I found myself in the curious position of not knowing what to do, while simultaneously being completely ignored.

"How'd this happen, then?" the Doc asked without looking up. She opened Suzanna's eye with one hand, moving the lamp back and forth with the other.

"Patchwork jumped us last night, clocked her one," I explained.

"How long ago?"

"Six, seven hours maybe."

At that, she looked up at me and stared. I couldn't tell what she was thinking. Finally she asked, "Have ye any medical trainin', Captain?"

"Um, I know some basic first aid."

"Then I'll thank ye to leave me to me patient."

I really hoped she wasn't going to be a bitch for the whole year ahead, otherwise I would wind up regretting my luck at cards. I left the surgeon's quarters, but she called after me.

"I'll be needin' that equipment, Captain."

I didn't turn back. "I'll send it up to you. Anything in particular?"

"The locked box and the second smallest trunk. For now."

"I'll see it done."

On the way to the staircase I paused at Serena's door. I closed my eyes and for a second I felt her mind, just a few feet away, at the edge of my awareness, like a soft fluffy blanket of peace and quiet. I could feel myself responding to her vampyric slumber, making me sleepy too. I yawned and shook my head to clear it, then headed back toward the mess. I spotted Restless in the corner and waved her over.

"Hi Restless," I said. She said she was thirteen, making her the youngest member of our crew, and of course her real name wasn't Restless. But she couldn't keep still for love, threats or money, so that's what everyone called her. And if she was a day over eleven I'd be stunned. She was smaller than Padmini, with long dark hair she wore straight and parted in the middle. But where Padmini already had a woman's curves, just built on a smaller scale, Restless was all gawky skinny legs and bony arms. She insisted she was thirteen though, and no one could contradict her. Her parents had been killed by the slavers we'd rescued her from, and she'd literally begged me to join the crew.

"Afternoon, Captain," Restless said, grinning, shifting her weight from one foot to the other.

"Shouldn't you be doing something?" I asked. Everyone asked Restless that question. She got distracted easily.

"No, Captain, nothing, I swear," she answered. One by one, she popped the knuckles on her right hand. I knew from experience she'd do the left one next, and then back to the right, and so on, unless someone told her to stop. "Anything need doing?"

"Yeah," I said, heading over to where I saw Hilda supervising some other girls putting out the midday meal. We might be a night shift crew, mainly, but people always needed to eat. Anyway. "Go find Gigi and Miss Merryweather, let them know we'll be heading out day after tomorrow, or the next, depending on how long it takes to round up all our crew and get everything ship-shape. Tonight I want to have a meeting with all the crew chiefs, decide where we're going to go."

We had a rough idea of what we wanted to do, namely continue to take out slavers. But that meant knowing where to find slavers, and that meant leaving Libertia and going hunting. No slaver would ever come to a town dedicated to the idea of complete freedom.

"That all, Captain?" Restless asked, bobbing on her feet, eager to have something to do.

"When you're done, come find me," I said, then turned to Hilda, not bothering to watch Restless run off. "How's it going, Hilda?"

"Goot, Captain, sank you," she answered, just barely stopping herself from curtseying. It had taken me two weeks to break her of that habit. Instead, she kept her focus on the job at hand, pointing out an empty spot on the serving table to a girl carrying a tray of fresh vegetables, raw and ready to eat. I snagged a carrot as the girl passed me.

Hilda wiped her hands on her apron. "How can I be of azzistance, Captain?"

"How's Inga finding her quarters?" I asked.

Hilda's blonde eyebrows rose in surprise. "I, well, zat is, I believe she finds zem adequate, Captain."

"Because you two seemed to be getting friendly, is all."

"Ya, zat is true, Captain. She is a fascinating woman. So many stories! So much adventure in her life."

Not that I'd know it. Inga hadn't said more than five words in a row to me since we'd hired her on. "Oh, well, good, then. I'm glad she's making friends."

Hilda's attention was distracted by a girl carrying a sliced pork roast. "No, not zere! Ach, zese girls. Excuse me, Captain?"

"Sure."

I watched her go deal with whatever unknown gastronomic infraction the girl had committed. Hilda was a great person, friendly, lively. Her help all obviously loved her, and a small jealous part of me that I hated with much hate wondered if the crew loved me the same way, and if they loved Hilda because they were all terrified of her mother, Brunhilde. Brunhilde ran the kitchens like her own private fascist dictatorship. I was the only person she would defer to. Everyone else lived and died under the threat of the wooden spoon she was never without and always eager to dispense with swift, spoony punishment. Whereas Hilda was always smiles and jokes and loving admonishment. How she'd resulted from Brunhilde was anyone's guess.

If things were different, I would have liked to be friends with

Hilda. She was just the sweetest thing. Everyone just got happier, more relaxed, whenever she was around. But I was the captain and she was the cook's assistant, and apparently that meant she didn't think we could be friends.

Except for Serena and Gigi, I was pretty much alone on a ship full of women. Serena was unconscious during the day, and Gigi was usually in the engine room, not exactly the best place for conversations.

I missed Eve, suddenly and fiercely. I wished I knew what had happened that night, when Doc Sweetwater had said something, some kind of verbal command, and Eve had gone all blank-faced and she'd flown away with him, leaving Molly and me on a crashing airship to die. I knew she wouldn't have left us like that, not willingly. Not Eve. She'd been one of my first friends here on Ayrth.

But she was gone, and no amount of wanting it otherwise would change that. I grabbed a couple slices of roast pork and some veggies and sat down to a cold meal washed down with Hilda's lemonade. World's best, I swear, and perfect against the day's heat. Here, in the Repair Hangar, the sun beating down on the corrugated tin roof high above us, streaming through the three huge bay doors set in the ceiling for airship launches, letting out the worst of the day's heat. Wind blew off the sea to our south-east, through the gigantic double doors set in either end of the hangar, cooling the rest. And still, it was hot enough that I felt sweat trickling down my back, soaking the blouse where it met my corset.

Our berth lay off in the deepest shade we could afford, since we ran a mostly night shift. Even so, a lot of my crew would wake up tired and cranky from a hot, sweaty sleep. Still, better that than outside in the open sun, cooking us crispy.

Most of the day shift would be settling down to their siesta soon. Even Market Street would mostly shut down, drapes drawn across windows and doors, people catching catnaps in the shade of alleys, under awnings, wherever they could escape the punishing sun.

Too restless to sleep, too restless to sit still, even, I needed to be up, out, moving. So long in port was making me stir crazy. I decided to go for a walk to clear my head.

On my way down through the ship to our gangplank, I ran into Restless again. "Find Gigi?"

"Yep, and Miss Merryweather, too," she grinned. "Anything else?"

"I'm going for a walk." I always made sure to tell someone whenever I left the ship. The first and only time I hadn't, Tring and her Open Hands had scoured Libertia for hours. But I mean, it's not like Serena didn't know exactly where I was. If anyone had bothered to ask her, she could have led them right to me.

Restless followed me down a ladder. "Can I come? Please, Captain?"

How could I resist those big brown puppy dog eyes? "Okay, sure," I laughed.

"Thanks, Captain!"

She tagged along as I left The Furies. Restless wasn't very good at most jobs, because she'd get distracted and wander off. Unless you gave her a very specific task with a clear, easily remembered goal. Most of the crew had adopted her as a kind of permanent younger sister, and some of the older women clearly saw her as a child in need of guidance and discipline. I saw her as a member of my crew, and expected her to earn her keep. She seemed to respond to that kind of recognition, and appreciated me not treating her like a kid.

Still, because she was always all over the place, talking to whoever wanted to talk, she was kind of a font of gossip.

"So Hilda and Inga are getting along pretty well," I prompted. It was usually all she needed.

"They sure are, Captain," Restless said. "No one else seems willing to even talk to Inga. You know what they call her, right? Doom. Inga Doom. She's blown away fifteen airships! Fifteen! And survived six crashes! No wonder they call her that. Some of the old ladies think maybe she'll be bad luck, what with all the crashes? I think she'll be good luck, with all her kills."

"Well, hopefully we won't need to kill too many people," I said, uncomfortable at the idea. Killing people was bad for business, every pirate I'd talked to said so. Too many murders and the Atlan Aerial Forces would come down hard on everyone. Terror was the way to go. People who were scared of losing their lives wouldn't fuss too much at losing their money.

I toured the ship, walking all the way around it. She looked ready to go, to my untrained eye at least. We'd scoured away the grime Captain Crow had let build up, patching and repainting her hull. Her lines held taut, waterproofed and ready to be cast off and wound back onto her winches. Up above, I saw three glittery flickers zipping back and forth across the black-and-gold of the balloon, the pixies checking and rechecking her.

Restless kept up a steady stream of comments and questions that she answered herself, and she kind of faded into the background noise of the hammering of hulls, the hiss of balloons filling with gas, the shouts and jokes of the crews around us, repairing their ships. Then something she said caught my attention.

"Wait, hold on," I said, stopping to look at Restless. "Say that again."

"Um, which part, Captain?"

"Something about Serena?"

"Oh! Well, she got back just before dawn, like always."

"Yeah?"

"And she looked like she'd been in a fight. At least that's what Mrs. Shorty said, she'd been up late, or early I guess, and she wanted to see if there was another way to organize the shelves in the Booty Hold."

"What happened to Serena?"

"I don't know, Captain, she went straight to bed. Though she did tell leave word with Padmini to tell Tring that we needed to double the guard."

I stared at her for a full five seconds, trying to keep my temper in check. Something in my face must have showed, though, because Restless kept quiet those full five seconds. It wasn't her fault. It wasn't. She was just the messenger. I closed my eyes, willing myself to calm down. Through clenched teeth, I asked, "And no one told me this, why?"

"Uh... I don't know, Captain."

I walked away, needing some space to think. Someone should have told me Serena had been roughed up. I should have known, over our link. But I hadn't. I'd let her go off on her own, hunting that patchwork attacker, while I'd gone to sleep. I should have gone after her.

Then something broke through the guilt and I realized if Serena had really been seriously hurt, I would have felt it. She couldn't be that badly off. I was overreacting.

I took a deep breath and looked up. Serena was okay. It still pissed me off that no one told me we'd doubled the guard, but part of having crew chiefs was letting them take care of things without consulting me. Back before we'd had specific crews, everyone had come to me for every little thing. I spent all day and all night making decisions without the information or the education to back them up. It was pretty stressful. So we'd come up with the specific crews and made crew chiefs for each crew to make things go smoother and make my life easier. I had to trust that Serena knew what she was talking about when she ordered Tring to double the guard. Of course, that meant there was a *reason* to double the guard, but I'd have to wait until Serena woke up at dusk to find out.

"What a beautiful lady," a man said behind me, his voice deep and his words Atlan. I turned.

He was tall and lean, with broad shoulders and curly dark hair. Maybe twenty five years old. He was dressed simply but on him it looked dashing. A plain linen shirt with the laces undone against the day's heat revealed his well-toned nearly hairless chest. Just enough for some friction, my best friend back home, Monica, would have said. Tight black pants showcased his muscular legs. He even wore those folded-over boots and had a small gold hoop in his right ear, completing his pirate look perfectly.

He wasn't looking at me, though. He was looking up. I glanced back up to see what he was talking about. Oh right, our new figurehead.

The figurehead gleamed, even in the shade, almost as if she drank in whatever little light there was and let it seep out of her slowly. He was right. She was beautiful.

"Thanks," I said, switching to pure Atlan. It's amazing how fast you can learn a language when you're surrounded by it all day and all night. And a good teacher helps. "She's brand new."

"So I see," he replied. "What an unusual design, too. Wings from her shoulders, fantastic!"

One of the things that really, really freaked me out about Ayrth was they had no legends, no myths. Not even any religion! Science was everything, here, and had been for the past two thousand years. So no one had known what I was talking about when I'd described what I wanted for our figurehead. "Like an Angel of Wrath," I'd said, and everyone had looked over at our nurse, Angel. They hadn't known what an angel was, what a goddess was. It was supremely weird.

So anyway. Totally hot guy was talking to me. And as I think I have mentioned, I tend to spaz around totally hot guys.

"Yeah, fantastic," I said, giggling nervously. *Oh please*, I thought, *please let me hold it together for five frickin' seconds.*

"An Eire-made ship with a Hispanian figurehead, how unconventional," he continued. Finally he looked at me, and my heart stopped. His sea-green eyes just filled the entire world, and my brain fell right out of my head. Somewhere, deep inside of me, I disgusted myself.

"You must be Sunset Val," he said, holding his hand toward me. "Captain of The Furious, is that correct?"

"It's The Furies," Restless corrected him. I was still wondering why he had his hand out.

"My mistake," he said, those incredible eyes never leaving mine. "Aloysius Tempest, Captain of the Stormgazer."

I finally clued in to the fact that he wanted to take my hand. I reached out and managed to say "Hi," without sounding like a complete idiot.

He took my hand in his. It was rough, the hand of a man who wasn't afraid to do hard work. The familiar calluses of sword work ridged his palm. My heart pounded in my chest as he leaned over and kissed the back of my hand, his lips, those perfect lips, lingering against my skin. My mouth was so dry, a desert, a wasteland, I'd never have enough saliva to dampen it again.

He let go of my hand and the universe plunged into darkness. He smiled and suddenly the world filled with light again. Yep, pretty embarrassing. "I wondered, Captain, if you and your first mate would do the Stormgazer the honour of your presence at dinner this evening? Say, eight bells?"

"Sure," I said immediately. "Absolutely. Yes."

His smile got broader, more glorious. "Excellent. We're in Berth 29, above."

"Okay, yeah, awesome," I said, nodding. Twenty Nine. What an amazing number.

He turned to go. "Until eight bells, then."

I think I would have said or done anything to keep him from leaving, if Restless hadn't grabbed my sleeve and tugged at it.

"What, Restless?!" I hissed at her.

"You alright, Captain? You took an odd spell."

Right. I'd been a total spaz. Great. How was I supposed to get through an entire dinner with him?

"Should we go wake up Miss Heartlace, Captain?"

"What? Why?"

Restless gave me an odd look. "She was invited to dinner, too, Captain, remember?"

"What? Oh yeah. I mean, of course she was. What I meant was, why wake her up?"

"Well, she'll be needing to get ready for dinner, won't she?"

"It's like, six hours away, Restless. Plus, she's vampyri. She won't wake up until the sun sets."

"Oh, right. Sorry, Captain."

"It's okay." I shook my head to clear it. He was completely gorgeous. I didn't have a chance. *Get it out of your head, Val*, I told myself. *It's not like back home, where people just ask each other out or whatever. Here, they go courting, if they're serious. And you're not the love 'em and leave 'em type. Besides, you're still just a kid. He'd never court a kid like you.*

Chapter Six

A Heart to Heartlace

"He's courting you," Serena said when I told her.

My heart raced. Serena laughed, hearing it beat from clear across the room.

Even after twelve hours of slumber and having gotten into a fight the night before, she looked awesome. The slumber had tussled her hair, messing it into sexy perfection. Her eyes were half-shut still, but it came off as alluring instead of sleepy. She threw off the covers and slid out of bed, her nightgown (daygown?) short enough to reveal her pale muscular legs and surprisingly slender, delicate feet.

"Not romantically, Wal, I'm sorry," she said from behind her changing screen. The nightgown was tossed with casual aim onto the bed.

My heart stopped and all hope died with it. "Oh."

"I am surprised it took so long, actually."

"What did?"

"Courting us. Ve are a new player in the skies. New allegiances can be forged vith us, upsetting the existing circles of power. New players are always a source of interest to pirate society."

"This is that thing you were talking about before we got here, right? How pirates don't have any organization, but they do have agreements between each other? Territorial boundaries, that sort of thing?"

"Exactly. And no one knows us. Ve could be an important piece in the continual struggle for dominance. Ve could be Atlan spies. Ve could even be escaped, rebellious slaves who slew our masters and took over their ship, as preposterous as that might sound."

"So?"

"So every pirate captain vill vant to be making sure that ve vill side vith them instead of their enemies. Or at least, agree not to interfere vith their plans."

"And no one has even tried to talk to us, even though we've been here for weeks."

"You vere attacked so close to our upcoming departure, and clumsily too. And then ve receive this invitation. It is a curious coincidence."

"Who knew we were leaving? And why attack us? And, clumsily? Suzanna still hasn't woken up from that patchwork's punch." Dr. Westmore had given Suzanna about a fifty/fifty chance of ever waking up again.

"An assassin who knew vhat he vas doing vould not have attacked in so clumsy a manner," Serena said, stepping out from behind the screen. As always, she was immaculate. Burgundy pants so tight they could have been painted on encased her long legs. A pristine white silk blouse enshrouded her arms, ensnared at her torso by a tight red leather vest embroidered with pink hearts. And somehow her long, straight, pale hair was combed to perfection.

She sat on the edge of the bed to pull on her thigh-high black boots. "An assassin who vas serious about it vould have finished the job. This vas a varning of some kind. There may be others."

"You didn't catch him, then?"

She made a face that clearly spoke of her self-disgust. "No. He escaped into the sea docks. I lost his scent in that stench."

Down by the ocean, there were actual docks for actual sailing ships. They were usually reserved for fishing boats, which explained the stench she'd referred to. I'd been down there only once, sightseeing, and the smell of fresh fish, rotting fish, fish blood and fish guts spilled out all over the dock under the tropical sun, well, it had been pretty bad. To someone with vampyric senses, though, it must have been terrible.

"So who was warning us, and what about?"

"Captain Crow might have had friends here, like that Captain Caliper," Serena said. It wasn't the first time she'd mentioned it. "Or, if not friends, people who didn't vant to see him dead. They might have recognized the ship as The Carrion, despite the new paint and newer figurehead."

I grinned. "Do you like her?"

"She is something to behold, it is true. Anyone seeing us on the attack vould think twice about resisting."

"Good. The more surrenders, the better."

She grinned, wide enough for me to see her razor-sharp inch-long fangs. "You are learning!"

I rolled my eyes. "What, how to be a pirate?"

"No, how to be a hunter. It is more fun vhen the prey runs or fights, but more vork, too."

Serena stood and strapped her sword belt around her waist. Then she pulled her sword out to study it. A thin blade three feet long, a rapier, it gleamed silver-gold in the lamp light. A beautiful cage of brass encased her hand, protecting it from an attacker's lunges. An adept fencer could even use that cage to disarm their opponent, risking damage to their hand to gain the advantage.

Her sword apparently passed her inspection. She returned it to its sheath with a single deft move, then turned to face me. "Come, Wal, let us get you dressed for this dinner. It should be enlightening."

Chapter Seven

Guess I'm Coming to Dinner

The airdocks were reached one of two ways. We chose the less exciting, more dignified way – the elevator, a box of brass and wood that caged the monkey animan elevator operator. Perched on his stool, he held the operating lever in the 'Up' position, getting us to the 20s Berths.

There were ten berths for airships per level, starting with Berths 1-10 at the very top of the tower. Berth 29 was pretty high up there, which meant that Captain Tempest had money, or some kind of pull with the Dockmaster. Or both. We'd been assigned to Berth 74, just one level up from actually landing the ship, until we bribed the Dockmaster to let us stay in the Repair Hangar.

"Twennies," the operator slurred. He'd probably been drinking, something that wasn't all that rare in Libertia. I tossed him a coin, which he caught with his bare foot.

We stepped out of the elevator car and onto a curved platform. Wind pulled at my dress and cloak. I'd wanted to wear pants and a coat like Serena, but she'd insisted that I get all dolled up. Adina had been thrilled to actually put her hairdressing training to good use, and almost for nothing, as the wind threatened my elegantly coiffed and curled hair. It was all ringlets suspended from an intricate bun high on the back of my head, now, instead of its usual barely-constrained pigtails shoved under a hat or cap.

Serena chuckled as the elevator doors closed. "That vas an Atlan sovereign."

"So?"

"So, probably a month's vages for him."

I shrugged. "Whatever. We'll just get more."

She shook her head, but she was smiling.

I reached down and lifted the hem of my dress with one hand, the other hand holding my cloak closed. The dress was a deep blue taffeta with about a hundred petticoats. The corset, worn over the dress pirate-style, was a bright sky blue leather. A couple of sapphire earrings sparkled in my earlobes. According to everyone aboard The Furies, I looked amazing, and I have to admit it, they were right. Still, I felt that heart-racing, can't-quite-breathe feeling that Captain Tempest had made me feel earlier that afternoon, and we hadn't even reached his ship yet.

"Just breathe, Wal," Serena murmured as we walked along the curved landing. Large signs carved in the shape of numbers hung from cast iron electric lampposts. *Twenty two, twenty three...* "He's just a man."

"Just about the most gorgeous man ever," I answered. *Twenty five, twenty six...* "One who turns me into a drooling ninny."

"You'll have me there this time," Serena said. "There is not a man alive who vill charm us both."

"Uh huh. Sure," I answered, my heart pounding, my mouth dry. Twenty nine, carved from a single plank of wood, painted red with gold trim. "This is it."

The berth itself was a wooden dock that jutted out from the curved landing, maybe twenty-five feet long by ten wide. At the end of it floated the Stormgazer.

She was a beauty, alright, sleek and lean. Not quite the size of The Furies, being less wide, less long, and with less decks, she still gave the impression of raw power, like she was straining at her lines to get back into the open air. By the light of the electric lamps at the end of the dock I saw she was painted dark blue with silver trim. High above her, her balloon was a greyish sausage disappearing into the night sky.

A crewman waited for us at the end of the gangplank, sitting on a wooden chair on the dock. "You'd be Captain Val, then?"

"Permission to come aboard?" I asked.

"Granted!" Captain Tempest called down. I looked up and wanted to die.

Somehow he was even more gorgeous in the lamplight than he was in the day. His eyes sparkled, his teeth shone, his skin glistened. His movements as he hurried down the gangplank to greet us spoke of strength, agility, and an absolute control of both.

Don't trip don't trip don't trip, I thought as I stepped onto the gangplank. I didn't trip, so maybe the universe didn't hate me after all.

Then he took my hand and kissed it again and everything spun.

Suddenly I realized the gangplank had no rails, and that we were very, very high up. I started to lose my balance and fell forward into his arms, just like the kind of drooling ninny I despised.

"I'm sorry," I said into his chest. *Don't look up don't look up don't look up...*

"I'm not," he said, and pulled me closer.

Now, okay. I've had exactly one boyfriend in my life. Miles Fletcher. Seventh grade. For all of two weeks. We held hands twice and I kissed him once. He barely knew to kiss me back, it was over so quick. Then he dumped me for Sylvia Sutton, a total tramp who'd started developing in like, the fifth grade or whatever. So that's all I had to go on about boys. Monica, my best friend back home, always had five or six boys drooling after her, and she toyed with them like puppets. I couldn't even get through this entire evening stammering and fainting. I had to do something, something Monica would do.

I looked up. Through my eyelashes, coyly. Or at least, what I hoped was coyly. I smiled.

"Thanks, then," I said, then fought every instinct I had to stay right there safe in his arms and pushed away. I wasn't a helpless drooling fainting ninny. I was Monica. Men were mine to toy with. Riiiiiiight.

"Welcome aboard my ship," Captain Tempest said with a grin. Monica? Monica who? No! Monica! Right.

He led us up the gangplank then waved us on board. Serena gave him one of her coldest looks, like she wasn't impressed in the slightest.

"You'd be First Mate Heartlace, then," Captain Tempest said to her, offering her his hand. She rested her fingertips against his, and he bowed over and kissed her hand, his lips barely brushing her marble-pale skin. Then he said something in a language I'd only heard Serena swear in.

She seemed surprised, and asked him a question in the same language. He answered back, then laughed. Serena smiled, despite herself.

"And this is my crew," Captain Tempest announced, waving an arm to take them all in.

There were quite a few of them, mostly Europans, some Africs. A handful of animen, which surprised me, and very few women, which didn't. Captain Crow only had three or four women on his crew of nearly thirty, a proportion I later found out was pretty typical. There were a couple of other female captains here in Libertia, and they tended to hire on more women than the male captains, but as far as I knew, The Furies was the only ship entirely crewed by women.

The crew of the Stormgazer nodded their welcomes to us. Some even touched their foreheads, a kind of salute.

"My first mate, Dan'el Monsoon," Captain Tempest said, and a huge lion animan stepped forward. He stood head and shoulders taller than Serena, dressed in nothing but a pair of leather pants and a leather vest. He and Serena stared at each other for a long moment, his huge amber eyes locked onto her own icy blues, then he bowed his head slightly. He turned to me and looked down, way, way down. One eyebrow rose, amused.

"Such a little thing," he rumbled. "Welcome aboard, Captain Val."

What would Monica say? C'mon, Val! "Big enough to take you down, Goliath. Thanks. Nice ship."

"She is a beauty, isn't she?" Captain Tempest said, dismissing the crew with a wave of his hand. "We can offer you a tour after dinner. Our cook's whipped up something special, and no mistake."

"Tempest, Monsoon... a trend, Captain?" Serena asked as he led the way to the captain's mess.

"Something like that," Tempest said. "After all, many folks turn pirate to escape who they'd been, don't they?"

"Some don't have the choice," Serena replied coolly.

"All my crew are pirates by choice," Tempest answered, taking my cloak and hanging it on a peg near the door. The Monica part of me smiled appreciatively. "I'll not have any pressed men aboard, hiding out during an action and claiming unfair shares. Everyone works, everyone fights, aboard the Stormgazer."

The mess was anything but. Elegant crystal goblets, fine china, and what looked to be solid gold cutlery were spread around a seating for five.

"Who else is joining us?" I asked, the words out of my mouth before I had consciously thought about speaking them. C'mon, be less Val and more Monica, dammit!

"That vould be me," a woman said, joining us from a side door.

Tall, dark haired, dark eyed, curves to die for, she was dressed in a red taffeta dress with a black leather corset over top. Gold bracelets glittered at her wrists, a gold locket dipped into her cleavage, gold hoop earrings dangled from her ears. She was simply stunning.

"My wife, Tatalia," Captain Tempest introduced, and I died inside. Of course he was married. Of course a man as gorgeous as him would have an equally gorgeous wife.

He took her hand and kissed it deeply. She smiled at him, perfect white teeth flashing from between luscious lips. The perfect couple.

Tempest looked away from his stunning wife. "May I introduce –"

"Sunset Val, Captain of The Furies," I said, not waiting. I stuck out my hand to shake hers.

She took it. Firm grip. I forced myself to look her in the eye and smile.

"And this is my first mate, Serena Heartlace."

Tatalia Tempest looked over at my first mate and her smile faded. Then she said something in Serena's language. I really needed to have Serena teach it to me.

Serena answered back, cold but polite. Tatalia glared at her husband.

Who had the good grace to look apologetic. "I'm sorry, darling, I should have thought."

"Yes, you should have," she snapped.

"Is there a problem?" I asked, completely out of the loop.

"Mistress Tempest is Romanista," Serena explained. "From my homeland."

"For centuries her kind kept my people as..." Tatalia paused, looking for the right word. When she spoke, her voice was thick with bitter sarcasm. "Vould you say, pets? Playthings? Tell me, Nightmistress, vhat vord vould you use?"

Serena's reply came flat and cold. "In our language the vord translates as 'food slave', Romanya. As you vell know."

"And I am Romanya no longer, as you must vell know."

The only expression on Serena's face was a slight raising of one eyebrow. "Because of your choice of husband, I assume? An odd custom. But your people vere always odd."

"Come now, ladies," Captain Tempest said, trying to keep the peace. "Surely we can let ancient history lay dormant? No need to dredge up a past none present can remember?"

Tatalia's eyes never left Serena's face. "Some memories are longer than others, my husband."

"My mother's mother was the last of my folk to keep Romanista," Serena stated simply. "Three centuries ago."

I couldn't help myself. "Three cen... How old are you?!"

Serena gave me a half-smile. "Still young, yet. Von hundred and seven."

"Ladies, please," Tempest said, going to the sideboard and pouring four glasses of wine. He poured a fifth glass from a different bottle, a darker red liquid, thicker than wine. "Let us toast. The past behind us, and a glorious future ahead."

We each took a glass. The crystal was thick and heavy in my hand, but in Dan'el's huge paw it seemed like a fragile child's cup. The fifth glass of red liquid he handed to Serena; she hesitated before drinking, taking in the bouquet. Apparently it met with her approval, because she raised it to salute Captain Tempest.

We toasted, the crystal glasses chiming as they touched. I took a sip. I wasn't all that keen on wine, though getting drunk to drown my sorrows sounding like a reasonable way to spend the evening. But I'd be damned if I let him see it. Plenty of time to get drunk and stupid back on board my own ship.

"Come, let's sit," Tempest said, leading us over to the table. He held the chair for his wife; Serena held mine. Then Dan'el held Serena's as Tempest sat at the head of the table.

"So," Tempest said, reaching over to pick up a dainty little silver bell and ring it. "Let us, in the manner of sailors the world over, swap tall tales. I was born in a hurricane, aboard this very ship. My father was captain, and his father before him, though in grandfather's day the ship had been a merchant vessel. My father had gone pirate, and I followed in his air stream. You?"

"Me, oh," I said. We'd practised my cover story before even getting to Libertia, but it had been a while and I wanted to make sure I got it right. "Born of lightning and science, you might say. My grandfather had been a pirate, and with his death, well, as his last heir I took command. My own Dad was taken by the blight, and Mother died of grief."

I still didn't know what the blight was. No one I asked would talk about it, scared to even mention it beyond a passing reference.

"How terrible," Tatalia said sympathetically. At least she'd stopped glaring daggers at Serena, opting instead to completely ignore my first mate's presence.

"So each from pirate families, eh? Seems strange we'd never run into each other before," Tempest said, reaching out to refill our glasses. He barely had to add any to mine, I'd hardly touched it.

"Oh well, Grandfather was sort of the black sheep of the family. Dad was a chemist, a terrible disappointment to Grandfather. And worse, he married a dedicated land dweller, another scientist. She dreamed of harnessing the power of lightning itself – but, you understand, always from the safety of the ground. But me, I always dreamed of the sky. Couldn't hardly believe my luck when the letter from the barrister came. And now here I am."

"Here you are," Dan'el rumbled. "And quite the crew, too. Most of 'em shipped with your grandsire, then?"

I laughed. "No, that scurvy bunch of dogs took off without a by-your-leave! And took everything that wasn't nailed down in the bargain. Took me the rest of Grandfather's fortune to refit The Furies."

The meal arrived by way of two crewmen carrying silver platters. One held a huge roast bird of some kind, the other was piled high with roasted vegetables. Captain Tempest stood to do the carving, portioning out slices to his wife and me, then handing the entire leg over to Dan'el. Serena wasn't offered any food. Instead, he brought her the rest of the bottle of blood.

"An interesting wintage," Serena said as he topped off her glass. "Mostly pig, I assume."

"Not entirely," he replied with a grin. "I have a friend who knows a man who procures the rare and unusual. I suspect it's only about half pig's blood."

"Fascinating," Tatalia said, serving herself another glass of wine. "Shall we toast?"

"Yes," Tempest said, picking up his own glass. "To new friends!"

"New friends," I repeated, sipping from my glass. Tempest was quick to refill what little I had drunk.

We ate, trading stories of the pirate life. Tempest told us of his first action, taking a merchant vessel while a volcano spewed ash into the air, a thick noxious smog that confounded his crew so badly that at one point they'd taken their own ship. Tatalia explained how she'd met her husband, trading the roaming life of a Romanista, which I figured out was some kind of gypsy, for the high-flying life of an airship pirate. Dan'el told us a story about an island of animen, where he'd been born, where his parents, a dog animan and his turtle wife, had chosen to gift him with the strength and size of a lion, and how disappointed they'd been when he'd gone off to join the crew of an airship.

"'If we'd wanted you to fly, we would have made you an eagle', my father yelled," Dan'el said, chuckling at the memory.

"That's awful," I said.

He shrugged. "Parents want what they think is best. What they think is best and what actually is best for the child don't always match up."

"And you, Captain Val?" Tatalia asked. "What story do you have to tell?"

The meal was mostly over and it had been delicious. I had no idea what had been on the potatoes but they had been amazing. I'd had a double serving and now all I wanted to do was take off my corset and relax.

"Oh well um," I stalled. What was I supposed to tell them? That I'd come from another world? A world without airship pirates, animen, vampyri, or even an Atlan? "I'm not a very good storyteller."

"Nonsense, every pirate worth his salt can spin a yarn," Tempest said. "Have some wine, loosen that tongue."

The part of me that wanted to copy Monica and flirt with him probably would have said something about finding better uses for my tongue. Luckily, that part had died a hideous death when I'd met Tatalia. At least I wasn't crushing on a married guy. That was one part of my spazziness that I was grateful for – as soon as I found out the guy I crushed on was unavailable, the spazzing stopped. That's how I'd been able to take all those lessons with my fencing instructor, Raoul, who was pretty much hotness incarnate.

"No, I know one," I said. "Our first action. We'd been trawling along the Afric Straight, looking for some plum merchant ship. No luck, of course, and most of the crew green too. Three weeks, then nothing. Suddenly, there's a ship. Too small for a merchant but the crew are grumbling. So to it, I decide. It's go time.

"The ship were slavers, fresh with a hold full of prime stock, headed for the Neptopolis markets. Mostly young ones, so likely the pleasure houses for them. We pull up alongside, pulling a wounded dove. They think they're about to take us. We slip aboard, free the slaves. Outnumber them, see? Took the ship, the stock joined our crew, we marooned the slavers. All's well that ends well."

They applauded, even Serena. It wasn't a great story, but it had the benefit of being at least partially based in truth, so it sounded a little convincing, at least.

Now, I know what you're thinking. I sounded a little off, telling my story. Not like my normal self, I mean. See, I'd practised using pirate terms like 'action' and 'stock'. And it wasn't just using the right words, it was using the right style. Pirates all talked big and acted bigger, is what I mean. So I pretended to be one of them by talking their way. Because let's face it, if they found out I was actually just some seventeen year old high school kid from another world, there's no way I'd get any respect out of any of them. It was tough enough as it was.

"So how long have you been attacking slavers?" Tatalia asked, when a knock came at the door.

"Come," Tempest said.

A tall girl with curly blonde hair stepped into the room.

"Jenny Squall, my bosun's mate," Tempest introduced us. "What is it, Jen?"

She said something in heavily-accented Atlan, too quick for me to catch. Guess Miss Merryweather's lessons hadn't covered everything.

"Excuse me," Tempest said, getting up from his chair. Dan'el followed.

Serena leaned over to me, one hand on my shoulder. "Ve should go," she whispered.

"What is it?" I whispered back, acutely aware of Tatalia watching us both.

"Could be nothing," Serena answered. "More likely? Trouble."

I turned to Tatalia. "You'll have to excuse us. I should be getting back to my ship."

"As you vish," she said, standing.

Serena and I stood too, then left. I grabbed my cloak as we headed out the door. Outside the officer's mess, the crew hurried back and forth. Tempest and Dan'el both gave orders in calm, decisive tones, but it was pretty clear they were freaked.

The Stormgazer wasn't the only ship suddenly bustling with activity. Both ahead and aft, the ships berthed there teemed with crew hauling lines and storing stuff. The Stormgazer rumbled and shuddered, its huge engines coming to life. At least, that's what it would have been aboard The Furies. For all I knew, Tempest had a captive tornado in his hold.

"Captain! What's going on?" I called after him as he headed below, presumably to his wheelhouse.

"You'll have to excuse me, my dear Captain," he said. "Seems an Atlan warship is patrolling a little too close for comfort, you know what I mean?"

"Actually, no," I said, but he was already gone.

"Ve're casting off," Tatalia explained. "I suggest you do the same."

"Everyone's casting off?"

"Captain, ve must go," Serena said, grabbing my arm.

I let her drag me off the Stormgazer. "Okay, fine, but tell me what the big deal is."

"Atlan varships never wenture this far vithout extensive support," she explained as we headed back toward the elevator. "And never vithout a wery good reason."

"So, what, they're going to attack? We haven't done anything!"

Serena glanced at me. "Ve are pirates, remember?"

"Oh yeah."

"Interrupting the slave trade, as vell."

"Right."

"And ve are not the vorst criminals in Libertia," she said. "This has to be the beginning of something much greater."

"So everyone's just going to run away? Fly away, I mean?"

"He who fights and flies away, lives to fight another day."

"But they're not even fighting," I said, stopping to watch a ship fly away from its berth. It was amazing that something so huge and awkward-looking could be so graceful. It soared out into the night sky like a swan gliding across a pond.

A pond filled with piranhas. "Hey what are those?" I asked, pointing at the small dark shapes flitting across the sky.

Toward us.

Serena turned. "Vhat the... No!"

Suddenly they were everywhere, and the ships' crews went into a panic. The dark shapes were men, made small by distance. They flew by way of leather bat wings jutting from backpacks strapped to their backs, belching out back smoke that only added to the confusion and chaos. Ships began to throw off their mooring lines, desperate to escape, not caring which ship was in their way. I saw one prow sink right into the balloon of a lower ship before Serena pushed me down and under her.

Then the world was suddenly a noise so huge that nothing else existed, a light so bright I saw the veins in my eyelids despite being under my first mate at the time. The explosion rocked the entire Docking Tower.

Serena was already on her feet, saying something. I could barely hear, barely breathe. I coughed and coughed, trying to catch my breath, but she hauled me to my feet before I had a chance to get my bearings.

A ship wouldn't have blown up like that. A rapid burn, sure, a slow drop and a sudden stop, absolutely, but that kind of explosion had to have been a bomb.

Off to my right, another ship blew up, lighting the night as clear as day. Flaming wreckage tumbled to the streets below. I glanced down.

Not far from where the fires were already burning lay the Repair Hangar.

Chapter Eight

'Flight' Also Means 'Running Away'

"We have to get back to the ship!" I said, hiking up my skirts and running for the elevators.

Serena, with her vampyric speed, was there ahead of me. Or more like, got ahead of me and stopped short, two berths from the elevator doors.

Five men were working on opening the elevator shaft's brass doors. They were uniformly dressed in black leather jackets, black leather pants, black leather boots, and black leather aviator caps. Goggles hid their eyes. On their backs they all carried those huge backpack things. Thin trickles of black smoke seeped from the exhaust pipes of each backpack, and funny leathery capes hung from either side. It took me a second to realize those were the wings, folded up. Airborne commandos with retractable wings. It would be really awesome, if they weren't trying to kill us and everyone else in Libertia.

And trying to destroy the Docking Tower, I realized, seeing the fairly large bomb one of the men was setting up.

The sound of metal rasping its way out of its sheath startled me. Of course Serena had her sword. And I had nothing.

Serena must have sensed my thoughts because she reached behind her, under her coat, and pulled out a main-gauche. Twelve inches of steel wasn't much, but it was better than nothing. I pulled off my cloak and wrapped it around my off hand. I'd never fought cloak-and-dagger style before but I'd seen it done.

Five against two doesn't seem like very good odds, but one of our two was a swordmistress of the ninth order, ready to graduate to the eighth, and I was pretty good, too. I'd gone from practising a couple of hours once a week to practising a couple of hours every day, and Serena was a much better instructor than Raoul ever was. Sorry Raoul, but it's true.

Serena didn't even say anything, just waded into them, sword dancing, dealing death. I followed in her wake, trying not to get killed.

They were good, these guys, I'll give them that. No shouts of surprise, no confusion. Serena killed the first one and by the time she'd disengaged her sword the others had armed themselves and leapt to the attack, four against one.

Four against two, I thought, jumping in. I stabbed one guy through his sword arm and he didn't even moan or grunt or anything, just switched his sword to his off hand and turned to face me. That was almost the last time I drew any blood in that fight. It was all I could do to keep his sword from skewering me. I kept tripping over my damned dress as I batted at his attacks with my cloak, trying to get close enough to jab or slash at him with the main-gauche.

He grabbed my cloak and hauled me close, catching me off-balance. I stumbled forward. He held his sword high, poised for the killing blow. Serena's sword blade erupted from his stomach, spattering me with blood. He stared at it, stunned. I got my balance and slashed at his throat. More blood sprayed everywhere. My dress was ruined. I laughed at how stupid that seemed, compared to five men who lay at our feet, dead. Serena had taken out four while I'd distracted the last one long enough for her to save my butt. It's hard not to be a little jealous in times like that, but I managed to bury it under a pile of extreme gratitude at being alive.

Explosions lit up the night sky around us. Smoke rose up from fires throughout the city below. Distantly I heard the clanging of firebell alarms as people rushed to save their homes and businesses.

There didn't seem to be any more of the batwinged attackers. I handed Serena back her main-gauche. "I was wondering why you were keeping your back so stiff," I said. "I thought you were just pissed off at Tatalia."

"I vas pissed off at her," Serena said, wiping blood from the blade before sheathing it under her coat. "They cannot let go of a blood debt, Romanista. It haunts them. It vas ancient history before I vas even born, I should bow and scrape and beg forgiveness the rest of my life?!"

"You're still pissed off at her."

"At them all!" She shook her head. "Come on, let's get back to the ship."

"Yeah, but I bet the elevator operator made a run for it."

"Ve cannot vait for the elevator," she said, leaning in to inspect the bomb. "Ve have three minutes to get off this tower."

There was a clock wired in to the mechanism set on the outside of the metal barrel that made up the bomb. It was counting down. Three minutes left. Less now.

"Okay," I said. "Bat wing things?"

"Bat ving things, yes."

We yanked the backpacks off the dead guys. I grabbed a set of goggles off of one guy, pulling his cap off in the process. His head was shaved bald, a line of tattoos running from his left eyebrow to the back of his skull. A trident, a skull, a star, others. Serena hissed.

There wasn't time to ask her what was wrong. I hauled the backpack on and strapped myself in. It weighed almost nothing, surprising me. I'd never tried one of these things before, but then, what choice did I have?

Serena explained. "This lever for the wings. Pull the right handle to turn right, the left handle to turn left, both handles to bank up, yes?"

"Okay, sure," I said. We headed for the railing. "Wait!"

"Vhat? Ve don't have time!"

"I know!" I yelled, heading back to grab the bomb. "Get back to the ship, get her in the air!"

The bomb was heavy, but I heaved it up and held on.

"Leave it! Wal!"

"We can't let the Tower be blown up! Go!"

"Vhat vill–"

"Serena, GO!"

I didn't wait to see if she listened to me, just flipped the lever to extend the wings and jumped over the railing.

Pulling on both handles to bank up was a lot harder with a bomb ticking away in my arms, but the threat of dying gave me all kinds of strength I didn't know I had. The wings pulled at the night air, fighting to climb despite the weight. I caught an updraft over a burning building and used it to climb up, high over the city. Then I turned and got myself aimed at the ocean.

Libertia was built on the shores of a hook-shaped bay on the eastern edge of Merinasy. Normally it glittered silver with moonlight. Now it glowed orange-yellow from the fires that raged through the town. I caught a lungful of smoke, sparks of fire shooting up all around me, and lost precious seconds coughing so hard I couldn't steer. I didn't dare look at the clock.

The bay filled my whole field of vision. I concentrated so hard on it that I didn't notice the bat winged commandos until a lucky updraft knocked me into an aerial somersault. Then I saw them. Three of them, behind me, knives out. One had a pistol.

Me, I had a dress. And a bomb. Not the best weapons for aerial combat.

The one with the pistol took aim and shot, two, three times. I didn't check to see how good his aim was, I just turned and dove for the waters of the bay. I wasn't bleeding, that much I knew, at least.

They chased after me. So stupid. What point was there in chasing after me? So they could put the bomb back on the Docking Tower? There wasn't enough time. Funny what you think about when you're being chased through the air over a burning city while carrying a bomb with seconds left to detonation. Well, anyway, take it from me.

I heard a weird farting rip noise and suddenly started spinning to my left. I glanced over and saw my wing had torn. Guess the gunman hit me after all.

Luckily the bay was under me. I dropped the bomb into the water and tried to pull up and away, but my left wing wasn't working very well or, you know, at all, so I kind of just flew in a wide curve while the air commandos swooped in for the kill.

Then the bomb went off.

The blast caught the air commandos and they went flying. The blast threw me probably a couple of hundred feet, landing hard in the water. The backpack filled up and I struggled to get it off but the straps were tangled and my dress suddenly weighed a hundred pounds and I was being pulled deeper and deeper into the water and I couldn't breathe and I had just enough time to think, *Oh well.*

Chapter Nine

Safer Underwater

Did I tell you about the mermaids?

Okay, so. Mermaids. Not quite pink-skinned redheads with strategically-placed shells on their human halves, you know? More greenish skinned. Beautiful, in that perfect should have been a supermodel but kind of weird underwatery try to forget she has a fish tail sort of way. But definitely, absolutely, without a doubt not dolphins or manatees. Big dark eyes. Long seaweedy hair. Webbed hands with wicked long sharp nails. And the requisite scaly fish tails.

Supposedly pretty common in the Europan Sea, what I would have called the Mediterranean back home. Did you know Mediterranean means 'centre of the world'? But since Atlan is the centre of this world, not so much. So, Europan Sea. Where the mermaids come from. But they're all over the world, now, like you can find Europans in Merinasy and Africs in Atlan and animen all over and whatever wherever.

Mermaids. In Libertia Bay. Thank goodness.

Three of them swam up to me and one of them kissed me. Yes, I kissed a girl, get over it. Did I like it? Not really. First of all, her breath tasted like fish guts. And her human bits were covered in a kind of slimy grease, like her sweat was made of margarine or something. But she was putting oxygen into my lungs, so I wasn't about to complain, you know?

The other two untangled me from the backpack and then undid my corset and dress, pulling me out of it, stripping me right down to my thin cotton chemise and bloomers. Finally able to swim, I started for the surface. The mermaids followed me up.

I broke through the surface and gasped, gulping in huge amounts of air, coughing up water, incredibly grateful to be alive. The mermaids surfaced and chattered at me in their dolphin-like mermaid language. I smiled and coughed and smiled and nodded and coughed some more, thanking them.

Why did they save me? Well, fishermen are constantly catching young mermaids (and mermen, I guess they must exist too, though I've never seen one and no one I ever talked to knew anything about them). Catching them in their nets and hauling them in, you know? Before they're old enough to know that the fish caught in the nets aren't just a free lunch. So the fishermen of Libertia have a kind of deal with the mermaid, throwing back any mermaids they caught. In return the mermaids help out anyone who managed to fall overboard.

Anyhow, they stayed with me as I swam for the nearest dock. I think they were amused with my feeble dog-paddle. I've never been much of a swimmer. I reached the dock, hauled myself up the ladder, waved goodbye and thanks again to the mermaids. Then I lay down and passed out.

Not for long, though. Fires still raged in town when I came out of it. Airships dotted the night sky, lit from below by the town's fires. Once in a while a volley of cannon fire would blast from one or another of the airships, trying to shoot down the Atlan warship.

With the smoke from the cannons and the smoke from the fires, it was hard to make out our attacker. I had glimpses of a long metallic cylinder, gleaming gold and red from all the fires. It didn't have a ship hanging from rigging suspended beneath it. Instead, it seemed to have the ship's cabins built directly into the balloon framework. A golden trident was painted onto its tail fin, the Atlan insignia.

Then the sky was blotted out by two dark silhouettes. Man-shaped silhouettes. Air commando-shaped silhouettes. Dripping wet air commando-shaped silhouettes.

One of them grabbed me, hauling me to my feet, holding my arms behind me. The other, a woman, slapped my face, hard. Any dazed confusion I might have had left over from the flight and the fall and the drowning and the rest disappeared, replaced with red-hot rage.

The woman hauled back to backhand me and I jumped up and planted both feet in her gut, kicking her as hard as I could. Unexpectedly forced to lift my entire weight, the one behind me stumbled forward. He let go of my arms to stop himself from landing on me. I wrapped my legs around his neck and heaved, pulling him off balance.

Yes, Tring taught me these moves. She'd sworn never to teach a non-Zhou anything about the Open Hand but I had bugged her until she'd agreed that I needed to know some basic self-defence if I was going to stay alive in Libertia.

I kicked at his face and throat, hoping that my three inches of heel would find something soft and vulnerable to make him think twice about getting up, then I got to my feet and started to run just in time for the woman to tackle me. She punched me, hard enough to make me see stars. I grabbed at her aviator cap, raking at her goggles with my clawed fingers, hoping to dislodge her headgear long enough to get her off me.

It worked. I pulled at the goggles with my left hand and they moved just enough that she didn't see my right hook until it caught her square in the jaw. Problem was, I didn't have much leverage and it didn't have much force. What it did do, though, was make her let go of me long enough for me to step back and make a break for it while she adjusted her headgear.

I ran. Hard and fast as I could. Legs pistoning, lungs sucking in air. I didn't look behind me. I was dripping wet, bleeding from somewhere, filthy from rolling around on the dock, wearing only a chemise, bloomers and my ankle boots. My elegant hair was a wreck. Half of the city was on fire. High above, the Atlan warship was busy blowing pirates out of the sky. I had no idea if my ship or my crew were alright. It was a complete nightmare.

I didn't slow down when I left the docks for the cobbled streets of the burning city. Over the crackling roar of burning buildings, the whines and whinnies of wounded animals, the alarms of amateur fire-fighters, the bonging of bells, the clamorous cannons of the airships above, over all that chaos and confusion, I was convinced I could hear the hard soles of my hated attackers. Yeah, still with the alliteration, I know.

When I turned a corner that I knew would lead me into town, toward the Docking Tower, I risked a glance back, and wished I hadn't.

They were barely twenty feet behind me. I doubled my speed, tripled it, convinced that at some point they would have to stop, have to give up the chase. Right about then I was pretty close to panic. My legs were made of lead, my head dizzy, my lungs burned. My sides ached with cramps. Tears streamed down my face, streaking the filth there. Burning wreckage from a downed airship blocked the road. I ran out of options, and darted into the nearest open door I could find.

The room was filled with women. Most were in various stages of undress, covered in soot and ash. They were tossing buckets of water onto everything they could find, even themselves. A line of them were handling full buckets of water out of a back room and up a circular staircase.

I fell to the ground, utterly spent. I didn't have anything left in me. The Atlan air commandos were going to kill me, and I didn't have the strength to even beg for help.

The pair of them charged into the room, black-clad death desperate for the kill. I panted in exhaustion as one of the women – a pleasure girl, I finally realized, I'd run into a pleasure house – knelt to help me.

A buxom redhead dressed in a red three-quarter coat, black gartered stockings and six inch heels stepped up to the commandos. "What's this then? Not enough you torch the town?" she yelled at them, hands on hips. Her Atlan was coarse but understandable.

"Stay out of this, mistress," the male commando said. "We just want the girl."

The lady got right into his face. "Mistress?! I'm a madam, and I'll thank you to remember it! Madam Helen de Lainzy, bucko!"

The male commando raised a fist to punch her and stopped at the heavy metallic *ch-chunk!* sound of rifles being primed. He looked up.

I looked around. Half a dozen women in their underwear had rifles aimed at him.

The female commando said, "We just want the girl."

Suddenly a dozen pleasure girls were standing between me and the commandos. "Which one?" someone asked.

"The soaking wet filthy one," the male commando said. "In her underthings."

The pleasure girls laughed. The only women in the room who weren't soaking wet, filthy, and stripped down to their underthings were Madam Helen and the female commando.

"Ya'll have ta be more specific," one of girls said.

"Could be he wants all'a us," another laughed, to the general amusement of everyone but the commandos.

"Dunno if'n he could take us all," a third joked, to more laughter.

The female commando put a hand on her partner's arm, shook her head, and left. He waited a moment longer, spit on the floor, then followed her out.

The girls with the rifles went to stand near the front door while the rest of the girls returned to their bucket brigade. Madam Helen came over to me.

"A lot of trouble for such a little thing as you," she said in Anglic.

"Yeah, tell me about it," I said, then I seriously passed out hard.

Chapter Ten

She Ain't No Lady

I woke up in a bed that smelled like roses and charcoal, probably the softest bed I've ever slept in. Someone had cleaned me up, bandaged my cuts and scrapes, and even combed my hair. Also they'd taken my soaking wet clothes away and left me a simple cotton dress hanging on the back of a chair, the only other furniture in the room.

Through the window slats I could see an orange sun hanging low in the sky over the bay, which meant it was just past dawn. Distantly, across the psychic connection, I felt Serena's sudden wave of relief, one I answered. Serena was alive and out there somewhere. How she felt me through the slumber I don't know.

I got dressed and opened the window. I soon realized that the room wasn't the only place that smelled like charcoal. Smoke hung in the air. What little wind there was coming from inland did little to clear away the smell of a town that still burned. I looked up and down the street. In one direction lay the wreckage of that downed airship, the one that had blocked my way, its fires spent. In the other direction were bodies of animals and people. The smell of death was everywhere.

Out in the bay, I saw the Atlan warship. Somehow it had been shot down. Ships floated all around it, moored and anchored to it. People moved along the wreckage, scavengers picking over their prey.

I closed the window and shut the slats, horrified but somehow numb. One airship had caused all this death and destruction. No wonder Captain Tempest had been in such a hurry to leave.

The bedroom door opened and an Afric girl dressed in a bright orange blouse and brown pants stepped into the room. "Oh, you're up," she said in Atlan. "Good. Madam Helen wants to see you."

"Um, okay," I answered, following her out.

She led me down tastefully-decorated corridors. Only some of the paintings and pictoriographs were even remotely risqué. Most of the pictoriographs were of Madam Helen in a variety of outfits.

The girl, who couldn't have been more than nineteen or twenty, led me to a room with an elegant desk and two chairs. A bookcase stood behind the desk, a small sideboard along the wall. Seeing the bottles of liquor reminded my body that I hadn't had anything but seawater to drink in hours.

I went to the sideboard and tried to see if there was anything non-alcoholic. Everything definitely was.

"Not too early, then?" Madam Helen asked in Anglic, entering the room and seeing me at the sideboard.

"No, it definitely is," I said. "For me, anyway."

"Sit down, sister," Madam Helen said, sitting down herself. "These heels are killing me. Gem!"

I sat down. The Afric girl popped her head through the door. "Yes, Madam?"

Madam Helen stuck out her booted foot. "Come boot-jack for me, will you?"

As Gem came over to help with the boots, Madam Helen asked me, "So what's your story, sister?"

"My story?"

"Why's a pretty girl like yourself getting chased by a couple of Deathwing Guard?" She gave a little moan of pleasure as Gem got the first boot off.

"Deathwing Guard? Is that who they were? I don't even know what that means."

"Means powerful trouble for you," she answered. Pulling out a thin cigarillo from a case in the desk, she offered me one. I shook my head. "Very elite Atlan special forces. Special training, blood oaths. One of their most sacred oaths is if any of them are killed, they will find the killer and have their revenge."

I rolled my eyes. "So that's why they were chasing me."

Gem got off the second boot. Madam Helen sighed with relief. "Thanks, Gem. Take those to my room, please?" She gave Gem an appreciative look. "And... wait for me there."

Gem grinned. "Okay," she said enthusiastically, then carried the boots out of the room.

Madam Helen got out of her chair and went to the sideboard. I was surprised to see how short she actually was, shorter even than me.

Somehow it made her impressive figure even more so.

She lit her cigarillo with a match from the sideboard, then poured herself a drink of something honey-coloured. "So you killed one? Accident, was it?"

"Well, um, no, actually," I answered. "There were the five on the Docking Tower, then three more chased me across town and over the bay... I guess the bomb must have taken one of them out, and the last two chased me here."

"Six?!" Madam Helen stared at me, her blue eyes wide, stunned. "You killed six Deathwings?"

"My first mate and I did, yeah."

She looked impressed, smiling at me. "Who are you, again?"

"Sunset Val. Captain of The Furies."

"Oh, right," she nodded. "That all-women crew."

It was my turn to be surprised. "You've heard of me?"

"Whole town has," she said, sitting down again. She took a long pull of her drink. "Whole crew of women, people will talk. Especially when the captain's a wee thing like you."

"We've got smaller girls aboard," I said, crossing my arms.

"Sure you have," she agreed. "But none of 'em's captain, are they?"

"What's my size got to do with anything, anyway?"

"Size and age, sister. Is it true you keep a vampyri as a pet?"

"Serena's not my pet, she's my first mate."

Madam Helen laughed. "Very nice. Well done."

"Um, thanks? Listen, I've got to get back to my ship."

She put the cigarillo between her teeth. "Well, as to that, there is the small matter of payment."

I looked at the thin dress I was wearing. "I'll send someone with money. How much for the dress?"

"Not just the clothes, sister. Last night's lodgings. Protection. Medical treatment. It adds up," she said, blowing out smoke, spreading her hands in a what-can-you-do, I'm-just-a-businesswoman gesture.

"Okay, how much?"

"Oh, call it two sovereigns."

Two month's salary for an elevator operator seemed a bit steep to me, but I wasn't exactly in a position to argue. "Like I said, I'll send someone with money."

"Now what kind of businesswoman would I be if I just let johns walk out the door on credit?" Madam Helen said. "No, I was thinking maybe you'd work it off."

Chapter Eleven

Back to The Furies

A long pause followed her words. My mind was a complete blank. How do you answer something like that?

Madam Helen's face was an unreadable mask of expectation. Then, to my utter and infinite relief, she cracked up. "You should see your face!" she laughed, slapping the desk between us.

I laughed too, though I didn't consider it all that frickin' funny. Some joke.

"None of my girls work against their will," she said, wiping away a tear. Her nails, I noticed, were extremely well-kept, cleaned, polished, and lacquered. "Nor against debt. Too many houses keep their girls by getting them indebted to the manager. Not me."

"Great," I said, not really sure what to say. "So I'll just go find my ship and send you some money, then."

"I'll send along a couple of my girls to help you search for your ship," she said. "And help you keep an eye out for any more Deathwing Guards. You killed six of their number, they'll be wanting your head mounted on their wall."

I stood and reached out a hand. She shook it. "Why are you being so nice to me?" I asked.

She settled back into her chair, feet up on her desk. "You owe me two sovereigns. And Madam Helen's House is a safe place for women. No one roughs anyone up in my house. Especially not two Atlan bastards come to burn my town."

"Fair enough. Thanks, Madam Helen."

She raised her glass and downed the rest in one shot, then saluted me with the empty glass. "You're welcome, Captain. Be seeing you."

I left her office and found two women waiting for me, a tall blonde Europan and an even taller Afric. Both looked muscular enough to be professional athletes, but I got the impression their sinewy curves weren't the result of working the night shift at Madam Helen's. When they moved to lead the way out, they moved more like Serena. Like jungle cats on the prowl.

"Where was your ship?" the Europan asked in passable Atlan.

"Repair Hangar," I answered.

We stepped out into the street. Survivors of the night's attack were picking through the rubble of what had been houses, shops, homes. Smoke drifted from burnt buildings. Everyone moved like they were dazed. Everyone was filthy, covered in soot and ash. I felt somehow guilty for being clean and wearing a new dress. Well, new to me, at least.

My guides fell into step to either side of me. I never did get their names, but from the catlike way they moved I thought of them as Liona and Panthra. It would be fun to see how they stood up against a real cat animan like Gigi.

Liona led the way whenever we reached a place that we could walk side by side. I noticed that her and Panthra's eyes never stopped to look in one place for very long. I guess the threat of the Deathwings coming back kept them on their toes. I found myself copying their behaviour, trying to see every direction at once.

Then we came to a sight I wished I'd never seen, wished I could scrub from my eyes.

The Repair Hangar was destroyed. The Docking Tower seemed to be okay. Well, ships were berthed all along it, at least. But the Repair Hangar was just a burnt-out shell, metal support beams corkscrewing into the sky like ribs of some slaughtered beast. Inside those ribs, like great charred organs, lay the remains of ships.

I couldn't extend the analogy for the blackened bodies of the unfortunate souls trapped inside the Hangar.

It took me a minute to get my bearings. A pair of steel support beams, bent and blackened, must have been the great door frame. That meant that The Furies would have been...

My eyes followed what remained of the catwalks and supports, trying to sort out where my ship might have been. We walked carefully through the ruined Hangar. Pieces of the catwalks croaked and groaned as their supports gave way, twisted and warped by the intense heat of the burning building, the burning ships, and all that burning gas.

I reached up to place a hand over my mouth and nose, to try and block some of the stink, and surprised myself. My face was wet with tears. I hadn't even realized I'd been crying.

Off in the corner furthest from where the hangar doors had once stood overhead, that was where The Furies had been berthed. The ceiling hadn't entirely collapsed there, making a kind of shelter from its corrugated metal. Maybe The Furies had weathered the firestorm in the lee of the …

No. Nothing could survive the heat. Everything was still hot, and the fires had been put out hours ago. The superheated air would have been sucked from their lungs, broiling them from the inside out.

I sank to my knees, not wanting to go any further. I couldn't stand the idea that my crew had died here. I couldn't begin to imagine sorting through all the blackened rubble, trying to figure out who was who. I couldn't.

Then I was tackled from behind.

Chapter Twelve

A Happy Reunion

Some bodyguards, I tell you. Liona and Panthra didn't even see my attacker in time to prevent me from sprawling face-first into the ash and soot. They did, however, pull the attacker off of me. Not much comfort in that, really. If Restless had had a knife and wanted to kill me, I would have been dead.

When I turned and saw her, I burst into fresh tears, leaping forward to grab her out of Liona's grip, pulling her into a fierce hug. Restless hugged me back, hard enough to hurt, each of us babbling out our joy at seeing the other.

"Where's the ship?" I asked, when we'd both calmed down enough and wiped away tears and snot. Restless was an incredibly messy crier.

"Out in the harbour, Cap," she answered, hooking a thumb over one shoulder. "Couldn't buy a berth on the Docking Tower for love or money. And after what we done, too."

I got to my feet, heading out of the burnt shell of the Repair Hangar as fast as I could. "Done? What happened?" The ship was alright. My crew were alive.

"Well, Miss Heartlace come on board on them mechanical bat wings, telling us to batten down and prep for lift off," Restless said, jogging to keep up. "We barely got out at all, everyone crowding to get out the bay doors in the ceiling, like. So Molly takes the wheel from Argenta and steers us under 'em all." She demonstrated the manoeuvre with her hands. "And BOOM! Inga blows the doors clear off the hinges. Others started following us out, and good thing they did. Every last ship trying to get out the ceiling doors got caught in the blast from when that ship fell on the Hangar from the Tower. Whole Hangar went up, then. We was already high up, high enough to see what was happening.

"Then we seen the warship, right? And Miss Heartlace is out for blood. Well, you know what I mean. She wants them dead. She orders all cannons at the ready. I'm running back and forth to the gun deck with orders, so I know what happened. Miss Heartlace orders Inga to aim for the balloon. Inga tells her, a blast that big will destroy the whole city. Lead her out to the bay. Miss Heartlace, she's plenty smart. She orders shots across the bow. Try and take out the wheelhouse. Well, Inga likes that much better. The whole port side fires, not all at once, no! One at a time! With Inga on each cannon, giving the order to FIRE! FIRE! FIRE! One after the other, see? All at the same place! Our cannons take out the wheelhouse, shatter it into splinters and kindling!

"So now we got the warship's attention. It starts after us, all guns firing, firing, firing. We get boarded by these black-clad bastards, begging your pardon Captain, all with bat wings! Well, Lady Tring, she ain't having none of that, is she? No ma'am. She and her Open Hands take out half of 'em, and the rest of us get in our licks. Miss Heartlace was something fierce to watch, I tell you. Like she was gone in the head, you know? Not one of 'em bastards, sorry Captain, survived."

"How many?" I asked.

"Two dozen, near enough," Restless answered. "Now we've got ourselves a fair number of them bat wings they use."

"No, I mean, how many did we lose?" I didn't want the answer. A captain needs to know, though.

"Hardly a one! I swear, that Dr. Westmore, she's something else! A true healer she was! Three girls lost arms, one a leg. Plenty of scars to go around, too."

"How many dead, Restless?"

She looked away, like she didn't want to answer. "Two, Captain."

Two dead. Four maimed. More wounded. But somehow that was a relief. It could have been so much worse. When we'd been slaves and revolted, we lost a lot more than that.

"What happened with the warship?" Liona asked, curiosity overtaking her natural lack of conversation.

"Oh, well, they're coming after us and Molly is dodging cannon fire like it weren't nothing to worry about. Never saw anyone so calm in a fight. She's giving orders to the engineers and Miss Gigi's doing everything she can just to keep up. Anyhow, Molly leads the warship out over the bay. Other ships start noticing what's going on and join in. Miss Violette, the new navigator? She's sending flashes to the other ships, telling them not to fire on the balloon over the town. Some of 'em weren't listening too good, though. So Moonchance and her pixies fly all over everywhere, getting the other captains to listen.

"Then just like that we're over the bay and Miss Heartlace gives the order, FIRE AT WILL! Inga just lets loose as fast as she can, her crews loading and firing, loading and firing, loading and firing! So all that training was good for something I guess."

I laughed. Inga had put her gun crews to work the day I'd hired her.

We were nearly at the bay and I could see the results of the night's handiwork. Ships still floated all around it, people were still picking it over for whatever salvage they could find, but I only had eyes for one thing – The Furies. I couldn't see it anywhere.

"Where, Restless?"

Restless grinned and pointed.

I'd been looking in the sky, even though she'd told me The Furies was berthed in the water. Or rather, by the water; she wasn't built to get her hull wet. The sight of her brought fresh tears to my eyes, just when I was about sure I'd used them all up.

I ran the length of the waterfront, trying to get to the pier where she was tied up. Finally on the pier, I couldn't hold myself back, even if I'd wanted to. I forced Liona and Panthra and Restless to run to keep up. My ship. My crew.

I swear I hugged everyone at least twice. Not a single person on the crew was without bandages of some kind. Everyone had something to say, everyone babbling at the same time. I got Mrs. Shorty to pay my protectors and give them a little extra for their efforts. She looked shocked when I told her who they were and what I was paying for. A night's lodging at a pleasure house while the rest of the crew had been in the firefight of their lives? I promised them all the whole story as soon as I could. First I needed to find Serena.

Chapter Thirteen

More Than One Surprise

Just off of the wheelhouse was a small room, barely bigger than a walk-in closet. Mostly filled with maps, which was why we called it the map room. That's where I found Serena.

She looked exhausted. A huge tankard filled with blood was gripped in one hand. A piece of tarp had been nailed up, covering the porthole window.

"How come you're up?" I asked.

"Velcome back, Captain," she answered wearily, yawning. "I can put off the slumber vith enough blood, for a vhile. Not something that I enjoy doing, you understand. Vith your permission I vill return to my quarters, and leave the ship in your hands."

"You're crazy. You could have left command with Molly or Miss Merryweather."

"I needed to see you back aboard," she answered, smiling. She stood, leaning against the wall for support. "Ve vill talk vhen I vake."

I helped Serena to her quarters, making sure to avoid the few beams of sunlight that pierced through to the main corridor of the crew deck. Not that there was a lot of sunlight; outside, the sky was still cloudy with smoke. Ash drifted down from the sky like grey snow.

I went to my cabin and changed into my own clothes. Domina picked out a tight pair of black pants, a crimson shirt and black leather corset to go over top. I pulled my hair back into my customary pigtails.

Then I went down to the surgeon's quarters. I found Dr. Westmore and her nurses covered in blood, none of it theirs. I mean, literally. Their aprons were once white; now they were dark red.

Women crowded the small room, sitting quietly on the floor. Some of them were sleeping. All of them were wounded, some very badly. Blood soaked bandages were piled high in a bucket. As I watched, Angel took the bucket out of the room. I had to step out into the corridor to let her pass.

"Help ye, Captain?" the Doc asked. She didn't look up from the slash in one girl's thigh she was sewing up.

"I was about to ask you the same thing," I said. "Is there anything you need?"

"Another set of hands, eight more hours in the day, a proper hospital to work in, and a cup of tea would be nice," she answered, glancing up at me. Behind her spectacles and the dark circles under her eyes, I could see she wasn't upset. She was … not quite enjoying this. In her element, I guess.

"I can get you the cup of tea," I answered, smiling at her. She not-quite-smiled back. "Can we put some of these girls back in their quarters, free you up some space?"

"Aye, that y'can," she nodded, then went back to work on the wounded girl. One of Tring's Open Hands. "Doc's taking good care of you, Li?"

"Yes, Captain."

"You'll be fine," I said to her.

One by one, I helped the girls back to their beds. Some of them could walk. Others waited while I got Domina to help me. Padmini found us and went off for more help. The amputees needed to stay in the surgeon's quarters so Doc Westmore could keep an eye on them for infection or fever. We converted the quarters closest to the surgeon's into a sick ward. The nine bunks filled up quick, so we threw some mats down on the floor for the rest. It took a couple of hours but soon the surgeon's quarters were empty of wounded.

Doc Westmore dismissed Mary and Angel, telling them to get food, a shower and some rest. Only once they'd left did she sit down with a moan. She removed her spectacles and rubbed the bridge of her nose.

"Little more than any of us bargained for," I told her. She chuckled.

The tea had gone cold so I stepped out into the corridor and sent Padmini for a fresh pot. Then I went back inside the surgeon's quarters. My sense of smell had died a long time ago. I wondered how Serena could stand it, all this blood, without going crazy. I sat next to the Doc, who had shaken her long black hair out of its bun. It made her look even more tired.

"I don't know how to thank you enough," I said. "You saved a lot of lives today."

"Sure an' I lost two, though," she answered.

"You saved more," I argued. "That's what counts."

She nodded, an odd expression on her face, like she wanted to believe me but couldn't – or wouldn't – let herself. She reached over to a small drawer and pulled out a silver flask. I watched her unscrew the cap and raise it in salute. "Yer very good health, Captain," she toasted, and took a sip. Then she passed it to me.

I raised it to her. "And yours," I answered, sipping. Eire whisky burned its way down my throat. I coughed a little. She snickered and took the flask back, capping it and replacing it in the drawer.

"Listen... Regan," I said. "This... What happened last night. I know it's more, much more than you signed on for. It's more than I signed on for. I never expected anything like this. So if you want, you can consider your debt to me paid."

She went very still, her face a mask that would make any six-card player proud. After a long pause, she answered. "That's very generous of ye, Captain."

"Yeah, well, you saved the lives of my crew, that puts me in a generous mood."

"And as much as I'd love to take ye up on it, I've patients need doctorin'."

"Yeah, but, I mean, Mary and Angel can handle them from here, right?"

"Mary and Angel are good girls, but I doubt they've two years of actual medical trainin' between 'em."

"What? They said they went to the University of Albion!"

"Sure an' I'll wager they did. Probably even in the medical school. But graduate? I'm doubtin' it."

"Great." I shook my head. I'm sure they had their reasons for lying to me. I'd have to remember to ask them about it later. Then it sunk in. "Wait, you mean you're staying?"

"That I am, an' against my better judgement, too," she said, standing up wearily. "If ye'll pardon me, Captain, I'll be takin' my leave and gettin' some sleep. If you see Padmini or Miss Merryweather tell 'em someone needs to be watchin' th' wounded, and t' wake me if there's any change in any of 'em at all."

I stood up too. She took off her blood-soaked apron and tossed it in the replacement bucket one of her nurses had put in the corner of the room. Even so, her dress was ruined with blood, too. At least it was black, the stains would barely show.

She didn't have far to go, what with her personal quarters right next door.

"Hey Doc," I called after her. "Thanks."

She waved a tired hand over one shoulder, then went into her room.

A couple of women were washing down the corridor already, scrubbing the planks with heavy square stones and water laced with lye. The bloodstains on the deck would be worked out, eventually. I wasn't sure if the stones would work on my conscience.

Chapter Fourteen

Go Time, or Time to Go?

We held a simple burial at sea just after sunset. Three women in total died. Two during the attack, and Suzanna. The patchwork's punch had done too much damage to her brain, Doc Regan explained sadly. Suzanna had died while the doctor was asleep, and I think Doc blamed herself. But with so many wounded to watch, no one noticed Suzanna had stopped breathing.

I didn't blame Doc Regan. I blamed the patchwork. He'd killed one of my crew. He'd tried to kill me. Serena hadn't found him, but I would. Then he'd pay.

For a brief moment, I understood the Deathwing Guard, and their vow of vengeance.

No prayers were said, though most of the crew broke into reluctant song. I'd learned enough Atlan to understand the hymn they sang. The words basically said, life is a mystery, death is a mystery, we'll figure it all out eventually. Science will triumph, blah blah blah. Not exactly comforting, but better than nothing, I guess.

My parents hadn't raised me to be very religious. Vaguely Christian, in a general sense. I mean, we celebrated Christmas and Easter and Thanksgiving. But we never went to church or anything. But on Ayrth, they didn't even have the option of not going to church. There weren't any churches to not go to. I think I'd rather have the option of not really believing in something, rather than really have nothing to believe in. Except science, of course. Like I said, I guess that was better than nothing.

No one said anything. The bodies were dropped off the flight deck. I forced myself to watch them fall all the way, watch the tiny splashes as they hit. My tears weren't the only ones shed.

I invited the crew chiefs to my cabin. We sat around the long table I had. Serena sat to my right, looking exhausted and hung over. All the blood she'd had to drink to stay awake, countering the slumber, had taken its toll. Next to her was Molly, our self-appointed chief pilot.

Violette Verdigris, our new navigator,was a tall brunette with an hourglass figure and a fondness for jewellery. She held her back straight and head high, a kind of nobility about her that somehow didn't come off as arrogant. "Wine, anyone?" she asked, heading for my sideboard. I kept a couple of bottles there, even though I didn't drink myself, and everyone knew they were welcome to it. Domina joined her there and started pouring glasses of wine, handing Violette the first.

Miss Merryweather and Mrs. Shorty had become good friends, sitting together opposite Serena and Molly. Then poor Brunhilde, who always seemed so out of place at these meetings. It would have been funny, watching such a big woman try to make herself as small as possible, if it didn't make you feel sorry for her first. But as Chief Cook she needed to know what the business of the ship was going to be, and that meant she had to be at these meetings.

I'd started hosting the meetings when it became clear that rumours were taking the place of actual communication. Also, I got tired of answering the same question from four or five different women all the time. This way, all the crew chiefs could find out at the same time what was going on, and they could tell their crews what their crews needed to know. It worked out surprisingly well.

Inga sat next to Brunhilde, somehow looking even more out of place. She was wearing a leather vest that showcased her heavily muscled arms, and her pale hair was still in twin braids from the night's action.

Domina brought me a glass of watered-down wine as the three pixies pushed and shoved for place on one chair. I would have thought our rigger and sailmaker would report to our aeriologist, but apparently not. Finally Moonchance gave up trying to take the central place on the chair and fluttered up to sit cross-legged right on the table. Apple and Wren, realizing their view was blocked, joined her, sitting to either side. Domina handed them brass thimbles filled with mead.

Tring sat at the far end of the table, looking like she'd rather stand. Her arms were folded into the wide sleeves of her brilliantly white shirt. Gigi sat to her right, next to Inga; Doc Regan sat on her left, next to the pixies.

"Ladies," I said, raising my glass. I waited until they'd all raised theirs. "To our fallen friends. Suzanna, who died saving my life.

Adina, putting out a fire and swallowing too much smoke. Marika, by a Deathwing's knife. A high price to pay."

We drank our toast. The wine tasted bitter in my mouth.

"Now then," I said once everyone finished. Domina moved to refill any glasses that needed refilling. "Gigi, how's repairs?"

"We took some damage last night, nothing major," Gigi answered. "A couple of days at the most. And that internal communication system you asked about finally arrived, just before the attack came."

I nodded. "The intercom, right." We'd ordered it from an electrician in town who happened to have the parts and was more than happy to sell them to us, but he had to find them in his massive pile of spare bits and pieces of electrical systems he'd pulled out of derelict ships and bought as salvage off of other pirates. No one seemed to see the value of such a thing. Not having to have a runner carrying orders back and forth through an airship seemed like a no-brainer to me. Even Gigi, who normally loved gadgets, seemed sceptical. "Wheelhouse to engine room first, please."

Gigi nodded. "After the repairs?"

"Yeah. You'll get whatever help you need from anyone on shift. Not sure where we'll be able to work, with the Repair Hangar wrecked."

"Are we staying?" Violette asked, surprised.

"Why not?"

She shrugged, looking at the rest of the women. "I assumed we would be taking off, running from the Atlan forces. Last night's attack was most likely a training exercise for their newest recruits. It's standard procedure for Atlan Aerial."

"What, attack some defenceless folks ain't done no one no 'arm?" Moonchance asked, indignant. She was rolling herself a tiny cigarette out of a scrap of paper and two or three shreds of tobacco. I caught Domina's eye and looked at the window. She read my mind and went to open it.

"Attacking known enemies of the Atlan Empire," Violette corrected. "Merinasy holds a special place in the Atlan world view. It's not worth conquering, so they leave it be. Libertia is a known pirate haven, though. Pirates who prey on Atlan shipping lanes, Atlan merchant ships, and forgive me Captain, Atlan slavers. Hence, known enemies of Atlan. The Merinasy government turns a blind eye to our existence so long as we don't cause any trouble and handle our matters internally. In deference to that, most pirates leave Merinasy ships alone. It's a handy little arrangement that benefits both sides. But the Atlan forces have no reason to respect that arrangement."

"And should ve attract trouble, the Merinasy vill not feel obliged to protect us," Serena added.

"Already there have been signs of resistance to our presence," Mrs. Shorty said. "I saw just this afternoon a riot nearly break out. Pirate crews were trying to collect the stores they'd bought from the merchants here. Food, mainly. The merchants wouldn't let them have it, returning their money. Merchants! Returning money! Unheard of. And yet, I saw it with my own eyes."

"Why would they do that?" Molly asked, tapping her metal fingers one after the other against the table. Anyone else, I would have suspected rude impatience, but I knew she was just practising her fine motor control.

"To resell it to the townsfolk at higher prices," Mrs. Shorty said with a shrug, as if it were obvious. "People will be hoarding their food, not sure when or if another attack will come."

"Oh, it'll come," I said. "Those Deathwings aren't going to take so many losses lying down. Even if they were recruits."

"All the more reason to take to the skies," Violette said. "Why stay? Surely there are other ports where we can make repairs."

She had a point. There wasn't anything really keeping us in Libertia. But something made me hesitate. It didn't seem right. We pirates had brought the attack to the town. Now that the attack was over, we were just going to leave? And not be here when the next attack came? That wasn't right, not at all.

"There are people here," I answered. "Townsfolk who live here. We brought the Atlan Aerial Forces down on them. They shouldn't have to pay for us."

"They've already paid," Miss Merryweather said calmly. "Nothing we do can change that."

"They shouldn't have to pay again," I corrected myself. "The next attack will come and they'll find the town deserted of pirates, who scattered like rats from a sinking ship. But the Atlans won't care. They'll pour their vengeance down on the town from up high, and all the merchants and pleasure girls and tavern keepers and everyone else we've met who lives in this town will die. Because there won't be anyone left to defend them."

"Can't they defend themselves?" Doc Regan asked. "Or ask Merinasy for help?"

"Libertia ain't nuffink t' 'em," Moonchance said, blowing out a tiny plume of smoke. "Ain't ya been list'nin'?"

"We cannot do it alone, Sunset," Gigi said. "The Furies doesn't have enough guns to take on a fully operational Atlan warship, run by seasoned veterans."

"Why do they even have warships?" I asked. "They conquered the world, didn't they? Who's there left to fight?"

"The Zhou," Tring said quietly. "There are battles, though no open declaration of war. They are reported as mishaps, miscommunication. Unfortunate accidents. But the thrice-favoured Emperor of Zhou knows a war is coming, and sooner rather than later."

"Not just them," Violette added. "The Amazonia military is every bit as ready for war, and much closer to Atlan itself."

"And there are others," Serena said. "People who vould rise up, should the circumstances present themselves. People who vould attack, if they sensed veakness in Atlan. So, the ships. The training missions. And people die for Atlan glory."

"All the more reason to stand and fight them," I decided, and only realized that a decision had been made once I'd made it. "If there are so many countries ready to fight against Atlan, if only someone has the guts to lead the way, I say, bring it. They're just a big bully, pushing everybody around like they own the whole world."

"Wait, wait, wait," Violette said, waving her hands. "What are we saying here? Defending ourselves against attack is one thing, but violent revolution is something for, well, revolutionaries. We're pirates, remember?"

"No reason we can't be both," Miss Merryweather said. "It's high time someone stood up to the Empire."

"If we're to end the slave trade, it would stand to reason that we'd have to take out the main source of demand," Mrs. Shorty added. "No more demand, no more trade. Simple."

"This is... well, it's more than I signed on for," Violette said. "I thought we'd be trawling for slavers, sure, and maybe once in a while a fat merchant ship. Make some coin, have some fun, see the world. Overthrowing an empire is something entirely different."

Moonchance flew to the window and tossed her tiny cigarette into the bay. "How much coin y'think them scavengers out there're gonna make, sellin' off that military salvage?"

I could hear the *ch-ching!* in Mrs. Shorty's brain from where I sat. The military had all the best equipment, like those bat-winged backpacks. She'd already asked me if we could sell them, and I hadn't decided yet. I had an idea they might be useful, one day.

Violette thought about it, nodding reluctantly.

"Alright, then," I said, raising my right hand. "We'll put it to a vote, before we put it to the crew. All in favour of staying here and defending Libertia against the next attack?"

Gigi, Mrs. Shorty, Miss Merryweather and Serena all put up their hands. Moonchance, Wren and Apple stood up, each holding both hands raised. Brunhilde joined in after a couple of seconds.

"Gigi was right, Sunset," Molly said. "We can't do it alone. We need the other captains."

"Forgive me, Captain," Domina said. "I had thought to mention this after the meeting, but it seems pertinent to the discussion."

"What does, Domina?"

"A conclave has been called, tonight at midnight."

"What's a conclave?"

"A meeting of captains," Miss Merryweather explained.

"I only received the message as you were all headed here," Domina explained. "It's why I was late."

"Okay then," I said. "I go to this conclave, convince the other captains to stick around, we fight off the next attack we all know is coming, no problemo."

"You make it sound so easy," Serena said.

I looked around the table. Molly, Violette, Doc Regan and Inga hadn't voted for my plan. Technically they were outvoted, but I wanted everyone on board on this.

"Tactically unsound," Inga said suddenly, surprising us all. Gigi actually jumped. Inga's voice was pretty high for such a big, brawny woman. And loud. I guess that's to be expected from someone who spent all night on the gun deck. "Fly away is better. But if other captains agree, maybe we have chance. Next attack, not so lucky. But, better prepared? Ya, maybe."

"So your vote is...?"

Inga crossed her arms. "Get other captains to agree. Then I agree, too."

Molly nodded. "What she said."

Violette shrugged. "Alright then."

I looked across the table. "Doc?"

"I can't be in favour of more bloodshed, Captain," she answered, not looking me in the eye as she said it. "But I'll go wi' th' majority."

Chapter Fifteen

Arguments, Asses and Other Unpleasantness

The conclave was set to meet at midnight, in the great hall of the Docking Tower, which was actually underground, a huge circular room with stadium-style seating ringing around it. Overhead, a chandelier made of a ship's wheel glittered with electric lights. I took a seat; Serena sat to my left. I looked around, trying to see Captain Tempest, the only other pirate captain I'd met.

I wasn't the only one who'd brought their first mate. Or at least, I assumed so. There were a lot of people in the room, anyway, more than the number of airships docked at the tower and in the bay combined. I guessed the number of people at somewhere around sixty or seventy. Maybe some of those folks were from the town, but I doubted it. From what Serena told me, conclaves were pirates-only business.

A tall lanky man in an awesome green-and-gold three-quarter coat strode in, black leather knee-high boots ringing out loudly against the polished wood floor with each step, even over the murmur of people's voices. He was missing one eye. The replacement was something like Molly's, a glass lens set in a brass casing, mounted directly into the socket. He had wavy ginger hair and wore a ginger goatee. I guessed his age to be about forty or so, which was pretty old for the pirate profession.

When he spoke, his voice was as rough as a hurricane, in accented Atlan. "Sit down, sit down, let's get this started!"

"You called this conclave?" a brunette in a green dress and tricorn cap asked.

"I did," he answered, moving to the centre of the room. "Maybe there's some of you's don't know me. Captain Farthing Lawless, of the Highwayman. I called this conclave to talk about last night."

"Didn't think you'd called it to talk about the weather!" a fat, bearded man in black called out. People laughed.

I didn't. I was so nervous I could barely keep still. Serena kept having to stop my knee from jerking up and down. I'd never liked public speaking. I mean, I was good at it, sure, but that didn't mean I liked it. And I had to convince all these people to stand and fight when I was sure most of them would rather run. And it looked like I was the youngest person here.

It was weird, me giving orders to women who were so much older than me. Mrs. Shorty, Brunhilde and Miss Merryweather were older than my mother, but they took my orders just like Padmini and Restless did. Doc Regan and Violette were in their late twenties, trained professionals, and they followed my orders just the same. It amazed me just about every time I gave an order and someone actually followed it.

But this was different. I hadn't saved any of these pirate captains from a lifetime of slavery in some Atlan manufactory or pleasure house. They had no reason to listen to me.

Serena's hand rested on my knee again. "Be calm," she said. "It vill be alright."

I smiled at her, but there wasn't much joy in the smile. "Sure hope you're right."

"Last night's attack was the beginning of something," Captain Lawless said. "We all know it. We've been too long without a proper cut-up. They've let things get out of hand, and we've grown bold in the process. But no longer! An attack on Libertia is sure to be the sign of some greater assault."

An Afric man stood up, dressed in a riot of zigzagged colours. "Captain Jackal, of de Scirocco," he introduced himself. "What proof d'ye have? Could be jus' a trainin' mission."

"They don't send Deathwings on a training mission," Lawless answered. "We all saw them. One of Atlan Aerial's most feared battalions!"

I stood up. "We took them out easy. Too easy!"

Lawless looked over at me. "And you are?"

I felt blood rush to my face, burning. "Oh. Right. Captain Sunset Val, of The Furies."

"Why'd you say too easy, Captain?" he asked.

I took a deep breath, willing my heart to stop beating so damn hard. "My first mate and I killed five of the Deathwing Guard, prevented them from blowing up the Docking Tower. Three more chased me across the bay. One of them bought it in the waters, but his buddies chased me into a pleasure house. The girls there held them off, no problem. If the Deathwing Guard are so fierce, how could a bunch of pleasure girls fight them off?"

"It's true," a woman said, her Atlan heavily accented with the familiar tones of Anglic nobility. She had a monocle held in place, like an eyepatch, and wore a black top hat and red swallowtail coat. "Captain Tallyho, the Tallyho Sisters. I saw the fight from my own ship as we were casting off. The Deathwings were planting a bomb, don't you know. Beastly thing. Captain Val and her mate there snicker-snacked the blighted scallywags, lickety-split. Then off she goes with the bomb. Didn't see what happened next, sorry."

Serena stood up. "Serena Heartlace, First Mate of The Furies, requesting permission to address this conclave," she said formally. Since she wasn't a captain, she didn't have an inherent right to speak. Captain Lawless nodded and waved at her to continue. "Two against five are not such terrible odds vhen vun of those two is a swordmistress, as I am. But these Deathwings vere not so fierce as they might have been, had they been weterans. And their tactics are not in keeping with previous Deathwing attacks."

"She's right," the fat man said, not bothering to heave himself into standing. "Remarkable Jones, Captain of the Mistress o' Merit, for anyone who doesn't know me." There were chuckles at that. I guessed he was kind of famous, even though I'd never heard of him. Which actually wasn't saying much. "Deathwings come in stealth, at night, the sound of those batwing packs of theirs the only warning. Silent and deadly, killing with subtle accuracy. Targets chosen out beforehand, well planned, executed flawlessly. Last night was chaos, disorder, sowing the seeds of terror, eh? Why is that, d'you think?"

"To get us to scatter to the seven skies, is why. Captain Ali al Anniz, of the Scimitar," he said, kissing his fingertips and touching them to his chest. "Then they pick us off, one by one."

A strangely-dressed woman on the other side of the room stood. She was wrapped up, like a mummy, in scarves of various shades of green. Her face was hidden behind a gold mask of a woman's face. Her hair was the only part of her that wasn't hidden behind the scarves. It had been dyed shades of green, too, and dreadlocked, long enough to reach well past her waist. She didn't say anything, just waited to be recognized.

"Captain Python," Captain Lawless said, nodding his head to her in respect.

"Lemurisian," Serena whispered to me. "Snake lovers. Wery strange people."

"No kidding," I whispered back.

The Lemurisian captain put one hand on her companion's shoulder, a woman with her head shaved on one side. The other side's hair was long and braided. She wore a simple sleeveless dress of pale green with a scale pattern embroidered on it.

"My mistresss wisshess to exprresss herr concerrn that an Atlan invassion of Merrinassy would give them an ideal sstaging grround forr an attack on ourr beloved home," the woman said, her Atlan accented with odd esses and rolling arrs. "Ssuch a thing would incrreasse theirr powerr a hundrred-fold."

"Everyone knows the Lemurisian islands, may they know sun and rain in equal measure, are both rich and powerful," Captain al Anniz said. "But such a possibility is not the purpose of this conclave."

I stood up again. "Yes it is. We're all here to figure out if we stay or if we go, right? Isn't that what this is really about? If we go, then you're right, Captain, they will pick us off one by one. But if we stay, we make ourselves a target. That's what we're afraid of, isn't it?"

Rumbling filled the chamber; pirates didn't like being reminded they get scared too.

"See, here's the thing," I kept going. *Go time*, I thought. "If we leave, the hammer will still fall, and the people of Libertia will pay the price. But if we stay, we can organize and fight back!"

There was a lot of laughter this time. My cheeks burned red. I could feel Serena's back stiffen next to me, without even looking at her.

"Organize?" Captain Jones said. "This lot?"

"We organized last night," I answered. "Four other ships followed our lead, and together we shot down that warship. If we did that with just five of us, imagine what we could do with fifty!"

"Following who's lead, yours?!" a voice from my nightmares said. I turned to face it.

Tyr Ebonfury stepped down, out of the crowd, followed by Dr.

Enerva. He still looked as fearsome as ever, broad-shouldered and eyepatched. His single blue eye glared at me, filled with hate and rage. Enerva looked good, for someone who'd had her arm torn off. She'd found herself a new one, a graceful thing of gleaming brass. Her sneer was as hate-filled as Ebonfury's eye.

"I thought she was dead," I muttered to Serena.

Serena snorted. "She vill be, vhen Molly finds out she's here."

"Do you know who this little bitch is?" Ebonfury raged to the crowd, pointing at me. "Do you know what she's done?"

"Here we go," I said, shaking my head.

"This *slave*," and he put a lot of sneering contempt into the word, "rose up against her master, my captain, and killed him. Stole his ship. Calls herself a pirate? All she does is attack slavers! And now this backstabber wants to lead an assault on Atlan Aerial?"

"I never said anything about leading an assault!" I answered.

"What about de rest?" Captain Jackal asked.

Everyone looked at me, curious, eager, bloodthirsty, cold, calculating, indifferent. My throat was so dry I barely could swallow. I lifted my chin and looked around the room.

"Yes. It's true." If everything fell apart because of this, might as well come clean about it. "I was taken by a slaver. I led a revolt. I killed the captain and took his ship."

Murmurs. Some laughter.

"So that's who she is," Captain Lawless said to Ebonfury. "And who might you be?"

"Tyr Ebonfury, Captain of the Relentless," he said, still glaring at me.

"Alright then, Captain," Lawless said. "Seems you two have bad blood between you. So, what of it?"

Ebonfury turned to look at Lawless, stunned. "What are you talking about? She's a slave! One who overthrew her own master!"

"I 'overthrew' my own father to take my ship," Captain Jones laughed loudly. "Should have seen the look on his face!"

People laughed, but Ebonfury was like his ship, relentless. "She preys on other pirates! What's she up to this time? Get in good with Atlan Aerial by getting us all to agree to her insane plan, and lead us into a trap?"

"He's got a lot more faith in my charm than I do," I muttered to Serena.

"I say, this is all a little off topic, isn't it?" Captain Tallyho asked. "We still haven't heard from Captain Lawless as to why he called this conclave."

"Take a seat, Captain," Lawless said to Ebonfury. "Captain Tallyho is right."

"But!"

Lawless cut him off. "We'll address it in a moment. Captain."

Ebonfury and Enerva took a seat opposite the chamber from us, glaring the whole time. I was beginning to wonder if he could do anything else with that one good eye of his.

"I called the conclave to suggest that we leave Libertia off limits for the next year, to keep Atlan attention away from it, but it seems that's a moot point. Now the question seems to be, do we stay and fight, or cut and run? Since we seem to be assuming Atlan's heading back for more blood."

"How long before that warship's declared overdue?" Captain Jones asked.

Captain Jackal stood. "Axum is de nearest Atlan Airbase. Two days for any survivors to get back dere. Dey'd send a corvette scout down to find out what happened to dere warship. Dat's a day trip for one of dem. Fast bast'ds. Den dey mobilize, maybe a day. T'ree days to get down here and pummel us into de ground."

"Assuming they don't already know and aren't already on their way," Ebonfury said.

"And how dey do dat, Capt'n?"

"A traitor among us," he said, still glaring at me. "Someone who makes a living from the blood of honest pirates."

"Not all slavers are pirates, and not all pirates are slavers," Lawless said. From the way he said it, I got the impression he was getting fed up of Ebonfury. A glance around the room told me Lawless wasn't the only one. "Still, if this supposed traitor managed to send off a corvette to get a message back to the base at Axum, we'd have three days. If not, we have a week."

It still amazed me that on a planet with engineering advanced enough to mass produce fleets of airships, a world where genetic engineering could produce animal-human hybrids with casual ease, a place where sentient robots were so common they were used as domestic help, that in such a place of everyday miracles and feats of mechanical wonder, no one had yet invented the radio or the telephone. No one had even invented the telegraph! You could get small intercom systems, like the one we'd installed on The Furies at my insistence, but no one had tried to use it on a massive scale. I couldn't figure that out. I'd have to remember to talk to Gigi about it.

Captain Tallyho stood. "It seems to me, chaps, that if we vote to stay and fight, in three days we'll know if there's a traitor amongst us. If no attack falls then, well, we'll have all that much more time to lay our trap, wot?"

"Lay a trap, split the booty," Captain Jones said. "All that military machinery, fit into our own ships. Can't say I'd object to that."

"It would make us quite a force to be reckoned with," Captain al Anniz agreed, and I could see a lot of other captains imagining their share of the spoils.

"Call de vote, Capt'n Lawless," Captain Jackal said. "Any more talk about dis is a waste o' time."

Chapter Sixteen

An Attack Earns Me Allies

"I can't believe it!"

Serena grunted. It wasn't a pleased sound.

Almost a third of the captains had voted to run. A third. That meant only twenty-eight ships remained to face whatever Atlan Aerial was about to throw at us.

"I mean, can you believe it?" I asked Serena. We were walking down to the docks. I needed the air to clear my head. Plus, all the cabs and rickshaws and carriages were taken up by the other captains, and I wasn't riding an elephant bird again.

Serena was just as upset as I was, but she tended to internalize her frustration. At least, that's what I got off the link we shared.

Our heels clacked against the cobblestone streets. Somewhere, a bell chimed three times. Three bells, or three in the morning. I was way too angry to be tired, and anyway living on a night shift the previous month and a half had gotten me used to being up so late. Or early, depending on your point of view.

I stopped ranting for a second and thought. I wasn't so much angry, I realized, as appalled. Appalled that so many captains would value their own skin over protecting the people they called their friends. Some friends! A dozen captains, Tyr Ebonfury included, had voted against staying, preferring instead to run away. Unbelievable.

We walked along for a couple of minutes in annoyed silence, when the clatter of metal hooves and rattle of a carriage behind us made us step off to one side of the road, to avoid being run over.

The steam-driven horse automaton stopped with mechanical precision, so suddenly that the carriage rocked hard forward. Women's voices rose in Anglic complaint from inside.

"I say, driver!" one voice complained louder than the others.

"Forgiveness, mistress," the automaton replied in Anglic, its voice surprisingly human.

"Gah!" I jumped. I didn't know some automatons could speak, much less the not-human-looking ones.

The auto-horse's head swivelled toward me in exactly the way a real horse's head didn't. It looked at me with glowing yellow eyes. "Forgiveness..." a whir and a couple of clicks and the glowing eyes flickered "...mistress."

"Yeah, sure, no problem," I said. From our link I could feel Serena's amusement.

"Halloo?" a familiar voice called from the carriage. I turned to see Captain Tallyho leaning out the window, one hand on her hat. "I say, Captain Val, bit of a long haul to the docks, wot? Climb aboard, ducky. Captain Tallyho will get you there, lickety-split."

I glanced at Serena. She gave a shrug so small only I could have noticed, her face a perfect mask of indifference. I turned to Captain Tallyho and gave her a grin. "Sure, thanks."

She pulled her head and hat back through the window and the door opened. I climbed in, Serena right behind me. If this was a trap, she'd be on our attackers in a second.

Inside, lit by soft electric lights, Captain Tallyho sat next to a woman who was her perfect double. The only difference between them I could see was the double wore her monocle on the opposite eye. Across from them, riding backwards in the carriage, was Captain Jones.

"Welcome, welcome," he said, patting the bench next to him. He rapped his walking stick against the floor of the carriage. "Sit here, Captain, and Guinevere and Gwendolyn will make room for your mate."

As the carriage started to move again, I squeezed in next to Captain Jones while Captain Tallyho and her sister shifted themselves to either side.

"Saw you walking along and simply couldn't let a kindred spirit suffer the night chill," Captain Tallyho said, pointing to a small circular display screen set in the carriage wall over Captain Jones' head. I stared at it. It was a television screen! Tiny and flickering greenish and grey, filled with static, the image jumping and jerking, with a weird distortion around the edges where the glass curved, but definitely a TV screen!

"'Let us stop and offer them succour,' I said, didn't I, Gwen?" Captain Tallyho went on.

"That you did, Guinny," said her sister, then turned to me. "That she did."

"Nice bit of speechifying you did back there, Val," Captain Jones said. "Good to see the younger folk working for something more than a quick sovereign and a few thrills."

"Oh, that?" I tried to shrug, but my shoulders were squished between the carriage wall and his massive... mass. "No problem. I'm just surprised so many captains voted against us."

Captains Tallyho and Jones had both voted for the stay-and-fight option.

Jones laughed. "Bah! None of 'em have the stones for a real fight. Rather prey on fat merchantmen out of Atlan or Amazonia. Surrender at the first sign of trouble. Backers all insured against loss, y'see? No money in putting up a fight. But the Aerial, now. That'll be something to tell our grandkids, just you wait!"

"Assuming ve live so long, Captain," Serena said. "There's no guarantee of wictory."

"Oh pshaw, Miss Heartlace!" Tallyho laughed. "A bloody good row is guaranteed, but I'd wager none of us entered the life expecting to reach a ripe old age!"

She was maybe thirty, tops. Captain Jones looked about forty or forty five. It was kind of hard to tell, here on Ayrth. Back home, I would have put their ages at much older, but they hadn't lived their entire lives with skin creams and health food readily available. I'd learned from my crew to adjust my age guesstimates downward.

Still, thirty and forty-five seemed to be pretty good ages for pirates to reach. Lots of my own crew hadn't made it nearly that old, and never would.

"All the same, Gwen, it might be nice to have some kind of plan in mind for this cut-up," Jones said. "Something a little more organized than 'wait for 'em to drop the hammer on us'."

"Well, obviously, Remy, I mean I'm not a total ninny," Tallyho answered, sounding miffed. "I can think of a few captains who might like to be in on the planning, wot?"

"I bet they all will," I said. They all laughed like I'd just said the funniest thing they'd heard all week, but I wasn't joking.

"Very true, very true," Jones said after he'd caught his breath.

"So should we maybe all get together tomorrow sometime and talk about it?"

"Absolutely! Just the thing," Tallyho said. "I do hope we'll be," she started, but she was interrupted by a huge thump which was almost immediately drowned out by the much huger crash of the carriage turning onto its side, and then the shock of the impact and the angry metallic rattling scrape of the carriage wall sliding along cobblestones. Yeah, I know, it surprised me too.

I was lucky that I landed on Captain Jones, instead of the other way around. The Tallyhos and Serena went over in a jumble of long legs and tangled arms, but I had a soft landing, at least. The running lights inside the carriage flickered and went out.

"Everyone alright?"

"What the bloody blight?!"

"Wal?"

"I'm fine," I answered. Concern and confusion pulsed along the link I shared with Serena.

She, of course, had found her footing and reached up to open the carriage door that was suddenly overhead. With a jump like a pouncing jungle cat, she jumped up and out the door. I heard the soft thud of her landing.

"Bit of all right, isn't she?" one of the Tallyhos said. In the dark, I couldn't tell which was which.

"Yeah, she does okay," I answered, craning my neck to see where she'd gone. "Serena?"

No answer.

"Serena!"

Still nothing. I reached up to climb out the carriage door when a huge hand reached in and grabbed me, hauling me out and slamming me to the cobblestones. All the air went out of my lungs and my head rapped hard, making me see stars.

"I say!" one of the sisters yelled.

I blinked to clear my vision. The auto-horse's eyes flickered at me from across the street. "Forgiveness, mistress," it said, then the lights flickered out.

Behind me, I heard the clatter of metal on metal I recognized as some kind of sword fighting, but it was so fast. I shook my head to clear it. Sharp pains jabbed me in the side with every breath. Rolling over hurt. Breathing hurt. I struggled to sit up.

Then I saw them. Serena fought with a huge patchwork, the same one who'd attacked me before. Long knives flashed in his hands. Serena had both her sword and her main gauche out, her face as calm as a statue's. I'd seen her like that before. She was in the zone, totally focussed on the fight.

The Tallyho sisters climbed out of the carriage. One came to me. The other pulled out a pistol and took aim at our attacker. The shot cracked out into the night, echoing off the walls of the adobe huts and ramshackle houses.

The bullet pierced the patchwork's shoulder and he grunted in pain. A glance behind him and he whirled, one huge arm swinging like a yardarm, catching the sister backhanded and slamming her hard against the carriage. She went down like a sack of potatoes. Her sister, who'd been checking me out, cried out and ran over to her.

The patchwork hadn't even slowed his attacks on Serena. She had her hands full just keeping him at bay.

Despite the pain I made myself crawl over to the sisters. I picked up the pistol from where it had been dropped, and took careful aim, holding it with both hands. From where I sat, there was a good chance that if I missed him, I'd hit Serena.

The remaining Tallyho sister leaned close to me, preventing me from firing. "Allow me, ducks. Let's finish this blighter."

I nodded and that made my head swim. I pulled my boot knife out of its hidden hilt. Tallyho moved off to the side to make sure she didn't accidentally hit Serena. I crawled toward the patchwork.

Captain Jones finally pulled himself out of the carriage with a roar for blood. A twist of the head of his walking stick and out came a sword. He jumped down off the overturned carriage with a surprising amount of agility for a man his size. He charged past me, straight for the patchwork.

We surrounded our attacker. One of his hands disappeared into his cloak and electricity arced across his body. He tensed, then flew into a frenzy of slashes and jabs, feints and ripostes, attacks and counter-attacks. I couldn't even get near him. He was too fast, way too fast. Serena lost her main gauche to a particularly violent prise de fer that had her snarling in pain. Captain Jones managed to stab the patchwork in the back, and lost his sword as a result. Tallyho shot the patchwork twice, once in the thigh and once in the chest, and it didn't even slow him down. We were dead.

A noise caught my attention, a mechanical, metallic clip-clop. The auto-horse's body was still trying to pull the carriage. I crawled over to it and used my knife to pry open the auto-horse's engine cover. Spending time with Gigi had taught me a few things about machines, enough that I was able to figure out how this auto-horse worked. An electrical fuel cell, basically a huge battery the size of my head, was positioned right in centre of its body, providing the energy required to boil the water to steam. The steam drove the pistons and rods and gears that made the legs move.

I yanked the battery out to a shower of sparks. I jammed my knife into it, causing even more sparks to shoot out of it. Then I stood up and yelled, "Hey ugly! Catch!"

I tossed the fuel cell at the patchwork and he caught it without thinking. The electricity arced all over his body again, and he roared in pain. Serena stabbed him again and again while he stood there, tensed up and spasming as the electricity coursed all through his body. Smoke billowed from his skin. Tallyho emptied the revolver into him and reloaded.

With an inhuman effort, he tossed the fuel cell away. The sparking continued for a couple of seconds, then died down. He panted in pain and frustration, glared angrily at me, and then jumped to a nearby rooftop.

Serena recovered her main gauche and moved to chase after him.

"Don't!" I yelled.

"Vhy not?!" she snarled at me.

"We can't stop him with normal weapons," I explained, then pointed to the unconscious Tallyho, "and she's hurt. We need to get back to the ship."

"He'll... be back," Captain Jones panted. "Sooner... than later."

"Are you alright?" I asked. He nodded, saving his breath. I went to the Tallyhos. "How about her?"

"She'll live," the conscious sister answered, and I finally figured out it was Gwendolyn, the first mate. "If we can find a competent surgeon, and right quick."

The razor edge of Serena's instinct to hunt and kill grated on my nerves like a saw blade scraped along steel. "And you?"

"Cheery, thanks."

"Okay. I'll help you carry her. Serena, Captain Jones, you keep a lookout for any more attacks. Serena, lead the way. Captain, if you'll follow?"

"Sound plan," he said, nodding. I noticed that neither Serena nor Captain Jones had sheathed their weapons.

The fifteen minutes that followed were filled with fear. Captain Tallyho was breathing badly, gasping gulps of air, and my side smarted something sharp. Serena twitched and twisted at every sound, and her caution contaminated my consciousness. But finally, finally, we found The Furies, berthed and busy.

Restless spotted us first, limping and twisting our way down the dock. One shout from her was all it took for the rest of the crew working away the night shift to notice us. They came running, and seconds later, we were safely aboard.

Chapter Seventeen

I Begin to Suspect my Crew Are Insane

Doc Regan shook her head. "Honestly Captain, there are easier, less painful ways t' get yerself killed."

"I wasn't trying to get myself killed," I answered angrily, then hissed in pain as she bandaged my torso a little tighter than I thought was absolutely necessary. Two cracked ribs. Fun stuff.

"Good thing fer ye, ye're not so well endowed as some," she continued.

"I wasn't aware verbal abuse was part of your bedside manner," I managed through clenched teeth, wincing.

"If ye think what I've t' say is bad, wait 'til Tring gets a hold o' ye," she answered. "Sure an' she's fit t' have kittens."

"Great," I muttered. "How's Captain Tallyho?"

"Her lung's collapsed is how she is, and more than a few broken ribs, too. Bastard must have fists of iron."

"Will she survive? Why are you here?"

She tied off the bandage. I didn't feel any better. It was about as tight as a corset, and less flattering. I reached for my shirt and a stab of pain reminded me that using my left arm was probably not going to be much of an option for a while. I turned and picked up my shirt with the other hand.

"Aye, she'll live. My girls're seein' to getting' her cleaned up and ready for the operation. I've released the pressure on her lungs, no fluid built up, at least. And I've a device in me things that will re-inflate the lung. Still, she'll stay the night and I'll keep an eye on her meself."

I pulled on my shirt, wincing and gritting my teeth against the pain. Buttoning it was easier, at least.

"Here," Doc Regan said, handing me a small green stoppered bottle. "Two drops of this in a cup of tea will help ye sleep. No more than two drops, mind, it's potent."

"Thanks," I said, honestly grateful.

"Aye, well, ye're welcome. Get on wi' ye now, I've a lung to re-inflate."

I left the surgeon's quarters. Through a porthole I saw dawn brightening the horizon. I needed to talk to Serena. I found her in her quarters.

"Captain Jones vent to his ship," she said, right to business.

"Fine thanks, how are you?" I joked, but it wasn't that funny, and neither of us laughed. "Good. Tring and the other Open Hands went with him?"

"He objected, and so did she, but I vas most insistent."

"The Tallyhos are staying until nightfall at least," I said. "Are you alright?"

"Yes, yes, fine. I am, as you vould say, pissed off."

"At me?"

"Vhat? No. At him! He shouldn't be able to move so fast."

"And that thing under his jacket that made him move faster."

"And that leap! If I did not know it vas impossible, I vould say he vas part wampyri."

"Why is it impossible?" I asked. The idea of a vampyri patchwork had never occurred to me.

"Bah. The process, it vas never designed for the flesh of wampyri. Ve are made of much different stock, my kind. Like vith animen, the patchworking cannot vork. The flesh is … rejected."

"Okay, so, he's not animan or vampyri. That's a relief. What else could he be?"

"I am beginning to suspect he is more than just a patchwork, if that is vhat you mean."

"Well, no kidding. Thanks."

"No, I mean, it is possible he has prosthetic replacements. Some kind of pistons in his legs vould explain his leaping from standing still to the rooftops."

"Oh man. You think he's got some kind of machine wired into him, making him faster, stronger? I mean, patchworks are all really strong, right? But this guy kills with one punch!"

Serena yawned. "Vhen I vake, ve can talk about this. Maybe vith the doctor, see if it is even possible."

"Okay. Have a good sleep."

"Thank you. And Wal? Try not to get killed," she said sleepily, pulling the covers over her head.

I snorted a laugh and left her quarters, headed for my own. I stopped at the wheelhouse on my way. Molly sat there, alone.

"Alright, Molly?"

"Morning, Captain," she said, not bothering to turn around to look at me. "Any orders?"

"Where's Argenta?" Our only automaton crew member was usually in the wheelhouse.

"Serena's ordered her to guard you," Molly explained, making a face. "Perfectly good pilot pulling bodyguard duty."

I stepped around the captain's chair and leaned cautiously against one of the control panels to look her in the face, trying not to sit on anything important. Behind me, the faint grey glow of dawn had brightened to brilliant gold and fiery rose. Red skies in the morning, airmen take warning. "Well, I guess I'll sleep better knowing she's there, but after what the assassin did to that auto-horse, I'm not sure what she'd be able to do if he did show up."

Molly nodded. She wasn't one for unnecessary talking, our Molly. Her mechanical hand curled itself into a fist, one finger at a time, then uncurled, reversing the order.

"You're getting pretty good with that," I said.

She glanced at me, her remaining human eye filled with bitterness. "Not much choice."

I realized then we hadn't told her about the conclave. "Molly... Enerva's alive."

She made a sour face and nodded. "That bastard Tyr saved her from my beating her to death aboard the Syren. Got her arm, though."

The sight of Molly casually tossing the bloody stump of Dr. Enerva's arm overboard wasn't exactly something I would forget easily. "No, I meant, she's here. We saw her, last night."

The bitterness in Molly's eye disappeared in a flash of pure hate. "What? Where?"

"At the conclave. Ebonfury's got his own ship, now. The Relentless."

Molly shot out of the chair and left the wheelhouse.

I sighed and went after her. "Molly, wait!"

"For what?" she spat. "My arm to grow back? My leg? My eye?"

I grabbed her shoulder and spun her to face me, wincing at the pain in my side. "No, wait, listen. They're here. From the way he acted at the conclave, we'll see them soon. We need to get ready for action. I need you to help get the ship ready for an attack. That patchwork isn't the only one wants me dead."

"What about what I want?"

"You want Enerva dead, I get that. And I'm sure you'll get your chance. But not right now. You were ready to wait when you didn't know where she was. Now you know. Just wait a little longer."

She didn't say anything for a long time. Nightshift crew getting ready for bed and dayshift crew just getting up saw us together and thought better about getting near us, just from the tension in her metal fist, gleaming brass in the dim electric running lights. I almost started to say something more when she spoke, quietly. "Fine."

"Talk to Tring, see what needs doing to keep us from being blown out of the waterfront."

"Triple the guard shift is all I can think of. Tring's not back yet."

"You see to it, then? Please?"

Molly rolled her eye and looked away, then nodded, mouth closed. I saw her jaw muscles clenching, knew she was probably grinding her teeth. When she left, frustration and rage were radiating from her. Crew wisely got out of her way.

Everything caught up to me all of a sudden and I felt the overwhelming need to sleep for oh, a hundred years or so. I turned back and climbed the metal spiral staircase up to my room. It took more effort than normal, a lot more. I thought I could safely blame exhaustion for that.

Argenta met me at the top of the stairwell and helped me undress. I asked her to close the slatted wooden shades on my windows, to keep out the day's heat and the gleaming sunlight, then slipped between the sheets of my bed and eased myself down. I quickly discovered there was no way to get comfortable lying on my back or my uninjured side, so I propped up a bunch of pillows. I dripped two drops of Doc Regan's painkiller in a glass of water, drank it quick, then sat back and hoped I could sleep sitting up

I shouldn't have worried about it. I closed my eyes and when I opened them again, the sunlight streaming in through the slats in my window shades had completely disappeared. Darkness filled the room, the only dim light the glow of Argenta's yellow eyes in the corner. Outside, wind rattled the shutters of my windows, rain lashing hard against them.

Lightning flashed, thunder cracking right after. The storm must be directly overhead.

"You are dead," a woman whispered, right in my ear.

I screamed and jumped away, my broken ribs making me gasp. A hand grabbed my wrist and pulled me onto the bed. Another hand clapped down hard on my mouth. My side screamed shards of agony.

Lightning flashed again and I saw who it was. Tring.

She shook her head at me. "An automaidon is no bodyguard."

I pushed her off, angry. "What is your deal?"

"In my land, there were warriors, proud nobles who fought great battles," she answered, setting back to kneel at the edge of my bed. "The greatest of them survived many such battles, died glorious deaths of honour and sacrifice. But sometimes, a warrior would weary of the dance of war. He would set aside his sword and armour, and step onto the field of battle, vulnerable to every attack. In moments, he would be cut down by any and all who dared strike him."

"So?"

"Is that what you are doing? Are you so weary of this life you seek to be cut down?"

"What?! You think I'm suicidal?"

"You are reckless. You treat your life as if it were yours to throw away. You are more than some mere girl. You are the captain of this ship. If you die, the ship dies. If you die, we all die."

"What are you talking about? If I die, Serena becomes captain."

"Not many will follow the vampyri. She does not inspire trust."

"The crew likes her," I said, defending one of my only friends.

"Like is not trust. If she were captain, she would lose many crew. How many of the women aboard would disappear into manufactories, into pleasure houses? How many would die, starving, in alleys? You hold them together. Give them purpose. Give them focus. You are too important to this ship. You hold the honour of the entire crew in your beating heart. If it ceases to beat, that honour will die with you."

I sighed. "Argenta, turn on the lights, please."

Argenta moved to light my lamps. As the room brightened, I slid off the bed and went to the sideboard for a glass of water. "So you scare me half to death to make a point?"

"I scared you to make you understand you are not scared enough. Many enemies seek your death. This mysterious patchwork assassin. Tyr Ebonfury. Captains of the slaver vessels you have destroyed. Captain Crow must have had some friends, friends who might have recognized this ship and asked the right questions of the right people. And now, Atlan Deathwings. Many enemies, and few friends."

"Okay, I get it."

"And yet you walk the streets, unescorted. You accept carriage rides from strangers."

"Captain Tallyho and Captain Jones risked their lives to save mine!"

"You did not know that, before the fight with the patchwork. You did not know they might prove themselves allies."

"I didn't think they'd try to kidnap me with Serena right there."

"You did not think. You need not say any more than that."

"Tring, what the hell?!"

She looked away, her dark straight hair falling like a curtain between us. "When you saved us from slavery, you took our honour in your hands. As long as you live, our honour lives. My honour lives. If you die, my honour dies with you."

She slid off the bed with easy grace, then bowed to me, folding at the waist, hands at her sides. "You will accept our protection from now on."

"Tring, I'm not trying to get killed. It's just a bunch of stuff that's happened all at once that makes it seem that way."

Tring still hadn't risen from her bow. "You will accept our protection."

"Okay, yes. I accept your protection."

"You will accept our protection."

"Yes, yes! I accept, geez!"

Unbelievably, that wasn't enough for her. "You will accept our protection," she repeated a third time.

I rolled my eyes. "Yes, fine, anything, just, stop bowing, okay?"

When she finally straightened, her face was wet with tears.

"Tring, I... I'm sorry," I said.

"Your life is my honour," she answered, not wiping away the tears. "I will assign shifts and notify you of who else has the honour of guarding you."

"I, um. Okay."

She bowed again, just a head nod like before all this weirdness, and left via my spiral staircase. Serena came up the stairs once Tring had gone.

"Good evening," she smiled.

"What was that about?" I asked.

"She vas most insistent. Who can understand the Zhou?" Serena said with a shrug. "How are you feeling?"

"Sore and confused. Also, pissed off at that patchwork. And Tyr Ebonfury."

"You think he sent the patchwork?"

"What? No. Not his style."

"I agree. Then who?"

"According to Tring, I have a lot of enemies. Any one of them could have sent him."

"Twice he could have killed you. Much more easily than a knife in the dark. A good enough rifleman could have killed us both before ve even heard the gunshots. No, I do not think this patchwork vants you dead."

"Then what?"

"I suspect he has been hired to kidnap you and bring you to his employer. To what end, I do not know."

"Great." I went to my closet and started pulling out clothes. I looked at all my corsets and sighed. "Guess I won't be wearing those for a while."

"Don't be so glum," Serena laughed, heading for the stairs. "Dr. Vestmore has something that might be of assistance. I'll send Domina up to help. From vhat I hear, the cure may be vorse than the problem," she said, then slid down the bannister, laughing.

"Is everyone on this ship crazy?" I muttered to myself.

Chapter Eighteen

A Cure Worse Than the Problem Itself

Domina helped me get dressed, just a loose cotton blouse, dark green pants and dark green three-quarter coat I left hanging open.

"There's another conclave tonight, Captain," she said, handing me my bowler. Without Adina around any more to help me control my hair, I'd reverted to braided pigtails to keep my hair in check. Domina had helped with that, too, since I couldn't lift my arms high enough to braid without gasping in pain.

"What time?"

"Nine bells."

I glanced at the clock on my mantel. It was just past seven thirty, and I was starving.

"I'll get something to eat first," I said. "Tell Tring I'm going to this conclave. Where is it?"

"The theatre," Domina answered. I didn't bother asking which theatre. I already knew.

Libertia's biggest theatre, The Palace, was something incredible. Imagine red curtains and gilded columns and marble floors and everything else you would expect from those old-style theatres you might see in old movies and you're about halfway there. The lobby ceiling soared nearly a hundred feet above our heads, mirrored and chandeliered to sparkling brilliance, the walls hung with paintings and pictoriographs as far as the eye could see. The grand staircases up to the three balcony levels were twenty feet wide and red carpeted. Every show was sold out, and sometimes two or three companies of players had shows all the same night. The people of Libertia and the pirates who visited them may not have had any police or formal government, but they sure loved their theatre.

We'd gone to a show, our second week in town, Serena, Domina, Gigi and I. Domina had literally begged us to come along. I'd never been to any live theatre in my life, and it sounded like a big deal, so we went.

The singers were amazing, even if I didn't understand a word of what they were singing. Domina wept. The comedians were hilarious. I swear I nearly peed myself. The acrobats were incredible, just jaw-dropping incredible. And that was just the warm up acts. The main attraction was a play, a story about an airship pirate who fell in love with a slave girl, but her owner was this incredible jerk who refused to sell her. Anyway, it all ended in tears, for the characters and for the audience. Domina wasn't the only one of us with a soaking wet handkerchief that night.

Anyway, all that to say, holding a conclave in the Palace was like holding a Girl Scout meeting at Carnegie Hall. It was an unusual choice.

Padmini found me in the mess hall, loading up a plate with roast ham and honey-glazed potatoes. I love my mom's cooking, and my dad knows his way around the kitchen, but neither of them could hold a candle to Brunhilde's roasts. She was some kind of kitchen goddess. My mouth had been watering from the second I stepped into the mess hall.

"Excuse me please, my Captain," Padmini interrupted. "But Dr. Westmore, she says you shouldn't eat anything before the procedure."

"What procedure?" I asked suspiciously. I put down my plate, pretty much sure I wasn't going to like the answer.

"Dr Westmore says she's found her ossificator."

"Her ossiwhatnow?"

"Ossificator. A bone knitting device. To repair your ribs."

"She couldn't tell me this last night?"

Padmini smiled in a way that said she had no clue. "She's waiting for you, if you please?"

I wondered briefly at who really ran the ship when everyone seemed keen to tell me what to do, then handed my plate to Hilda with reluctant regret. "I'll be back for that," I told her.

"Ya, zis is no problem, Captain," Hilda answered happily.

I sighed and headed for the surgeon's quarters. Captain Tallyho and her sister were just leaving when I got there.

"I say, don't look so down in the mouth, chum," Captain Tallyho laughed. "You'll be right as rain in a tick or two."

She didn't exactly look right as rain, but she looked better than she had the night before. "Feeling better?"

"Feel even better than this after a few rum toddies," she answered.

"No time for that, though. Have to get spiffy for the conclave, wot?"

"Yeah, I guess I'll see you there," I said.

"Captain Val," she said, offering me her hand. I took it and she shook it vigorously, pumping it several times. "You've a friend forever in the Tallyho sisters. I cannot express enough thanks."

"You nearly got killed because of me."

"Oh posh," she answered. "Bit of a cut-up like that? Spot of bother, but we've seen worse, eh Gwen?"

"That we have, Guinny," her sister answered. "One time we near lost our heads, wot?"

They both laughed at what was obviously an inside joke between them. Doc Regan stuck her head out her door and said, "Ye're next, Capt'n."

"Well, best of luck, Captain. See you soon," Captain Tallyho said, tipping her hat to me. I tipped mine back. We shook hands one more time. I clenched my teeth to keep from wincing as my ribs reminded me they'd recently been broken.

She grinned at me, thinking my grimace was a smile. "We'll save a spot for you at the conclave. It's open to crew, too, so I understand."

"Not all crew, obviously," her sister explained, "but those as need knowing what's to come."

"Oh so, engineers, cannoneers, aeriologists, that sort of thing?"

She nodded. "And navigators."

"Captain!" Doc Regan called impatiently.

"Right," I said. "See you later."

"Indeed."

"Quite so."

"Cheery-o!" they said together, then left.

I stepped into the surgeon's quarters. Doc Regan wore a huge pair of goggles over her eyes, magnifying them to grotesque proportions. "Sit down, please," she said, nodding toward the examination table.

"What's this ossificator thing?" I asked, pulling off my coat carefully.

"It stimulates the natural processes of bone knittery," she said, as if that explained anything. She handed me a beer mug filled with what looked like milk, but it had the thickness and consistency of white paint. "Drink this. All of it."

"What is it?"

"Liquid bone."

And I'd nearly put it to my lips, too. It sloshed against the rim as I jerked it away from my mouth. "What?!"

"It is a concoction made of the various minerals and nutrients that form bone," she explained. "The ossificator makes use of these nutrients to heal your broken bones."

It tasted worse than that, too. Vaguely like milk that's been sitting out all day, with a lemony aftertaste. I wanted to puke.

"Now hold this between yer teeth," Doc Regan said, handing me something that looked like a horse's bit. A copper wire snaked from either end of the bit to a machine next to the examination table, a suitcase-sized wooden contraption of dials and switches and knobs. She flipped a couple of switches and the ossificator began to hum.

Then she connected what looked like two cattle prods to the ossificator.

"D'ye like yer blouse?"

"It's alright, why?"

"Best take it off, then."

I pulled the blouse over my head with great pain and greater concern. I wanted my ribs healed, but what the hell, you know? I sat there, topless, bandages totally tight around my torso.

Doc Regan fiddled with a couple of dials on the ossificator and the hum increased until it was a loud, high-pitched whine. Satisfied, she nodded, then pressed a button on the side of her goggles. They began to pulse a bright, greenish white light, like a camera flash stuck on 'seizure-inducing strobe light'.

"What's with the goggles?" I asked, just before she stuck the bit between my teeth.

"They allow me to see yer bones. Hold still now, this'll sting a tad."

I clenched down on the bit as she stuck the cattle prods against my side. Electricity ran through my body and STING A TAD?! My side clenched up with crazy cramps. I could feel my bones. Feel them! Inside me! Something strange stirred in my stomach, a bubbling boiling burble that made me want to belch, bit or no bit.

Part of me was dimly aware of the fact that Doc Regan was tracing the cattle prods along my ribs, but most of me was OH GOD OW OW OW OW STOP IT OOOWWWWW!!!

After an eternity, it ended. The bit fell from my slack jaw.

"There now," Doc Regan said happily, shutting down the ossificator and removing her X-ray goggles. "Feel better?"

I threw up.

Chapter Nineteen

Off to the Palace

After that I didn't have much appetite. I changed my clothes. They reeked of sweat and vomit. New pants, new blouse, corset, jacket. On Serena's advice I picked my stiffest corset, a dark blue beauty of leather and whalebone and silver buckles. It would support my newly healed bones while offering my some protection from a knife or sword. Bullets, not really, but after Tring's bitching me out, I didn't want to give her a reason to do it again, so I would wear whatever protection I could find.

Then it was time for the conclave, so we flagged down a six-wheeled steam cab and piled in. There were quite a few of us. Serena, Inga, Violette, Gigi, Mrs. Shorty, Miss Merryweather, Moonchance and Tring joined me inside the carriage. Four of Tring's girls rode on the outside. None of us was unarmed, carrying swords, knifes, and six-shooters. Moonchance had two tiny little daggers she insisted would be more than enough. Serena refused to carry a gun, but Inga's arsenal more than compensated for her, the Open Hands, and pretty much everyone else. Apparently she didn't believe in reloading. If trouble came for us, we'd be ready.

When we got to the Palace, we realized we weren't the only ones who'd come packing. Everyone we saw was bristling with swords and guns, knives and rifles. Everyone stared at each other suspiciously. The low murmur of voices as we entered wasn't anywhere near the joking around, laughing, generally amused rumble from the previous conclave. I wondered what had happened while I was sleeping to change everyone's mood so much.

We found the Tallyho sisters sitting in a box on the third level of balconies. They'd brought a half-dozen crew whose names I forgot almost instantly. We settled into the box next to them, Tring and her girls staying standing in the corners, eyes darting in every direction, trying to spot trouble before it came.

I saw a contingent of women all clustered together in the benches down on the floor and recognized Madam Helen. It was then I realized that townsfolk had been invited to this thing, too. I tried to guess who was a pirate and who was a townie, based on how they were acting or how they were dressed. It turned out the townies were easier to spot than you might think: they had less weapons.

The red velvet curtains parted and revealed not Captain Lawless, like you might have expected – at least, that's who I'd expected, anyway – but Captain Jones.

"Alright then!" Remy roared, and the crowd quieted. "We all know why we're here. We're making a stand. Everyone has their own reasons to be here. Maybe you're fed up of Atlan tyranny. Maybe you're looking to pick the bones of some juicy military ships. Maybe you're just looking for a fight."

"And maybe we're all mad!" someone yelled, but not many people laughed.

"I wouldn't deny it takes madness to fly into a hurricane," Captain Jones answered. "And no mistake, this won't be a easy. In fact, it's likely to get a lot of people killed."

"So long as they're Atlan bastards!" another man yelled, and a lot of people agreed, murmuring and nodding.

"We need a plan! And right quick, too."

"We need a leader!" Captain Tallyho called out, leaning over her balcony rail to be seen by everyone.

"Flight formations!" someone else yelled out.

Captain Lawless leaned out of his balcony and yelled, "A command structure, hierarchy, flight formations, these are all the Atlan way of fighting. We fight them on their terms, they'll tear us to pieces."

"Ve fight them on ours, and ve'll all die," a familiar voice yelled out from above and to my left. I leaned forward and looked up.

Tatalia Tempest leaned out, her dress a tattered mess, her hands bandaged and bloody. Her gorgeous dark hair was pulled back in a ragged ponytail, mostly hidden under a red kerchief. "Most of you know me. Almost all of you knew my husband. He tried to fight on his terms, and vhat did it get him? A slaughtered crew. A ship in flames. An early death." On that last word, her voice cracked with emotion, barely held in check. From where I stood, I saw tears spill down her cheeks, washing away soot and ash.

That sailor who'd interrupted our meal on the Stormgazer, Jenny Squall, stood near. She put a hand on her captain's widow's shoulder. Tatalia glanced at her and squared her shoulders.

"What would you have us do, Mistress Tempest?" Captain Lawless asked. "Cut and run?"

"No!" she answered, chin held high. "Fight! Fight them to the death. Kill as many as you can. But vithout some kind of order, some kind of plan, ve cannot hope to vin."

"It's true," I heard someone say, then realized it had been me. Everyone looked at me. My mouth was suddenly bone dry.

"What would a backstabbing child like you know about war?" a voice said from the floor, and I saw Tyr Ebonfury sitting there, a smug look on his face. Dr. Enerva was next to him, and I felt Molly tense up behind me. Beside them was a ghost.

It was the only thing that made any sense. Diana had been a bitch and a pirate slaver, and I had marooned her with the last of the crew we'd captured when we took the Carrion away from Captain Crow. She had to have died a few days later. I didn't like to think about it too much.

But there she was, sitting next to Tyr, her eyes filled with hate, glaring at me.

Next to me, Serena cleared her throat, almost too quiet to hear. It shook me out of my shock.

"What are you doing here?!" I yelled back, ignoring the ghost beside Tyr. I must be seeing things. Too much action, not enough food, that ossificator had done something to my brain. "You voted against staying!"

"Never said when I'd leave, did I?" Ebonfury yelled back, leaping to his feet. "And who's to say I haven't had a change of heart?"

"Anyone here not completely on board with playing a part in the fight can leave right now," Captain Jones interrupted. "Or else."

"Don't want you running back to your Atlan buddies," I called down to Ebonfury.

He just laughed. "Spare me your pathetic attempts, traitor. Children should speak only when spoken to."

"Don't rise to his bait, Captain," I heard Miss Merryweather murmur behind me. She was right. I took a deep breath and addressed the crowd.

"Listen," I said, trying to remember my history of the American Revolution. "There was this army, right? Trying to fight for their independence. Against a tyrant across the sea. At first the army fought the same kind of war as the tyrant's better trained, better funded armies. And they got their asses handed to them!"

People laughed.

"But once they changed their tactics, they started winning! Hit and run raids, dead of night attacks, ambushes. Fighting on the same battlefield as the tyrant's armies, they couldn't win a single battle. By making the fight their own, they won the war. That's what we have to do! Fight Atlan Aerial the pirate way."

"What's the pirate way, then?" Ebonfury yelled. "Every ship for themselves?"

"No! We can work together, but not the way the Atlans expect!"

"How, exactly?"

"There's got to be some way to co-ordinate our attacks," I said. "We managed, against the warship."

"Heard about that," Captain Lawless said. "Not everyone has pixies in their crew."

"Messengers take too long," another captain stood and said. "In battle, seconds matter."

"I still can't believe no one ever invented radios," I muttered, mostly to myself.

"I think I might be able to work something, Sunset," Gigi said, leaning forward. "But it will take a lot more intercom systems, and hundreds of yards of wire..."

"Gigi, we can't fly into battle all tied together," Violette argued.

But then, fate intervened.

The doors at the back of the hall slammed open. Everyone was so on edge that a lot of guns and swords were drawn, pointed in every direction.

They shouldn't have worried. Or at least, they should all drink less coffee or whatever. Because what came down the aisle wasn't something to get twitchy about.

Five automatons of various designs rolled or strode down the central aisle, to the general WTF? of everyone. The biggest of them looked like a huge brass cylinder, stood up on end, rolling on six wheels. It had four thin spindly arms and a single huge eye lens set on a rotating mount, on top of the cylinder. The smallest was –

"Argenta?!" I nearly shouted. "What's she doing here?"

Gigi leaned forward, brilliant green cat eyes narrowing. "It's not her, Sunset. Same model, but look at the differences in her chassis. That modification to her shoulder mounts? And the way she walks, definitely some kind of hip upgrade."

I calmed down. I had no idea what Gigi was talking about. She looked exactly the same as Argenta, at least to me.

The automatons stopped at the foot of the stage. The cylinder one swivelled its head around and in a deep, emotionless, electrostaticked voice said, "The Union of Automated Gentlemen wishes to address this conclave."

Chapter Twenty

An Offer We Can't Refuse

"Well, that was weird," I said, later.

We waited outside the Palace for a free carriage. Tring and her girls effectively had me completely surrounded, trying to watch everyone at once.

"Vhat vas veird?"

I turned to Serena. "The whole thing with the Automated Gentlemen. I really didn't expect it to get so violent."

"People who value freedom dislike being told they're effectively slavers," Miss Merryweather said.

"Quite right," Captain Tallyho agreed, walking up to me. Or at least, as close as Tring and Li would let her. "Care for a drink? Night's early yet."

"Not tonight," I answered, patting my ribs. "Still sore from yesterday."

She laughed. "Oh come now, Dr. Westmore's contraption fixed me right up! Surely you're not going to let something like that slow you down?"

"Another night," I said. "Promise."

"May not have many left, dearie. Well, toodles!" she waved foppishly and went off with the rest of her crew.

"They had a point," Gigi said.

"You want to go out drinking?"

"No, the automatons," she answered, rubbing her chin, a sure sign she was thinking hard. "We treat them like property when it's been well established they have sentience of their own. Look at Argenta."

"Argenta's a member of the crew, not one of the engines," I answered, getting just as defensive as some of the people had gotten in the meeting.

"True, but how often do we consult her opinion?"

Violette gave Gigi a look. "She can't speak. She has no voice box."

"Only because she's been designed that way," Gigi argued. "I could outfit her with a new throat and voice box easily, if she wanted one, but we've never asked her, is my point. We treat her like equipment. She has no quarters of her own, didn't get a share of the booty."

"Okay, fine," I said, my head pounding with the argument. The townsfolk hadn't liked the Automated Gentlemen's offer, but the pirates had seen its merits right away.

Turns out someone *had* invented radio. Only the someone was a scientific research automaton named Zero One Zero. The other automaton, the cylinder guy, had called him Dr. Zero. The cylinder guy's name had been Golem Charlie; the automaidon, Alumina. The other three names I forget, but they hadn't said anything during the whole argument, though one reminded me of Tik-Tok from the Oz books, just a round copper ball head on top of a round copper ball body with spindly little arms and legs.

Anyway, radio. The automatons had it, and wanted to give it to the pirates. Well, by give, I mean sell. The price was all automatons everywhere had to be freed of their shackles of slavery. Just as Libertia had no slaves, neither would any automaton be forced to work against their will, nor would they be considered property. And the pirates had to swear that any automatons liberated in any engagements be brought to Libertia and set free, in perpetuity, which meant for all time. In exchange for their freedom they would sell the pirates and the townsfolk this new wireless communication device Dr. Zero had just perfected.

A lot of people were dead set against it. Maybe it was like Miss Merryweather said. Nobody wanted to be called a slaver, especially not by something they previously considered on the same level as their toaster. Some pirates, from what they'd said, were just more morbidly pragmatic. Automatons and automaton parts were worth a lot of money. Taken as booty, they were quite a find, and they'd sell for a lot of sovereigns, even more than a hold full of actual flesh-and-blood slaves.

There was a lot to think about, and I couldn't do it in the crowd. I wanted to get back to my ship and talk to my crew about the situation. But first, we had to get a carriage.

The crowd began to thin, a little, and I caught sight of Tatalia Tempest. She and Jenny Squall were standing off to one side, near one of the columns that faced the Palace, mostly ignored by the crowd.

"Somebody get us a carriage," I said, then headed over to Captain Tempest's widow. Tring and Li and the other Open Hands followed me, if someone can follow someone else by being in front of them.

Jenny saw me first and nodded. Tatalia caught the movement out of the corner of her eye and turned.

"Captain Wal."

"Mistress Tempest," I said, taking off my hat. I hoped, too late, that my hair wasn't too much of a mess. "I'm so sorry about your husband."

She raised her chin, her eyes going flat, emotionless. "Thank you."

"The whole ship went down?"

Her voice was quiet, stripped of the fiery temper she'd shown at the dinner we'd shared. "About half the crew dead. The rest have found bunks on other ships, here, or left Libertia altogether. The ship, destroyed. Not even enough to sell for salvage. I have nothing, now."

"Just the clothes on our backs," Jenny said quietly, her Atlan heavily accented with Gallic overtones. It was almost a whisper, really. Tears began to shimmer in her eyes.

"You're welcome aboard The Furies, if you need a place to go," I said.

Tatalia almost refused. I could see it in her eyes. Too proud to accept charity, the words almost on her lips, when Jenny closed her eyes, raising a hand to hide her tears.

"Thank you," Tatalia said, instead, every word dragged out of her like it caused her pain to say them. "Ve accept your generous offer."

Jenny shook her head. "No, Mistress," she said.

"Mistress no longer, Jenny," Tatalia said. "Ve are part of Captain Wal's crew now."

Jenny stared at her, then nodded slowly, sadly. She wiped away the last of her tears with the back of her hand, then turned to me. "Orders, Captain?"

"Let's get back to The Furies," I said. "We have some talking to do."

The carriage ride was crowded and quiet. Everyone was lost in their own thoughts. Gigi and Jenny spoke a little to each other in Gallic, but Gigi was distracted and Jenny not exactly forthcoming, from what I could judge from their vague questions and short answers.

When we got back to the ship, I sent out word for Argenta to join me in my cabin. I left Tatalia and Jenny in Miss Merryweather's very capable hands, and told the rest to gather the crew for three bells.

Argenta found me, looking at one of Violette's maps.

"Come in, please," I said to her, suddenly aware of how seldom I used that word when I talked to her. You don't say 'please' to the oven.

Argenta stepped into the room, her metal feet clanging against the hardwood floor. They were shaped like shoes, I noticed, maybe for the first time. Who had decided to give her two-inch heels? Why give a robot heels at all? Why shape her like she was shaped? All of her, every rivet, every gear, every steam-driven piston, had been designed. Even the fact that she had no voice had been a conscious decision on someone's part.

"Argenta..." I started, and didn't know what to say. To stall, I said, "Um, sit down."

Her metal skirt made it difficult, if not impossible, to sit on a chair. Why would you design a robot to look like she was wearing a French maid costume, anyway? Unless you intended for her never to be able to sit. But then, why would a slave need to sit, am I right?

Argenta settled for sitting on the edge of my bed, since I didn't have any benches for her to squat down on. She folded her hands in her lap and looked at me, yellow eyes glowing, unblinking.

"Argenta," I started again. "Are you happy?"

The yellow eyes flickered they way they did whenever she thought hard. Then she shook her head.

"You're not?" I asked, honestly surprised. I guess I assumed she would tell us, but then, why would she? How would she?

Again, she shook her head.

"Are you upset?"

Her head shook.

"Wait, what are you, then?"

She waited. I realized I hadn't asked her a yes/no question. I tried something different.

"Can you read? And write?"

She nodded.

I grabbed a stack of blank paper and a pencil and sat beside her on the bed. She took the paper and smoothed it out on her skirt, then took the pencil and wrote, in Anglic:

I am neither happy nor upset. My directivation does not include such sensations.

"You don't feel anything?"

Satisfaction at a job well done. It is my principle motivation.

"Do you consider yourself a slave?"

No. But neither do I consider myself a member of the crew. The Union of Automated Gentlemen seem to think I am one, or the other. This is a logical fallacy. There are many different positions aboard a ship.

I wasn't quite sure what she meant, but I didn't think I wanted to get into a discussion on logical fallacies, whatever that was. Instead, I asked, "Would you like to be a member of the crew?"

Her eyes flickered for a long time. Then she wrote:

Your mission to eradicate slavery is a worthy endeavour. To be part of that job well done would be very satisfactory. I accept your offer.

For some reason, I felt a tremendous amount of relief, like a weight had been lifted from my heart. I realized that if she'd wanted to leave, I would have missed her a lot. I hugged her, and she sat there and let herself be hugged.

"Listen, Gigi says she can upgrade you so that you'd be able to speak. Something about installing a voice box in your throat? Would you like that?"

Her hand went up to her stick-thin neck. Her eyes flickered for maybe a second, then she nodded.

I grinned at her. "That's great. We'll do that as soon as we can."

She stood up and nodded again.

I stood up, too. "Let's go talk to the crew."

Chapter Twenty One

Adapting to Change

Everyone in the crew saw the simple logic of the plan. Trade radio for a free Argenta, and any other automatons we captured from any other engagements in the future. It was a small price to pay for a chance at winning the battle.

"If we are all killed, it makes no difference," Inga pointed out. "If we survive, we free more slaves."

"And get some new equipment to play with," Gigi added. I could see it in her engineer eyes, she just wanted a chance to take their wireless communicator thing apart and see how it worked.

I had been expecting more of an argument, like we'd had at the Palace, but then, most of my crew had lived however briefly with the terrifying prospect of a lifetime of slavery ahead of them. Now we were all freed slaves. Freeing more slaves was the reason were were all on this ship. And the upcoming fight, we knew, wouldn't be easy. We'd need every advantage we could find.

Once the meeting was over, the day shift went back to bed and the night shift went to work. The ship still needed to be repaired from the last fight, and we had a new fight to get ready for. Every deck just about buzzed with crew going back and forth, running errands and completing tasks.

The biggest problem, actually, was the fact that everyone else ran on a day shift, and we were a bunch of nightrunners. The Tallyhos called on me for breakfast, which went way past my bedtime, lasting nearly until noon, when Captain Jones and Captain Lawless joined us for lunch. We talked tactics and strategies and probable responses from Atlan Aerial until I was yawning so much I nearly fell asleep at the table. Tring and her girls didn't seem to have any problem staying awake and alert. It made me wonder if maybe they were on something, some pill to keep them up. When I asked her about it later, Tring took offence at the very idea.

Gigi and the crew worked around the clock, scavenging parts from shipwrecks when we couldn't buy them outright from the townsfolk, most of whom were busy digging in. I mean, literally – people who owned homes were turning their basements and root cellars into bunkers. Riots broke out over food and supplies. A dozen people were killed in one riot over petrol. I gave the order that none of the crew was to leave the ship alone. I shouldn't have bothered, no one wanted to leave at all, and when we had no other choice, we went heavily armed.

It had only been a couple of days since the attack and what little civilization Libertia enforced had fallen apart.

Still, the one good, fun thing that happened came when the Union of Automated Gentlemen demonstrated their wireless communication device, which they called their radiophonic communicatron. I was determined never to call it that mouthful of unnecessary syllables if I could absolutely help it.

The demonstration took place in the morning at the Docking Tower. One unit – and I'll describe them in a second – was set up at the top of the tower, the other in the ruins of the Repair Hangar. The unit was a masterpiece of purely functional design. Nothing like the elegantly wrought wood-and-brass beauties that was every piece of technology I'd seen so far on Ayrth. It was a perfectly square steel box, riveted along the edges. A series of dials, switches, gauges and knobs stuck out of every face but one, and, I assumed, the bottom. Out of the top jutted a longish segmented metal tube, coiled like a snake. At the top's centre lay a circular wire-mesh grate, and a huge pair of wire antennas rose up from either side of it, like you'd see on older televisions, what they called rabbit-ear antennas. When they powered the unit up, electricity arced from one antenna to the other, rising slowly along the antennas to wink out at the ends, replaced immediately by another arc of electricity at the bottom of the antennas. A portable generator the size of a camping cooler stood nearby, humming and occasionally sputtering, hooked up to the radio unit by a thick cable sheathed in rubber. The whole thing looked like absolutely no effort had gone into making it look even remotely attractive. At least, not to the human eye.

Dr. Zero was something else entirely. From the way Golem Charlie and the other Automated Gentlemen had spoken about him, I expected some kind of tin man mad scientist. After dealing with Argenta and her incredibly human design, I even half expected him to have a sculpted metal beard and crazy metal hair. Instead, Dr. Zero was huge, like ten feet tall, a wood and brass box on tractor treads. Gauges displayed readings on each of his body's four sides. Eight arms, two on each side, ended in four-fingered pincer-like hands. And he had four heads, set on top of his body, each looking in a different direction. None of the heads was sculpted to resemble a human's at all, just a ball on an extendible neck, with two flickering yellow eyes and large round ears like satellite dishes. His heads never stopped moving, looking this way and that, ears swivelling constantly to pick out bits of conversation, pieces of information. Gathering data.

He'd been escorted by at least a dozen automatons, including Golem Charlie and Alumina. She was the most human-looking of the bunch. There was even an auto-horse, which made me feel really terrible about the one who'd been wrecked by the patchwork assassin. Or killed, I guess.

When Dr. Zero spoke, his voice echoed oddly. Deep and resonant, without any accent to his flawless Atlan.

"Fellow sentients," he began, "this humble radiophonic unit will change the way we communicate."

One of his arms reached out and took hold of the metal tube coiled on top of the radio, pulling it close to the speaker set in that side of his body. That's when I figured out why his voice echoed the way it did. He had four voice boxes.

"Ahoy the tower," he said into the tube. The electricity arcing between the antennas crackled as he spoke.

We waited for maybe two or three seconds. You could have heard a pin drop, everyone was so quiet, waiting for the reply. When it came, it was crackly and distorted, but understandable.

"Ahoy, Dr. Zero."

Suddenly everyone wanted to try it, talking all at the same time, coming up with ideas, ways to use the radiophonic communicatron to stay coordinated in battle, stay in touch out of battle, all kinds of stuff.

Dr. Zero waved his arms, trying to get our attention. "The range is limited at present to five miles," he said, answering someone's question. "And the radiophonic communicatron requires some training to use. The operator must be able to attune the frequency of the radiophonic waves, and maintain connection with the signal. Should you wish to install a communicatron aboard your ships, you will have to dedicate one person to its use."

Nobody cared about that. Everyone wanted one.

I turned to Gigi, who was practically drooling. "I know someone who wants a new voice box. Think we can convince her to use it over the radio?"

Gigi just grinned and nodded.

Installing the radio unit turned out to be pretty simple. We just had to piss off our navigator.

"Honestly, Captain, I must protest!" Violette raged at me.

I faced her, hands on hips. "Really? Why's that?"

"The map room is hardly big enough for myself and my map table!" she said, waving her hands at the doorway to the room in question. Inside, we'd removed a rack of maps and replaced it with our radio. Violette raised a hand to her forehead. "Placing this unit in my room and having another person in there with me at all times is simply... claustrophobic."

"First of all," I said, holding my temper with admirable restraint, "you're not in there at all times. In fact, the times you're most likely to be in there, we most likely won't need to have a radio operator in there. Secondly, it's not your room. It's not your personal property, Violette. I'm sorry you feel inconvenienced, but it's the only room close enough to the wheelhouse to be useful to us when we're in action. I can't coordinate with the other ships if the radio is on another deck, or thirty feet away. I need it close by. You do understand that, right?"

Violette looked away and nodded, reluctantly. "It's your ship, Captain."

"Yes? Alright? Alright," I said, and she walked off. Probably in a huff, I don't know. At that precise moment, I didn't care. I wanted the radio installed, I wanted the battle over with, I wanted to go home. I wanted a lot of things.

It took Alumina about fifteen minutes to set up the radio. Showing Argenta how to use it was another matter entirely. She spoke quietly to Argenta, explaining slowly so our automaidon's self-directivation learning tapes could record all the information.

Seeing them side-by-side, the differences between them were

obvious. Alumina had her voice box installed, for one thing. Her voice was high, very feminine, with an upper-class Anglic accent. Her lips didn't move when she spoke, since her voice came out of a tiny oval speaker set on her throat. She called Argenta "sister," and had learned a lot of human mannerisms, touching Argenta's arm with familiarity, shifting her weight from one leg to the other. The upgrades to Alumina's hips and shoulders allowed her a lot more relaxed attitudes, while Argenta was stiff, all prim and proper. There was something undeniably sexier about Alumina. It was like watching twin sisters, one a party girl, and one a bookworm. Totally weird.

Our radio not only had the circular metal grill on top as a speaker, but also came with a set of headphones, so that the operator would be able to hear what was being said over the roar of battle. Seeing Argenta with the headphones on, she looked like some crazy robot deejay, ready to drop some mad beats.

"You'll have to upgrade her shoulders for a wider range of motion," Alumina said to me. "To facilitate her use of the wireless communicatron."

"What she wants to upgrade is up to her," I answered. "Argenta's a member of the crew, with a full share of her own."

Alumina looked at me for few seconds, her eyes flickering. I wondered if I'd somehow offended her. Finally she said, "That's very enlightened of you, Captain Val. Would that more people held that opinion."

"Is the Union having a lot of opposition?" I asked, walking her out of the ship.

"Some," she admitted. "Mostly from townsfolk who object to losing their slaves and gaining very little. Airship captains can see the application of the wireless at once, of course, but to townsfolk, there is very little reason or benefit to coordinating actions."

"I guess, from that perspective, they have a point," I said. "What's the use of a radio, when what you need is someone to chop firewood or pull carriages?"

"Indeed," she agreed. "It is a problem. Dr. Zero is looking for better applications of the wireless, ways for the townsfolk to use it."

"You could broadcast music," I said. "Then everyone in town could enjoy the shows at the Palace."

Alumina stopped walking, her eyes flickering, deep in thought.

"That is an excellent idea. I shall inform Dr. Zero at once."

We shook hands at the gangplank and she left. I went back to the radio/map room. Argenta wasn't there. I asked around and finally found her.

Gigi was performing surgery.

Chapter Twenty Two

Changing to Adapt

I found Gigi and Argenta in Gigi's lab.

We'd converted the slave mess into a laboratory for Gigi to work on mechanical and technological stuff. It was where she fixed Molly's arm and leg, had put together the intercom system, and where she'd set up the aetheric portal, the machine that Dr. Sweetwater had invented that pulled me from Earth to Ayrth. It still didn't work, but Gigi put the pieces together, at least. It looked like a big brass circle about ten feet wide, laid down on the floor, with wires and cables and lights and gauges and dials all over it. The wires and cables all snaked back to a control podium, covered with switches and more dials and gauges. It looked impressive, but didn't work.

Anyhow, the rest of the room was filled with work benches and shelves, all covered with machine parts and Bunsen burners and glass tubes of some weird-looking liquids and pretty much everything you'd expect in some kind of mad scientist's lab. I really hoped Gigi didn't go mad.

She'd pushed together two of her work benches into an L shape. Argenta's body lay face down on one, her back opened up to reveal her directivation tapes. Her head rested on the other table, eyes dull and lifeless.

It had been easy to find a working voice box. When the Union of Automated Gentlemen found out we were looking for one for our automaidon, they'd given us one. "All automatons should be able to voice their opinions," Alumina had said when she'd delivered the radio unit. The voice box looked like Argenta's neck, only slightly bulkier, with a tiny speaker grill set near the base, where it would join at her shoulders. It came with directivation tapes and a thick spool of wire. The wire contained Argenta's new vocabulary. Unfortunately for me, it only came in Atlan. Alumina insisted we could pick up other language spools and install them easily, but unfortunately the only ones readily available were Atlan. If we wanted an Anglic one we'd probably have to go to Anglica.

Gigi had already removed Argenta's original neck by the time I got down to the lab. She wore a set of magnifying goggles to help her with the finicky little connections. Seeing her green cat eyes magnified to huge size made me jump a little when she looked up at me.

"How's it going?" I asked.

"Fine, fine," Gigi said, turning back to her work. "No trouble."

I picked up Argenta's new neck to look at it. Without looking up, Gigi plucked it out of my hands and put it back, exactly where I'd taken it from.

"Sorry, Sunset, but I'll be needing that soon,"

"I was just looking," I muttered. I went to Argenta's head and picked it up, unscrewing the metal 'bun' at the back. Inside was a dial that an automaidon's owner could use to set the language the automaidon would respond to, Atlan, Anglic, Gallic, and so on. We'd rigged it so that she understood them all, since so many people on board spoke so many different languages, and our own shipspeak slang pretty much used them all. Gigi had explained that it was tough on her directivation tapes, whirring back and forth to understand all the different languages, so direct orders to or conversations with Argenta were best to be done in just one language.

"Will we need to rewire this?" I asked Gigi, showing her the bun.

"No," Gigi said, sticking her soldering iron into Argenta's neck-hole. A whiff of smoke escaped as I watched. "She'll still understand all the languages, but she'll only speak Atlan."

"Alright," I said, screwing the bun back into Argenta's head.

I stepped away from the head and went to the other side of the work bench where Argenta's body lay, to get a better view of what Gigi was doing. I didn't understand what she was doing, but it made me feel better when I could see what was going on.

"She'll be fine, Sunset," Gigi said after a few minutes of quiet soldering. I looked up and realized my own face was only inches from Gigi's.

"I know," I said quickly. "I know. I trust you."

Gigi smiled. "It's never a matter of not trusting me. We've lost too many crew this last week, and you take that hard, I know. This is a simple procedure. Argenta will be up and running soon. Who knows? Perhaps we will have cause to regret giving her a voice. Perhaps she'll be a real chatter box, having been forced to be silent for so long."

I grinned back. "That would be hilarious."

Gigi nodded. "Now, hand me the language spool. please?"

We worked on it for maybe an hour, and by we, I mean Gigi worked and allowed me to hand her things. I had no clue what she was doing, but she seemed completely confident with it, so I basically just kept her company and appreciated her letting me feel useful. At any rate, after about an hour Argenta's neck was attached properly and we were reattaching her head to the new connectors when Restless found me.

"Captain, that wireless thing is making noise," she said. "Though why they call it wireless, I don't know. I mean, it has a power wire, doesn't it?"

I looked down into Argenta's lifeless eyes. Our radio operator was out for the moment. I made a mental note to get someone to assist her, once she was up and running again, so that they could learn from Argenta.

"Come help Gigi," I said to Restless, then left the lab, headed for the radio room.

People had gathered, listening to the hiss and crackle of the radio unit. As I entered the room, a woman's voice broke through the static, completely garbled. I sat down, plugging in the headphones and pulling them over my ears. I waved a hand at the women gathered around, shooing them away.

The hiss and crackle in my ears was bad, but the garbled voice coming through was somehow ten times louder, loud enough to hurt. I turned down the volume and fiddled with the dial, trying to make the voice clearer.

I pulled the speaker tube close to my mouth and raised my voice. "Say that again?"

"KKKKKKKKSSSSSHKKKK ay ahoy th zzzzzSSSSSHHHHHH zzzzzzmmmmmmmm this is the Tal PAH! zzzzzzzzzz," the headphones shrieked into my ears. I twisted the dial the other way and suddenly I heard the woman say in Anglic, "Do you read us?" though the static and distortion made it difficult to identify the speaker.

"Just that last part," I said. "Who is this?"

"Gwendolyn Tallyho, of the Tallyho Sisters," the voice said. She sounded so different from real life. It made me wonder what mine must sound like to her. "I say, to whom am I addressing myself?"

"Captain Val, of The Furies," I answered. "Our operator's lost her head, so to speak. What's up?"

"A cloudless sky, a full moon coming, but no enemies in sight, more's the pity. Care for a bit of coordinated flying? Get a leg up on the competition, wot?"

I nodded, then realized she couldn't see me. "Sure thing. Where?"

"One moment, please, Captain Val." I heard muffled murmuring over the headphones, like she was talking to someone else, then she came back. "Just the other side of the peninsula, what do you say?"

I glanced over at the map of Merinasy Violette kept on her table. She'd explained she liked to keep a map of wherever she was readily available. Libertia was built in a fish-hook bay on the north-east face of Merinasy. Across the peninsula lay the Hindyastani Sea. "Why so far?"

"Best not give any spies or saboteurs any ideas, don't you know. In an hour, then?"

"Sure thing," I answered. In an hour it would be sunset. Serena would wake up, Argenta would be back in business, and the night shift would be up and running. Night manoeuvres were never easy. All sorts of things could go wrong. Practice would get us back in fighting trim. "See you then."

"Toodles!" she answered, then the line went silent.

Chapter Twenty Three

We Should Have Gotten the One With Caller ID

An hour later, we were airborne, soaring out into the night sky. Serena had agreed with my idea immediately. The crew were all keen to be doing something, instead of just waiting in port. I was glad to be away from the dead fish smell. I did send a shiny thank you gift to the mermaids who'd saved me, by the way, I don't want you to think I didn't. Anyway, the fresh night air blowing in the windows put everyone in a good mood.

Argenta's first words to me were, "Thank you, Captain Val." Her voice was high and feminine, like Alumina's, but without any of her sister's subtle, emotional inflections. Gigi told me those would come in time, as the language spool loosened up.

"You're more than welcome," I answered in Atlan. Might as well practice, even though I knew enough to understand most conversations. "How's the neck?"

She turned her head left, right, up, down. And then surprised me by tilting it from side to side. "Better. Thank you for asking."

"You feel up to taking your post at the radio?"

"Of course, Captain."

Molly called me forward into the wheelhouse. She had a telescope up to her human eye. "There she is," she said, pointing at a blacker patch of night in the sky. Then the moon shone on her balloon from an angle we could see, a silver-grey oval hovering there, waiting. "Running dark. Going to make it hard to coordinate our flying."

I went to the intercom, flipping all the switches. Each switch controlled an intercom in another room, where my voice would be heard. By switching them all on, the entire ship could hear me. "Serena, to the wheelhouse, please."

Molly passed me the telescope. I gave the Tallyho Sisters a good look. Something struck me as off about her, but I couldn't place it.

I stepped back toward the wheelhouse door, leaning out to ask

Argenta, "Hail the Tallyho Sisters, please, Argenta."

"Ahoy, Tallyho Sisters, this is The Furies," Argenta spoke into the metal tube, holding it to her throat speaker instead of to her sculpted lips. "Ahoy, Tallyho Sisters? Can anyone hear me?" She turned to face me. "No answer, Captain Val."

I began to worry that something might have happened to them. I stepped back into the wheelhouse and said, "Bring us up alongside them, Molly."

Molly took over the wheel from Salia. Serena arrived in the wheelhouse, and I told Salia to go find Tring and ready a boarding party.

"Trouble?" Serena asked, looking out the window.

"She's not answering our hails," I explained.

"Perhaps their vireless is malfunctioning."

"No," Argenta's voice called out from the radio room. "I beg your pardon, Miss Heartlace, but their wireless is receiving our communications."

Serena leaned out of the wheelhouse. "How do you know this?"

"If there were no wireless to receive the signal, I would hear nothing. But I am hearing some noises over the headphones. This leads me to believe they have a wireless communicatron. They simply are not responding."

Serena turned to me. "Vhat do you think?"

"I think..." I looked out the window. We had pulled up almost even with her, maybe a hundred feet off our starboard. Her decks were lifeless, empty.

Some movement caught the corner of my eye. In the split second it took me to realize what it was, it was too late.

"GET DOWN!" I shrieked, diving for cover, as her cannons fired.

Chapter Twenty Four

Ambushed and Ambushed Again

Screams filled the air. Moans of pain, of confusion. Shrieks of metal bending and breaking, thuds of wood shattering, falling to the decks. Smoke everywhere.

"Molly!" I coughed, using the captain's chair to help me to my feet. "Get us out of here!"

Molly still hung onto the wheel, though blood was pouring into her face from a gash in her scalp. Broken glass littered the wheelhouse floor. She turned us hard to port, away from the ship. I prayed that the ship's gunners, whoever they were, wouldn't be able to reload in time to fire on us again.

I spun the engineering control to Ahead Full. No intercom would be loud enough to be heard over the ship's huge pounding engines. Molly spun the elevator control as fast as she could crank it. On an airship, the elevator was the flap thing on the balloon's tail that made the ship tilt up or down. By cranking the control forward, the ship would rise. Molly was trying to gain as much altitude as possible.

"INGA!" I yelled into the intercom, which I realized was still set to broadcast to the whole ship. I hoped that helped when I hollered for people to get down. "Get our guns loaded!"

A voice I didn't recognize answered back, "Inga's compliments, Captain, that's what she's doing."

"Okay, right, thanks," I said, switching off the intercom. The deck began to tilt under my feet, the ship's nose coming up.

"Bring us about to their bow," Serena said. Molly spun the wheel, heaving us back to starboard.

"Do we fire back?" I asked.

"They have indicated hostile intention," Serena said, her tone so dry it sucked the moisture from the air, I swear. Every time I think I'm a master of sarcasm, Serena shows me how it's really done. "I vould think it prudent to answer in like kind."

"What if it's the Tallyhos?"

Serena just pointed out the window. I looked.

Though her hull and balloon were similar enough to fool us, the Tallyho Sisters and our mysterious attackers' ship had one distinction difference – the figurehead. Where the Tallyho Sisters had a figurehead shaped like themselves, dancing with swords outstretched along the bowsprit, this ship's figurehead was a skeletally thin man dressed in black, black cloak billowing out behind him, like wings along the hull, arms stretching forward, clutching, grasping.

"It's Captain Crow!" Molly snarled.

"That vould be the Relentless, then," Serena added. "Eire-made corsair. Fast." She turned to me, grinning so fiercely I saw her fangs. "Not heavily armoured."

"This was all a trap," I said, feeling stupid. "The Tallyhos are probably still back in port."

"So it vould seem. Ve have more pressing concerns, though."

Outside, we saw the Relentless' nose rise.

"Gun deck to wheelhouse!" the intercom squawked.

I flipped the switch for the gun deck. "Wheelhouse!"

"All guns report ready, Captain!"

"Fire at will!"

The whole ship shook a second later as all our starboard guns fired. The noise deafened me for a second. Serena grabbed me by the shoulder and pointed out the window.

I stared at the Relentless, behind us off our starboard. I could just make her out. The nose of her balloon had a huge hole in it and was deflating fast. But Moonchance had explained it to me in excruciating detail. Airship balloons weren't just one big sack of gas, they were dozens of smaller sacks, separate one from the other. To truly blow a ship out of the sky, you needed to damage enough of her gas cells that she'd achieve negative lift. In other words, enough of the gas cells had to be emptied so that the remaining cells couldn't hold the ship up any more, and she'd sink. It was that kind of technology that had kept me from dying aboard the Syren, when we'd been captured by Captain Caliper.

All that to say, even though her nose was leaking, the Relentless wasn't out of the fight just yet. Even as I watched, dark shapes scuttled out over the tattered membrane, pulling sheets of cloth with them.

"Now those're sailmakers," a voice said in my ear. I jumped, startled. Moonchance had zipped into the wheelhouse while I was trying to see if our enemy had died yet. "Y'see now why I's so bloomin' insistent, like? Ain't no seamstresses gonna swing out over a leaking nose and plug up a bleedin' leak like 'at, not in a fight they ain't."

The Furies spun away from the Relentless, turning to port. Hopefully we could broadside her properly this time, instead of that volley we'd just lobbed at them.

"Alright, I get it! What are you doing here?"

"Come to tell ya that last volley din't hit nuffin' worth hittin'. Seen it wi' me own eyes. Them Eire corsairs'll fly with four gas cells half full. Need to batter the hull, take out the engines, and board 'er."

"If ve descend to her altitude she vill fire upon us. No, ve need to blast her balloons," Serena argued.

"She's taking the decision out of our hands," Molly said. "We're the ones on the run."

"How are we supposed to fight something that's behind us?!" I yelled. "We can't even see her!"

"Bring us about," Serena ordered. "Ve need to see her to kill her."

"She's already full rudder to starboard," Molly said, shrugging her shoulders toward the wheel, where her hands gripped it so tightly her knuckles shone bloodless white with strain. The deck had tilted to a dangerous angle. Shards of broken glass began to slide along the floor. If we didn't do something soon to shake her, the smaller ship's tighter turn circle would have her broadside to us in seconds.

Our main engines were already at full. We literally couldn't turn any sharper, or any faster.

"Dammit!" I swore, then left the wheelhouse. I ran up the spiral stairs to my quarters, then out onto the main deck. Moonchance followed me up, then passed me on the way to her beloved balloons.

Wind tore at my clothes. Tring and the other boarding party regulars stood at the starboard rail, watching the Relentless turn. Her gun ports were open, cannon muzzles glinting in the moonlight. I ran back down the stairs, yelling, "Hard to port! Hard to port!"

Molly was already turning the wheel when I arrived in the wheelhouse.

"All rudders to port, Captain," she reported. The deck began to tilt back the other way, glass shards skidding along the floor.

Long seconds ticked by. The thunder of cannons off our starboard side told me the Relentless had fired on us; the lack of screams told me she'd missed. I ran to the radio room, snatching the metal tube from Argenta.

"Hey, Tyr! Missed us!" I taunted. "Got a little too excited?"

"You'll beg for mercy before this day's over, murderer," a woman's voice snarled back over the speaker grill.

"Oh please, who's murdering who?"

"You killed my twin, you bloody bitch!" she answered. "I'll see you bleed!"

"Your sister? Wait, who is this?"

"Artemis Hawkmoon," she said. "And now I get my revenge."

"Artemis..." I remembered something from one of my English classes, or History maybe, when we were studying Greek and Roman myths. "Diana? Diana was your twin?"

"Yes! I can't wait to make you pay!"

"Captain!" Serena yelled from the wheelhouse.

"Hold on a sec," I said into the metal tube, then handed it back to Argenta.

"Vhat vas that about?"

"Tyr's got a new friend, and we have a new enemy," I said. "What's up?"

"She's nose on to us," Molly said, pointing out the port window.

Is a window a window if there's no glass in it? Anyway, off our port side, I could see the Relentless' bow, full on to us. We had her completely broadsided.

During the last few weeks, I'd learned a few things about aeronautical battles. In addition to the advantage of altitude, there was a little manoeuvre called "crossing the T". Basically it meant having our side to their nose, also called the bow, or their rear end, the stern. That way, our cannonballs would fly through the length of their ship, instead of their much narrower width. We'd do more damage that way, and they'd hopefully surrender.

I had a feeling Tyr and Enerva and Diana's twin weren't likely to surrender.

Anyhow, we had their T completely crossed. But they were way too far away for us to take advantage of it. And they were turning hard to starboard, trying to come about our stern.

I was about to give the order to come about to starboard when a huge explosion shook the entire ship. I lost my balance and fell to one knee, pain shooting through it as slivers of glass slashed through my pants and skin. The ship rolled with the blast, swinging back and then forward again, hard, like riding a wave. Then a second blast rocked the ship.

"What the hell is she doing?!" I yelled. The ship rocked even harder. Caught off guard, Serena tumbled out the open window. She snatched at the twisted window frame, shards of glass slicing through her palm.

"Look!" Serena answered, hanging on for her life by one hand while she pointed with the other.

Somehow, Inga had used the rolling of the ship to our advantage, getting just the little bit of extra angle or range or whatever necessary to hit the Relentless. Explosions rocked her hard, all along her balloon and decks. I cheered, yelling at the top of my lungs. From the gun deck below, I could hear more cheering.

"Molly, bring us about!" I ordered, helping Serena back into the wheelhouse. Molly spun the wheel to port so our starboard guns could fire on the Relentless.

But the Relentless had other ideas. Despite the fires raging on her decks and her deflating gas cells, she continued her turn to starboard, completing the turn before we came about. She turned her tail to us and made a run for it.

There were cheers from my crew. We'd been ambushed and now the enemy was on the run.

"We're not letting them go?!" Molly snarled.

"No way," I agreed. "Full ahead. Let's see how Inga handles those new guns she insisted on."

When she'd been hired, Inga had one look at our gun decks and declared the cannons barely adequate. We'd worked for a solid week, installing five new ones. Three jutted from our stern.

Now Inga rolled out our other two guns, a pair of huge cannons set in the bow of the gun deck. I swear I could hear her give the order to "FIRE!" from the wheelhouse. The entire ship rocked backwards and the world filled with a sound so huge I think I blacked out a little, like my brain couldn't handle a noise that enormous, so it shut down for a second to process it.

Serena said something but I couldn't hear anything over the ringing in my ears. Molly looked dizzy, clinging to the wheel for support.

Ignoring Serena for a second, I went to the intercom. "Gun deck! Hold your fire!"

I heard Inga swearing in background and someone said, "Uh... Aye, Captain."

I turned to Serena. "What?"

"You don't need to shout!"

"What?!"

"YOU DON'T NEED TO SHOUT!"

"Oh. Am I?"

"Yes."

"What were you saying just now?"

"The bow guns are directly under the vheelhouse. Perhaps next time ve fire, ve should evacuate first."

"Good idea." I went to the forward windows and leaned against them. I couldn't see if the bow guns had done any damage to the Relentless. They headed inland, which surprised me, north-east away from Libertia. We went after them.

Repair and clean up crews came to check out the wheelhouse, led by Miss Merryweather. They swept up the broken glass. A couple of minutes later Angel came up and bandaged my knee, Serena's palm, and Molly's forehead. I also had a gash in my left palm that I couldn't remember getting, and she bandaged that too, making me promise to come see the doctor at my earliest convenience.

"Angel," I said as she stored her gear back in her bag. "How's the crew?"

"Three dead, Captain," she answered quietly. "Twelve wounded, two severely. Dr. Westmore's done her best, but those two likely won't see the sun set again."

Five more dead. I didn't blame myself, like some captains might have. No, I blamed Tyr Ebonfury. Him, and the crew of the Relentless.

I glanced at the engineering control, still set to Full Ahead. I looked out the window. Slowly but steadily, the Relentless was pulling away.

"Looks like Moonchance was right," I muttered. "Eire corsairs can really fly." I turned to Serena. "Is there any way we can go faster?"

"Only way to go faster is to lighten our load," Molly answered for her.

"If ve empty our vater reserves, that might do it," Serena agreed.

"Don't we need them?"

"Ve can always refill vonce the battle is over. And if ve lose, vell, fresh showers and clean clothes vill be the least of our vorries."

"Alright, do it," I said. Serena left to carry the message to engineering. We'd need to figure out some kind of intercom system that would work over the pounding thunder of the engines. You know, if we survived.

The jungle lay beneath us, a sea of gently swaying black occasionally shimmering silver as the moon came out from behind the clouds that had rolled up during our brief encounter with the Relentless. I stared at our fleeing enemy for as long as I could stand it, probably only about two minutes, even though it felt like about two hours. I left the wheelhouse and went to Argenta.

"What's the range on our radio?" I asked.

"Five miles, Captain Val," she answered.

"Can you reach anyone in Libertia?"

"We are well out of range, Captain."

I glanced at the map on Violette's table and realized I had no clue where we were. "Where's Violette?"

"I have not seen Miss Verdigris," Argenta answered.

"Dammit, what are we paying her for?" I asked rhetorically.

Argenta answered me anyway. "To navigate, Captain Val."

"Yes, thanks, Argenta."

"You're welcome, Captain."

I went back to the wheelhouse. We weren't any closer to the Relentless. Below us, the coastal jungles had given way to inland plains. A herd of antelope, spooked at the sound of our engines, scattered. And a good thing too, because that was when the water reserves began pumping out.

We began to rise as we cast off weight, and Molly adjusted the elevators to keep us even with the Relentless. With the clouds rolling in, we risked losing her.

I turned on the intercom, switching all stations. "Violette to the wheelhouse, please."

I snapped off all the switches, but a reply came just seconds later. "Wheelhouse, Surgery."

I flipped that switch. "Go ahead, Surgery."

"Begging the captain's pardon," Mary said, "but Miss Verdigris's been injured."

All of the anger and frustration I felt immediately turned to guilt and worry. "Is she alright?"

"Broken leg, took some shrapnel. She'll live, but she's not happy about it."

"Can she walk?"

"She hasn't been fitted for a cast yet. Doctor's still busy."

"Somebody get her a walking stick or some help or something and get her up here. We need her to figure out where we are."

"I, well, that is... aye, Captain."

I turned off the intercom. Violette, hurt. Who else? How many more of my crew would be hurt? For what?

"Captain!" Molly yelled. I turned, and went numb.

Ahead of us, the clouds had parted, leaving a clear midnight blue sky, filled with stars. The moon silvered the highland plains below. In the distance, mountains were peaked with a thin line of snow, glowing by moonlight, a jagged line of silver white.

Between us and the mountains, a sight that turned my blood to ice water. Five huge fearsome forms flew toward us, soaring slow and steady, moving with malevolent motivation.

"What is that?" I asked, surprised my voice was so calm. Behind me, Serena returned to the wheelhouse, and immediately began swearing in the vampyri language.

"Atlan Aerial," Molly answered after I asked the question again. The skin around her eye lens had gone bloodlessly pale. "A whole division, from the look of it."

"Three Groupers, a Devilfish... and a Great Vhite," Serena, horror hissing her words to a whisper. "Half a dozen Barracudas, too."

I didn't know what she was talking about, but it didn't sound good. "And that means what, exactly?"

"Bad news for Libertia," Serena said. "This is an invasion force. Ve cannot fight them."

I looked out the window. The biggest of the ships looked to be like ten times our size. It had wings jutting out to either side and a vaguely pyramidal command tower built on top of its huge balloon, giving it a distinctly shark-like appearance. "No kidding we can't fight them." I tore my eyes from the five massive masses moving by moonlight and found the retreating rear of our recent foes. All thought of revenge melted in the face of the Atlan Aerial forces. "Molly, bring us about. Hard. Now."

"Aye, Captain."

I went to the wheelhouse door and saw Violette being carried in a chair by three girls, a rough splint around her right leg, bandages elsewhere, her clothes spattered with blood. She held an open bottle of wine in one hand, her face contorted with pain. She flinched and swore with every jostle, every bump. Every third or fourth bump she took a swig from the bottle. When she saw me, she asked, "What's so bloody important you can't leave me to my agony?!"

"Figure out where we are and get us to Libertia," I ordered. "Do it now or we're all dead."

The other girls went pale and set Violette down as gently as they could. She still swore and swigged, several long swallows. "Get me to the window, and find my equipment," she said, wiping her mouth with the back of one bandaged hand.

Two girls each took an arm, while the third went to the navigation desk and pulled out Violette's gear. Argenta cleared out of the way as quickly as she could. Violette shook off the two girls helping her and hopped to the window herself, using whatever support she could find. She glanced out the window and swore, violently and creatively. She looked at me, panic piercing her pain.

"Do it now or we're all dead," I repeated. She blinked once, twice, then nodded. Glanced out the window. Looked to her desk. Grabbed the compass and took a reading. Measured our movements on her map. Her lips moved in quiet calculation.

"Come to... one-sixty-five mark three," she said, and I repeated it to Molly, who didn't answer, just turned the wheel. Violette sank back in her chair and swigged her wine.

I went to Serena. "Tell me what those ships are."

"The Groupers are troop carriers. Like the Barramundi warship that carried the Deathwings."

"How many troops?"

"Hundreds. Perhaps a full battalion, a thousand soldiers. Three Groupers, potentially an entire brigade."

"Wow. Okay. Next?"

"The Devilfish is an ornithopter carrier. Perhaps fifty Piranha ornies, their pilots, accompanying support crew. A thousand airmen, at least."

"That's the big flat one?"

"Two dirigibles linked by their flight deck, yes."

"Great."

"And the Great Vhite. A dreadnought. The biggest airship in the seven skies. It has von purpose. Var."

"They aren't fooling around, are they?"

"Not even a little. And do not forget the Barracudas. Ship-killers. Designed for speed. No cannon, but plenty of personal wolley guns."

"Whatty what?"

"Volley guns," Molly answered. "They have many barrels, all loaded beforehand. Lock the barrel in place and they fire one after the other, no reload delay."

"So like a machine gun," I said to myself, nodding. "They use those to kill ships?"

"A hundred rounds pumped into a balloon at short range vill kill a ship faster than one cannonball. All those holes to patch, every gas cell leaking? The ship crashes before the sailmakers can even fly out a line."

"Are we sure they're headed for Libertia? Are they following us?" I asked, then ran up the spiral stairs to the main deck. I sprinted down the length of the ship. A crowd had gathered at the stern.

"Don't you ladies have something to do?" I asked, shoving my way through. "We won't be boarding them any time soon, trust me. Go below and find something to clean or whatever."

The crowd of boarders dispersed, none too happy to be sent back to cleaning duty. Tring looked like she had something to say, but didn't. I was sure I'd get an earful eventually.

Far off our stern, the Atlan Aerial force had turned off, not following us exactly. Their course would lead them north of Libertia. Maybe they'd sail past.

Yeah, right.

I couldn't make out the Relentless in all the flying shapes, but I knew they had to be there. Somehow they must have sent word back to the Atlan base, to send as many ships and soldiers as they could. Tyr Ebonfury had to be the traitor, I was sure of it. I just had no proof. Or even hard evidence. Might as well suspect him of sending the patchwork assassin after me. As much as I hated his guts, it really didn't make any logical sense to blame him for everything.

Sure made me feel better, though.

I went back to the wheelhouse. Adrenaline still coursed through me, giving me the shakes. Just the act of sitting in my chair made me realize how tired I was. Pain in my hand and my knee and the dozen other little cuts and bruises started making themselves more than just nuisances. Also, I was starving.

Domina showed up, limping a little, her shirt bloody, a thick bandage visible under it.

"You alright?" I asked.

"I'll live, Captain, thank you," she answered. "Permission to return to duty?"

"You should be resting, I bet," I said. "But unfortunately Atlan Aerial isn't going to give us that chance. Get yourself something to eat, if you can, and bring us something, too, please."

"Aye, Captain."

It was a tense, silent ten minutes. I almost nodded off, as my body tried to conserve energy. Domina brought food for Molly and me, and an entire bottle of blood for Serena. Molly locked the wheel in place and we dug in.

"Bring me four more," Serena said after taking a long drink.

I looked up from the most delicious ham sandwich I'd ever eaten in my life. "Really?"

"There vill be fighting, Captain, and soon. The sun rises in an hour. Ve cannot afford to have me slumbering."

"Yeah, but it really wrecks you," I argued.

"I vill be really wrecked if ve go down vhile I slumber," she answered, draining the bottle. "Four more, Domina."

"Aye, Miss Heartlace," she answered, and headed off to find more.

"You can't stay in the wheelhouse," I said to her.

Serena shook her head. "No. I vill go to the map room. Ve can tarp up the vindow easily enough. I can coordinate vith the other ships faster than Argenta."

"Captain Val," Argenta said from the map room. "We are within range of Libertia."

I scrambled out of my chair, bringing my half-finished sandwich with me. "Get the Tallyho Sisters on the radio, Argenta."

"Aye Captain Val."

Chapter Twenty Five

I Guess We're All Crazy

The sisters weren't dead. They weren't even hurt. They were a little curious as to where we'd gone, and when they found out, they were absolutely beside themselves with fury.

"No bloody blighter's going to use my bloody name to draw my friends into a bloody ambush!" Captain Tallyho swore over the radio. "They'll pay for that, or my name's not Guinevere Madelaine Evelyn Tallyho!"

"Too right, Guinny!" I heard Gwendolyn agree. "We'll show those miserable wretches what for, wot?"

"Too right indeed, Gwen! Now. What's this about Atlan Aerial?"

I told them everything I knew. They were heading north of Libertia. They had a lot of troops, a lot of ships, and a lot of guns. There was no way we could stand against a force like that. "Spread the word, fast as you can. Everyone needs to get out of town, like, right now."

"I say, that is disconcerting. We'll spread the word, don't you worry."

"And get the news to the town, too. Their basement bunkers won't do them any good, not against five thousand airmen and soldiers. That's like, a third the population of the entire town."

"More like half, I should think. We'll tell them. Do hurry back. Wouldn't want to lose you in the confusion."

"We're on our way," I promised, then signed off.

I went down to the Surgery. Doc Regan had her hands inside someone who was being held down by three other girls. I couldn't tell who the patient was. There was an awful lot of blood. Everywhere. On the floor, on Doc's clothes, on the girls, one bloody hand print on the wall where someone had leaned against it, probably when we were doing all those hard turns.

"Hold her still, blight take ye!" Doc Regan swore at the girls helping her. With a final pull, she extracted a piece of sharp metal about the length of my pinkie from her patient's gut. She dropped it into a waiting dish with a loud *clink!*, then said, "Angel, sterilizing solution."

Angel grabbed a pitcher of steaming cloudy white liquid and poured it very carefully into the wound while Mary held an electric lamp closer. Doc Regan leaned down and inspected the wound. "Right. I think that's it. Sutures."

Mary handed over a curved needle threaded with thick black thread, and Doc set to work. She glanced up, noticing me for the first time.

"Are ye wounded, Captain?" she asked.

"What? No. I mean, I am, but it'll keep."

"Fine then," she answered. "Mary, the laudanum."

Mary unstoppered a brown bottle and dripped some of the liquid into the patient's mouth.

"Is there anything you need?" I asked.

"Someone to help clean up," Doc Regan said. "And more water."

"We dumped the reserves," I explained. "To lighten our load."

She glared at me for a second, then grunted her reluctant acceptance. "We need water."

"I'll get it for you." I ran off, headed for the engine room.

Below the crew deck and the gun deck, the damage was much more apparent. I saw a hole in the hull as I ran through the maze of the Operations deck, Miss Merryweather already organizing a repair team to seal the breech with planks of wood. A metal plate would be welded on later, assuming we outran the Atlan Aerial forces approaching. I paused there, briefly, asking her to send a crew to the Surgery to clean up the mess. Then I slid down a ladder to the engineering deck.

Gigi had her girls running, inspecting every huge boiler's pressure, getting the stoker crews to shovel coke into the boiler whenever the pressure dropped below a certain point. Mostly they communicated by hand signals, since the pounding of the pistons and the turning of the great propeller shaft made too much noise for normal communication. I noticed there were fewer girls than usual.

I'd almost reached the point where I could enter the engine room without thinking about the days I'd spent there as a slave.

I waved frantically to get someone's attention. One woman saw me, got Gigi's attention, and pointed. Gigi turned and saw me, then ran over. I used to think I had cat-like reflexes until I met Gigi. Her cat animan physiology let her jump up the steps from the engine room floor to the engine room door in a single leap. We stepped outside the engine room and closed the door.

"We need water," I explained.

"You ordered the reserves dumped," Gigi answered.

"What about the water in the boilers?"

"We need that if you want to stay at full speed. We need maximum pressure in the steam pipes."

"Shit," I swore, scrubbing a hand through my tangled hair. "Any ideas where I can get some water?"

Gigi shook her head. "Sorry, Sunset. Ask Mrs. Shorty."

"Alright, thanks. How are things down here?"

"Fine. Some of the girls are helping out with repairs. I would be too, but you need full speed, so..."

"Thanks. If we survive the rest of the day, you can have all the time you need to finish up repairs."

"Deal," she grinned, then the smile faded. "Wait, survive?"

"Tell you about it later," I said, and went off in search of Mrs. Shorty. You're probably wondering why I was doing all this running around, instead of sending Restless or Domina or Padmini to do it. The truth is, I needed to be doing something. Sitting in the captain's chair waiting to see if we made it to Libertia before the Atlans behind us just killed me. Not, you know, literally. But I had too much adrenaline, too much energy, to just sit around waiting.

I found Mrs. Shorty in the Booty Bay.

"Take the ice from cold storage," she said, without any pause whatever, when I explained the problem to her. Then we organized a crew of girls to haul the big blocks of ice up to the mess hall, where a quick word with Brunhilde got us a great big pot on the stove to melt the ice in.

All that took about twenty minutes, so I went back to the wheelhouse to see what was going on. I passed Argenta in the radio room, but she just sat there, eyes flickering. From the muffled, tinny voices I could hear coming through the earphones, there seemed to be a lot of conversations coming over the radio.

I stepped into the wheelhouse. Cleaning crews had gotten the last of the broken glass off the floor and out of the windows, and even put up some metal grills in all of the empty windows except the two directly ahead. It didn't do anything to stop the wind, but at least we wouldn't be falling out the gaps any more. And we could see through the grills.

In the distance, the first faint lightening of the night sky began to hint at an upcoming grey dawn. It was an hour away at least, but I knew the slumber had to be starting to affect Serena.

Who wasn't in the wheelhouse. "Where's Serena?"

"Went to get changed," Molly explained without facing me.

"How are you doing?"

She shrugged.

"We'll get them, one day," I said, guessing. She was never very talkative, but since the attack and the Relentless' escape she'd been as quiet as the grave. "We couldn't go through that whole Atlan group to get them, is all."

"I want her dead, but I'm not suicidal, Sunset," Molly said quietly, flexing the fingers of her artificial hand. "Taking on that Great White alone would have killed us all."

"Yeah," I agreed, a little at a loss for something to say. Luckily Serena saved me the trouble.

She stepped into the wheelhouse clad head to toe in black leather; knee-high leather boots, tight leather breeches, a high-collared leather jacket, long-cuffed leather gloves. She'd bunned up her long blonde hair and encased it in a leather aviator cap. Goggles with dark lenses covered her eyes. She had a sword on each hip and looking insanely bad ass.

"All that will protect you from the sun?" I asked.

"Ve vill see," she answered, swigging from a bottle of blood. She wiped her lips with the back of her fist. "There are stories of wampyri doing as I am, holding off the slumber long enough to find shelter, clad in thick blankets and capes, hooded. Ve vill see if this leather is thick enough."

"What about your face?" Molly asked.

Serena held up a length of thick dark grey canvas.

"What is it?" I asked.

Instead of answering, she wrapped it four or five times around her face and head, scarf-like, securing it in place by tucking it into her jacket and up under her goggles. She didn't look bad ass any more. She looked downright terrifying.

"Wow."

"Mnk mm," she answered, then pulled the scarf away from her face. "Thank you," she repeated, drinking from the bottle again.

"Sunset," Molly said, drawing my attention back to the window.

I expected Libertia to be an ant's nest of activity, everyone awake and alert. All lights were dark, all chimneys smokeless.

But the sky swarmed with shapes. Ships by the dozen darted about. Smaller vessels fed supplies to larger ones, already afloat.

I went to the radio room. "Argenta, get me the Tallyhos, please."

"At once, Captain Val," she answered. "Attention Tallyho Sisters. This is The Furies, can you hear me?" A muffled tinny voice came over the headphones, which Argenta promptly took off and handed to me. "Tallyho Sisters, Captain Val."

I pulled the headphones over my ears, then spoke into the metal tube. "This is Captain Sunset Val of The Furies." Then, just to make sure, I added, "Too bad about that auto-horse."

"I say, wot?" a woman asked.

"The auto-horse."

"Oh! Yes. I dare say he lost his head, haw haw," she answered, and I knew it had to be Gwen. Still, just to be sure, I asked, "Gwen?"

"In the flesh, so to speak."

"Why aren't you leaving? There's a huge invasion force coming!"

"Oh, that. Bit of a bother, really. Once we'd put the word out, simply everyone was itching for a fight! Can't say I blame them."

"Alright, I'll get to the idiocy of that in a second. Why's the town all dark?"

"All lamps and cookfires extinguished. Can't risk a fire in the midst of a battle, my dear."

"Yeah, I guess a Great White dreadnought, a Devilfish, and an entire division of Atlan soldiers is enough to worry about. Like maybe too much? Like, how about everyone lives to fight another day?"

"Have to make a stand sometime, pet. Might as well be here. Else they'll take the town, enslave the women, patchwork the men, and hunt us across the seven skies. No, no, and again no. Besides, if we all go down in flames, at least someone somewhere will write a story about us."

"If no one survives, no one will be alive to write the story, Gwen."

A short paused followed my pronouncement, then she answered, "Hadn't thought of that. Best we win, then, eh? Listen pet, I'd love to stay and chat, but we do have a battle to get shipshape for, wot?"

"Yeah, sure," I answered, signing off. I handed Argenta the headphones and tube. "Get me Captain Jones, please."

Argenta twirled the dial around, speaking into the tube. I turned back to the wheelhouse, and saw Serena looking at me. "They're all crazy."

"Insanity vould be a great assistance in these circumstances."

I laughed. "Yeah." I stepped closer to her, checking to make sure no one was near enough to hear me. "We can't win this. They have to know that."

Serena nodded. "And yet, they stay. Who knows vhy? All that matters is, they stay. Vill they flee vonce they see the enemy? I hope not. It vill be much vorse to vait and then run. If ve run now, ve may get away. But if ve vait, ve cannot hope to escape. No, if ve vait, ve must fight."

The idea of staying to fight that huge invading force filled me with fear. But... the Tallyhos had waited for me. All these other people had stayed to fight. People smarter than me, more experienced than me. Crazier than me, true, but if they thought we had a chance, then maybe we did. And if we did, and I ran, then I'd be a coward. And if I ran, and they lost, I'd be worse than that. I don't know that I could live with myself if that happened.

It was stupid. It was crazy. I barely knew these people. There was a good chance I'd get a lot of my crew hurt, even killed.

"Orders, Captain?" Molly called from the wheelhouse.

I shared a look with Serena.

"We wait," I said.

Chapter Twenty Six

The Battle Over Libertia

That was the worst, the waiting. Not the running for our lives, not the chasing the Relentless, not the explosions and the screams. The waiting was the worst, and it was all Captain Jones' fault. He'd come up with a plan.

I could just imagine how it must have looked to the incoming invasion force. There's Libertia, all quiet. No lights, no cookfire smoke. Not a ship in the sky, or in port. Seems deserted, right? No sign of anyone, anywhere.

Maybe the Devilfish sends out its ornies. Maybe they land their Grouper troop ships, deploy their soldiers to investigate. The Great White circles the town, a predator robbed of its prey.

I suspect, though of course I have no way of knowing for sure, that when we all came out of the cloud bank we'd been hiding in, it took them by surprise.

At Captain Lawless' suggestion, we concentrated our attack on the Devilfish. The less enemy in the air, the better. We dove out of the clouds, steep enough that I had to hold onto the arms of my chair to keep from sliding off of it. The Devilfish lay almost directly beneath us, a huge flat expanse of floating airfield held aloft by two dirigibles. It was a beauty, and our job was to destroy it.

Ornies scrambled to take to the air. Nice thing about ornies was they didn't need much of a runway. Bad thing for us, but good for them, I guess. A few managed to take to the air before we opened fire.

Our pirate armada had split into three prongs: one for each dirigible, and one for the airfield, to take out as many ornies as we could. I ordered Inga to fire the forward guns at the airfield as we dived, covered my ears, and saw two huge holes appear in the otherwise seamless field. More followed shortly after, as other ships followed our example.

Then the sky was filled with explosions and ornies firing at us. I went to the intercom and flipped the Launch Bay switch. "Launch all ornies!"

I yelled, hoping they could hear me over the roar of cannon fire. Four ornies dropped out of our launch bay, all four-seaters. A pilot, a spotter, and two of our best sharpshooters rode in each orny. Sixteen women left our ship, and I hoped more than anything they'd all be back.

I flipped the Gun Deck switch. "Fire at will!"

A fierce roar from the women at the guns was all the answer I needed. Cannon fire rocked our ship, first from port, then almost right away from starboard. Fires erupted all along the Devilfish's airfield.

We finished our first pass of the Devilfish, then came about as hard as we could. I saw the other ships in our prong jostling each other, nearly colliding. Two ships did collide, explosions rupturing their balloons, their fragile frameworks collapsing, their weight surrendering to the pull of gravity. If we'd had the time to organize, to train together, it wouldn't have happened. Atlan Aerial hadn't given us the time to train.

"We can't see each other," I said to myself, then turned to Serena. "Get lookouts on the main deck, with runners to warn us. Our fastest girls, the best runners. And tell them to watch out for Atlan ornies! No, wait, give them the rifles! Shoot them out of the sky!"

She nodded and left without a word.

An explosion rocked the Devilfish's port dirigible, the ship immediately listing. Then the port dirigible went up in yellow-green flames. The Devilfish clearly had been finished off. It began its long slow crash into the bay.

And then we had bigger things to worry about. Or, well, smaller things, technically.

The sky filled with those smaller ships, the Atlan Barracudas. They bristled with guns and flew straight for us. Four pirate ships went down in the first pass, caught in a deadly hail of bullets from their volley guns and repeating rifles, their balloons shredded. The Barracudas were too fast to get a bead on, so we couldn't fire back. I sent the word for the sharpshooters who were left to start firing on them.

"I can't see a thing from here!" I said angrily.

Argenta stepped into the wheelhouse. "Captain Val, Captain Jones says everyone should come about to port."

"Molly!"

"Aye, Captain," she answered, already hauling on the wheel, hand over hand. The deck leaned hard. Argenta stumbled against the wall.

"Back to your post, Argenta," I said. "And thanks."

"Aye, Captain," she answered, and staggered back to the radio room.

We came about hard to port and found ourselves staring at the stern of the Tallyho Sisters. They'd taken some hits, from the looks of her. Their sailmakers were scrambling along the sides of their balloon, held by ropes, buckets of sealant glue and strips of balloon canvas attached to their safety harnesses.

A few ships pulled in below us, and a couple above, a wall of vessels, easy targets. I didn't know what Jones was up to, but it seemed to me that this was a great way to get a lot of people killed.

I went to the radio room. "Well?"

"Captain Jones says to wait until they're committed to the attack, then let fly, Captain Val. Double shot for range, if you please."

I went back to the wheelhouse and passed the word on to Inga. Whoever answered for her, just said "Yessum."

The Barracudas swept in for the kill, but this time we had them broadsided. I stood at the intercom, one hand on the switch. They flew closer, closer, closer. They'd turn at the last possible minute, and let fly a volley from all their guns, and we were just sitting, waiting for it.

Except we weren't, not really. Captain Jones' ship, the Mistress o' Merit, was just above us, and they fired first.

I yelled "FIRE!" into the intercom then flipped the switch to off and covered my ears. A half second later, the boom of the cannons rocked the ship. The Tallyhos were only a half second behind us.

The Barracudas were fast and they were agile, but they couldn't avoid an entire wall of cannonballs. They scattered, turning hard, but every ship hits, balloons and underslung cabins both. All six ships were shredded, their crew tumbling from the open volley gun doors, and I hoped they were dead before they hit the ground. Later, it would give me nightmares. Just then, I felt a savage, fearsome joy.

It didn't last long. In the east, over the ocean, the grey light of earliest dawn had turned crimson, painting the clouds a bloody red. Red sky in the morning, airmen take warning. Great.

Serena downed the last of her bottle of blood and tossed it out the window, then wrapped the scarf around her face, her movements almost too fast to see. "I'll be in the radio room, for now."

I nodded. She'd drunk enough blood to normally last her a month. "Stay away from the surgery until we can get it washed down," I said, worried.

She nodded, once, deliberately slow enough for me to see, then disappeared. For a second I thought she'd somehow gone invisible, but she'd just moved too fast for me to see.

I glanced back at the dawn, then saw a huge silhouette blot out the sun. The Great White.

I ran to the radio room. "Tell Jones we have to scatter!"

Argenta relayed my message, and I waited for about eighteen years before the answer came back. "Captain Jones agrees, and directs us due west, all speed, low as we can go."

"Molly, due west, bring her down now!" I went back to my chair in the wheelhouse. "There has got to be a better way for this to work," I muttered to myself.

The deck tilted forward and to port just as the Great White opened fire. Huge explosions rocked our pirate fleet. the Atlan vessel's giant cannons getting lucky hits on some of the bigger, unluckier ships. Fiery wreckage rained down on the docks of the bay, and I briefly hoped the mermaids had gone and hid somewhere. Like, Australia.

We avoided the Great White, but there was no avoiding what the Groupers had ready for us. Up ahead we saw them, huge and bloated-looking, compared to the sleek killing elegance of the Barracudas. One Grouper had landed and already discharged its cargo. Men and machines menaced the townsfolk who rose in riotous rebellion.

Another Grouper looked to be landing as well. I ran to the radio, snatching the tube from Argenta.

"Anyone headed due west, this is The Furies. Follow us in on that Grouper!"

Back to the wheelhouse. Glanced out the windows. Saw about a half dozen others flying alongside us. We began to pull ahead of them, the point of our attack spear.

Suddenly the air filled with dark fluttering shapes that I immediately recognized. The Deathwings had taken to the air. One actually landed on our nose and started to climb through the windowless front of the wheelhouse, only to meet Molly's metal fist to his face and a shot from her pistol. Blood spattered against the open window frame and he fell.

"Take us starboard of the Grouper," I ordered as Molly retook the wheel. "Then tell Inga to open fire."

"Aye, Captain," Molly answered.

I raced up the stairs to the main deck and found it in chaos. Deathwings had boarded us and run smack dab into Tring's Open Hands and every other woman aboard who'd been itching for a fight. I drew my sword and pistol and waded into battle.

It became immediately clear that the Deathwings we'd faced before were raw recruits. These guys were veterans. They fought well, working together, partnered back to back. They used pistols and daggers. My girls fought hard, but they were obviously outmatched by these professional predators. Too many of my crew fell, injured. Doc Regan would have her hands full soon.

Moonchance and her pixies swept down from our balloon, causing as much confusion as they could, pulling off goggles and poking Deathwing eyes, stabbing faces with needles, flipping switches to activate the Deathwing's mechanical wings, sending them flying uncontrollably overboard. But even their efforts were too little to do much good.

"Fall back!" I ordered, surrendering the main deck. The crew escaped into the lower decks, the Deathwings following us.

Right into Serena. Hopped up on all that blood, she was a whirlwind of death, like the Deathwings had walked into an invisible airship propeller. Wherever she went, she left dead Deathwings behind, killing and moving on to the next, almost too fast to see. We turned on them, too, but she did most of the bloody butchery. In seconds, our ship was scoured of the enemy.

Then the cannons roared, and I knew we were passing the Grouper. Distantly I heard other cannons echoing our volley, and then a huge explosion rocked us. I ran to the wheelhouse to see what had happened.

The Grouper had exploded, showering more yellow-green fire onto the town below. I went to the radio room.

"Tell everyone who followed us to come about hard and dump their water reserves onto that fire! We can't save the town from the Atlans only to lose it to fires."

"Aye, Captain Val."

We'd had just enough time to refill our own reserves with sea water from the bay before we'd had to hide in the cloud bank. I knew we'd need to keep some, for medical reasons, and hoped we'd have enough for both the surgeries and the fires below.

I grabbed Domina. "Tell Gigi to dump ninety percent of our water reserves," I ordered, and she ran off. Then I found Miss Merryweather.

"Get half the girls to help the wounded, then set the others to clearing these Deathwings."

"Aye, Captain. What should we do with the bodies?"

Part of me wanted to dump them overboard, but I figured dropping corpses on the town wouldn't exactly make us popular. Not that anyone would have noticed, I guess, what with flaming wreckage of ships already falling on the town. "Store them in the Booty Bay. Get Mrs. Shorty and her girls to strip the bodies of anything useful."

"Like those wings?"

"Yeah, exactly."

She nodded and went about getting our girls in gear. I headed back to the wheelhouse.

Another explosion rocked the ship, hard enough to knock me off my feet. We'd been hit!

"What happened?!" I yelled over my own ringing ears as I ran through the wheelhouse door.

"The Relentless," Molly snarled through clenched teeth.

Chapter Twenty Seven

A Relentless Fury

I leaned out the starboard window to get a better look, and pulled my head back just in time. Another volley rocked our ship. Screams of pain filled my ears, from every deck in earshot. Inga's crew returned fire. I saw the Relentless' hull take the full brunt of our volley. Then she rammed us.

Not head on, mind you. Side to side. I heard the yells of the girls on the main deck as they repelled the boarders trying to take us.

I flipped all the switches. "All hands on deck! We're being boarded!" I turned to Molly. "Can we get loose?"

"Our lines are tangled, and the helm's sluggish. I'm betting she took out our rudder. At least this close she can't take out our balloons."

"Leave it, then, and come get some payback," I said, pulling my sword from its sheath. Molly grinned fiercely at me, slammed the engine control to Full Stop, then followed me topside.

On the main deck, another chaotic melee had erupted as Ebonfury's crew tried to swing across the gap between our ships. The Furies had a pretty narrow balloon for her size, only about twenty feet wider than the ship itself. The Relentless had been built for speed and manoeuvrability, with a longer, thinner balloon, so in total only about fifteen feet separated the two ships. We were about two hundred feet up, though, so it made for a hell of a drop.

Their boarders swung across on lines as their sharpshooters kept us diving for cover. As soon as the boarders had crossed, though, their sharpshooters followed, which gave us a chance to fire back. A dozen boarders died in a blast of bullets and smoke, and then we crashed into the rest with screams of rage and howls of fury. We'd watched women get wounded, or worse. We weren't exactly in a forgiving mood.

I ran one guy through with my sword and emptied what was left in my pistol into a couple of straggling boarders as they swung across. I didn't watch them fall through the gap, turning to find the next boarder, and the next, and the next after him.

It was a blur of flashing swords and cracking gunfire. Something punched me in the left arm and I lost my main gauche, just as I slashed my epee across the throat of a woman who barely looked older than me. She fell to her knees, dropping her sword. Restless stabbed her in the back, tears streaming down her face.

She looked at me and grinned, then her eyes went wide with shock. "Cap'n, you're hit!"

I looked down at my left arm. My left hand was cold and numb, despite the heat of exertion and the coat I wore. Something red dripped from my fingers. I raised it and realized Restless was right.

"Ow," I said, surprised at my own lack of reaction. Then someone came at me with a knife and I used my sword to stop him, dead in his tracks.

Restless was tugging at my arm. It hurt. I couldn't seem to think straight. Why did my arm hurt? Oh, right, I'd been shot.

She was wrapping something around my arm, tight. It hurt like hell. I pushed at her hands to stop her. She was taller than me, suddenly. No, wait, I was sitting. When did I sit down?

Domina grabbed my other arm and together they dragged me below decks. My arm was nothing but pain from my shoulder down. Suddenly Doc Regan looked at me. Mary and Angel sliced open my sleeve. The sudden release of the pressure the sleeve exerted on my arm made the pain so huge and total and everywhere that everything sort of just evaporated.

More pain in my face brought me back.

"Don't pass out," Doc Regan said. "Sure, an' this is but a wee thing. In an' out, no harm done. Through the muscle, see?"

She poked a finger into my arm and I nearly threw up. Not from the pain, which was pretty intense, but from trying to wrap my brain around the idea that someone else was inside my arm.

"Do what you have to," I said, turning away. "I need to get back."

She wasn't gentle, but she was quick. Stitches went into my flesh. Some kind of powder sprinkled inside me, to fight infection. A cream smeared on the outside, and bandages.

"Drink this," Angel said, pouring some liquid into a teaspoon and sticking it in my mouth before I could object, or even ask what it was.

It tasted terrible.

"What was that?"

"Something for the pain," she answered.

I got to my feet. Restless and Domina stood nearby, to help in case I needed it. I felt shaky, but I could walk. I nodded to them. "I'll be alright," I told them. "Go see who else needs help."

"Aye Cap'n."

"Aye, Captain."

"Thanks," I said to Doc and Mary and Angel, but they were too busy with the other wounded to answer me.

I went to the weapons locker, grabbing another pistol. I made sure it was loaded and climbed the stairs to the main deck.

Just like the Deathwings, the boarders had managed to get below decks. Just like the Deathwings, they'd faced Serena. And just like the Deathwings, they'd died.

Unlike the Deathwings, we'd followed the boarders back aboard their ship. I saw fighting on the main deck of the Relentless. I spotted Molly, fighting against Ebonfury himself. Tring and her Open Hands were taking on anyone stupid enough to face them. Tatalia Tempest and Jenny Squall fought back to back, a blur of bloody blades. Gigi and some dog animan clawed and bit each other, surrendering to their animal sides. I even saw Argenta, grabbing and bending sword blades plucked from enemy hands.

Whatever Angel had given me, it worked fast. The bloom of white hot pain in my arm had faded to a dull roar. But when I grabbed a boarding line to swing across to the Relentless, the pain sawed through my arm again, bright and brilliant.

Unable to cross over to the fight, I settled myself behind the rail and drew my pistol. Using the rail to steady my hand, I fired all six shots, each a hit against one of Ebonfury's crew. None of them looked happy about it.

Then someone grabbed my hair and hauled me to my feet. I grabbed at the hand that held me, my left arm singing an aria of pain. I felt cold steel against the skin of my throat, and grabbed at that hand too. A familiar voice snarled, "Now you'll die, you bloody bitch!"

Out of the corner of my eye I caught sight of blonde curls. "Diana?"

"Wrong twin," she answered.

"Right, sorry, Artemis. Listen, don't you want to know how she died?"

"All I care about is that you killed her!"

I talked fast, faster than I ever had before. Which was saying a lot. "Technically starvation killed her. Or dehydration. I don't know, we didn't go back for her body. Anyway, before we made her jump, she begged me to let her take your pictoriograph with her."

A sob escaped my would-be killer's lips. I felt the knife ease away from my throat, a little.

An angry yell from behind us made her turn, wrenching my hair. The knife came away from my throat. Artemis threw me to the deck, threw her knife at her attacker.

Restless.

The knife caught her in the gut. She gave a little cry that sounded more surprised than painful and sank to her knees.

I grabbed Artemis' ankle and hauled on it, hard. Caught off guard, she fell to the deck, smashing her knee. I pounced on her, forcing her face to the floor, grabbing handfuls of curly blonde hair, slamming her face again and again against the deck. When she stopped moving, I scrambled over to Restless.

Tears streamed down her pale, bloodless cheeks. "I peed myself," she said, teeth clenched against the pain. "Don't tell no one."

"It's okay, Restless," I answered. "Lots of people do that when they get stabbed."

"Really?"

"Sure. Come on, Doc Regan will fix that in no time."

I spotted a couple of women helping the wounded and called them over. Together, the three of us lifted Restless and carried her down to the Surgery. Blood drenched Doc Regan to the elbow, staining her apron dark red. She looked at Restless and said, "Get her on the table."

I left then. There wasn't anything I could do. Not there, anyway.

The pain in my arm disappeared in the sea of rage I felt. It wasn't the fury of a storm. It was the clear white anger of a lightning bolt. I grabbed more ammunition from the weapons locker and headed topside. I found my gun and loaded it, then I started firing.

Not at the enemy. At their balloon. It was an easy target. I barely had to aim. I pumped round after round, bullet after bullet into their gas cells. There didn't seem to be any noticeable effect, at first.

Moonchance landed nearby as I reloaded for the fourth or fifth time.

"What?" I asked.

She seemed startled at my rudeness. "What is it ya think yer doin', Cap?"

"Take out the balloon, take out the ship, right?"

"Aye, Cap."

"Then stop squawking and take out their balloon."

She nodded, a fierce joy in her grin, and left with a quick salute.

I kept firing. I had no idea if it was working, until one of the gas cells collapsed completely, letting loose all its gas at once as the balloon fabric ripped. Did it sound like a fart? I don't know, I was too busy deafening myself with gunfire.

The Relentless lurched, hard, and I saw people on their main deck fall to their knees. They'd done some repairs on their balloon on the trip back to Libertia, but they hadn't found a new source of gas. They were going down, this time. Eire-made corsair or not.

Of course, I'd forgotten one little thing. Their lines were tangled in ours.

One of our lines snapped like a guitar string plucked one time too hard, a loud whiplashing thrumming snap. The Furies shook with the recoil. The Relentless shook harder, all hands abandoning the battle to grab onto something. Above, Moonchance had done something, somewhere, and their gas cells emptied even faster.

My crew began scrambling to get back onto The Furies, followed shortly after by the remaining members of Relentless' crew. Soon we had a boarding fight on our hands again, my girls swinging and jumping across the gap, climbing aboard, and turning right around to repel boarders. I emptied the last of my ammunition into a huge lumbering rhino animan then looked for my sword.

I found it where I'd dropped it, but there was no sign of Artemis. Great.

The ship shuddered again, and the Relentless definitely started to fall, dragging us along with her. I ran to the wheelhouse. "Gigi! Get our engines going! You rest, get out the axes and cut us loose!"

In the wheelhouse, I grabbed the wheel and hauled her hard to port, but Molly was right, the wheel was was sluggish, like trying to turn it through mud. Molly joined me and added her strength to my efforts, but it wasn't enough. There was no way we were going to avoid crashing.

The Furies hit the cobbled streets of Libertia only seconds after the Relentless ploughed through a bank of houses. Their collision slowed us enough to keep us from being completely wrecked, but it wasn't much fun. The noise was huge, enormous. It filled the entire world. Rocks and dust and dirt peppered Molly and me through the open window frame. The electric lights flickered out immediately after we stopped moving.

I picked myself up. Coughing the dust out of my lungs, I helped Molly to her feet. Somehow, miraculously, The Furies had stayed mostly erect, so the deck didn't lean too dangerously. We stumbled out of the wheelhouse and climbed the stairs to the main deck, where the reason for our stability became clear. The ship was leaning against a house. I looked through the fourth or fifth floor window of a little kid's bedroom. Huge eyes in a small face stared out at us, half-hidden by the window sill, stunned silent.

The crash had knocked the Relentless loose. She lay behind us in a heap of rubble, the ruins of the block of houses we'd destroyed in our descent.

Molly and I helped the other ladies to their feet. Together, we went below decks and started carrying the wounded out. Below, all was dark, lit only by dim drizzling daylight draining through dusty porthole windows, and the occasional distant flash of cannonfire or lightning. I found myself a battery lantern and lit it, then carried it ahead of me into the depths of the ship.

Everything was still and quiet on the Operations Deck. No hiss of steam in the pipes. No gurgle of water. No pounding beat of the engines below me. I spotted a pair of yellow glowing eyes staring at me, getting closer, closer. I almost drew my sword when Gigi spoke.

"Had to shut the engines down, or the whole ship might have gone up in flames," she said, stepping into the range of my lantern.

"Oh," I answered, not really knowing what to say. "Will they be alright?"

"The ship's taken a beating," Gigi answered. "It might take weeks to undo the damage."

"If ve survive the day," Serena whispered from the shadows, and Gigi and I both jumped out of our skins. "Then ve vorry about the ship. For now, ve should move the crew to the streets. The ship is just a target."

"Alright," I nodded. "Let's go."

"I vill stay and guard the ship," Serena said quietly. "Safe here. In the dark."

"Serena, are you alright?" I lifted my lantern to try and spot her. I found her in the shadow of a support beam, her face hidden by a curtain of hair. She'd lost her aviator cap and scarf. Her goggles rested on her forehead. She hissed and turned away from the light, but not fast enough for me to miss the smears of red on her face. Serena had been feeding.

"Go now," she snarled, her voice thick with warning. "Go."

Gigi had begun to back away, and I joined her.

"Stay safe," I said from the stairwell.

Serena nodded. "You too."

Gigi and I climbed out of the lower decks and found the wounded being transferred into the little kid's room. We gathered what supplies and ammunition we could, and joined them. Those of us who could still walk and fight gathered in the family's parlour, while those too wounded to go on filled the beds and couches and chairs and tables and even the floors of the house.

I looked into two dozen faces. We looked like hell. None of us had escaped injury. All of us were filthy and bleeding and soaked from the rain. And every last one of us wanted a fight. Anyone who didn't, or couldn't, stayed behind to help with the wounded.

We left the house and took to the streets. I left Mrs. Shorty in charge of figuring out what we needed from the family and negotiating how to compensate them.

"Which way?" Miss Merryweather asked. She walked with a limp, but she could still swing her sword.

Out in the streets, The Furies towered above us. Seeing her from this angle, seeing all the damage she'd taken, I wanted to weep. I couldn't imagine how we could ever fix those huge holes in her hull, how we'd wash away all the blood.

I looked away, unable to face her. Back up the street, the wreck of the Relentless lay in ruins. Down the street, though, I saw the Atlan soldiers who'd made it off their Grouper. They didn't wear the black leathers of the Deathwings. Instead, they had on brown uniform jackets, brown pants tucked into black boots, the golden Atlan trident emblazoned on their right shoulders. Round black helmets with metal crests shaped like a fish's dorsal spikes completed their uniforms. They carried rifles and swords, and looked like they hadn't seen a single second of combat.

Just when I thought my fury couldn't possibly grow any greater, it spiked white hot and blindingly brilliant.

"Come on," I snarled, pulling on the backpack I'd brought with me.

We all had. The last of my crew pulled on their backpacks, too. My arm knotted up with pain but I managed to get the Deathwing wings going, the leather flapping noise filling the street, echoing off the buildings. I rose about ten feet, then let out a shriek of pain and hate and thirsty vengeance. I soared down the street at the enemy, the soldiers who had brought war to this peaceful city. Behind me, I heard my cry echoing, and at first I thought it was my own shriek bouncing off the walls, but it went on too long, in too many voices. My crew had taken up my wordless cry, following my flight.

We landed in the middle of the group of Atlan soldiers. They had no idea what hit them, thinking, maybe, that we were Deathwings coming to help. Well, we had wings, and we brought death, but we weren't there to help. Pistols fired. Swords flashed. Blood spilled. When it was over, they were all dead, or so injured it didn't make much difference. We'd taken injuries, scratches and bruises mainly. No losses.

"What now?" someone asked. Domina, maybe.

"Now we find more of these blighted bastards to kill," I answered, and took to the skies.

We swept street after street, searching for soldiers or survivors. Locals looked alarmed as we passed. We found two more groups of soldiers. One group had been pinned down in a square, taking cover behind market stalls as the townsfolk tried to pick them off with their long hunting rifles. We descended like the mythical Furies we'd named ourselves after, howling for bloody revenge. Again, the Atlan soldiers didn't know what hit them.

Down by the docks, I found Madam Helen and her girls, defending their house from all Atlan forces. Piles of dead soldiers surrounded the house, testifying to her girls' accuracy.

"Well now, look at you!" Madam Helen called from a window on the third floor.

I flew closer. "Need any help?"

"We're fine and dandy, sweet thing. Though from the looks of things that might not last long."

She pointed behind me and I looked. Out in the bay at least a dozen pirate ships floated, in various states of destroyed. A quarter, maybe a third, of our forces, ruined, wrecked. Their destroyer was obvious enough. The Great White.

It had stopped circling the town and now headed inland, toward us. I couldn't see if it had taken any damage at all.

"Find a place to hide, sweets. That big bastard's coming to hand out a punishing." That said, Madam Helen closed the shutters to her window, and her girls did likewise.

I landed on her roof, and my crew landed nearby.

"What do we do, Captain?"

Moonchance landed on my shoulder.

"Any chance we can take that big bastard out?" I asked.

She laughed. "No chance at all. 'er balloon's covered in copalum mesh plates, armour-like. Keeps out most cannon shot, see? Not that there's anyone nearby can get a shot at 'er without being blown ta bits their own selves."

I laughed too, short and bitter. "Great."

"If we could knock off one o' her stabilizing fins, maybe she'd tip, but fat chance o' that."

I looked at her, not an easy thing to do. "What?"

She pointed at the fins sticking out to either side, slung low on her balloon. "Them fins, see? They keep her balanced, counterweight to the command tower on her back. Neat bit o' design work, that."

Little bits of ideas began to burst in my brain, like that thing they do in cartoons when the characters have a light bulb over their heads. I grinned. Only Gigi recognized the grin, and she grinned back. The rest of my crew looked at me like I'd gone mad.

"I have an idea," I said. "Come on."

Chapter Twenty Eight

Talk About a Barrel of Fun

We flew back to The Furies, only to find her under siege.

Atlan soldiers had surrounded her, despite the pounding they were taking by the few crew left aboard. My girls used their pistols, but ammo had run low and some of them had resorted to dropping cannonballs on their attackers. As we swooped in, the Atlans retreated without a fight.

I found Inga in charge. She'd stayed behind due to the huge bandage covering half of her face. She was in danger of losing that eye.

"What's going on?" I asked.

"They came. We attack."

Typical Inga. You'd think she had to pay for each word she used.

"Alright, fine. Good work. We need all the gun powder we have left."

That got through that icy outside. She stared at me, stunned. "All?! But why? We need that powder to keep them from taking the ship!"

"If I don't get that powder, we won't have a ship to keep. Pack it into barrels small enough to carry."

"Ya, ya, but they are already in such barrels. But why?"

I told her my plan. Inga grinned bigger than Gigi had. She even laughed.

"Ya. Ya!" She slapped me on the shoulder so hard I nearly lost my balance. At least it was my good arm. If it had been the injured one I probably would have passed out. "You will have it all. All! Girls! Come! Quick now!"

"Captain!" Padmini yelled from the stern.

I ran over. I almost asked, "What?" but it was obvious the moment I looked past her.

An Atlan machine was headed our way. I didn't know what to call it. My brain immediately decided on war-crab. It walked on eight legs, carried six soldiers. Two of them piloted the machine. Two others manned the volley guns mounted on its back. And the last two soldiers manipulated the giant pincer claws it had.

"Oh shit," I swore. Padmini just nodded, her eyes wide with terror.

"If she reaches us, those claws will gut the ship like a trout," Molly said beside me.

"Better make sure she doesn't reach us, then," I said. "Girls! Go time!"

We took to the air. I had no idea what to do besides charge them. Probably not the brightest idea. Luckily my girls were smarter than me. Most of them grabbed cannonballs on their way out, and as we flew overhead, we dropped them.

We were also lucky in that their volley gunners had been watching the streets and not the skies. They wouldn't make that mistake again. Well, they wouldn't be making any mistakes ever again, at all. A twelve pound cannonball dropped from twenty feet can do a lot of damage. Multiply that by two dozen, well...

The war-crab took a pounding. One of its legs snapped. Another bent awkwardly. Unfortunately it had six other legs. The soldiers manipulating the giant claws immediately put them to protecting the pilots, parking them in position. Then they jumped into the volley gunners seats, pushing their dead comrades out of the way. Their guns roared, echoing down the street.

I led my girls high into the air, hopefully out of range of the volley guns. I heard a girl scream and turned to see Padmini drop to a rooftop. Hilda followed her down.

We scattered, making ourselves less of a target. As I flew through the air, I saw the Great White had almost reached the shore. Its forward guns had already begun firing on the town.

I glanced down at the crab. We didn't have time for this!

Lucky for me Inga's nickname was Doom. A huge explosion dwarfed the sound of the war-crab's volley guns, and one of its claws exploded. I looked over at The Furies, and saw two cannon muzzles, pointing out of a huge hole in her stern, right where our stern guns had been blown away. Inga and the few girls who'd stayed behind had moved the enormous bow guns into position and as I watched, the second cannon fired.

Another direct hit on the war-crab! Machine parts and body parts rained down on the cobblestone streets. The war-crab's legs shuddered and it crashed to the ground.

"Yes!" I yelled. Then, "Girls! On me!"

My crew swooped in, following me back to The Furies. We flew through the hole in the stern, landing on the gun deck. Half of us grabbed barrels of powder, the other half fuses and lighters and other tools. I ran to the stairwell, heading for the radio room.

Argenta wasn't there, so I grabbed the metal tube and earphones and hoped the radio was set to the right frequency or whatever.

"Hello, hello, Tallyho Sisters, this is The Furies, can you hear me?" Seconds ticked by. It might have been my imagination, but the boom of the Great White's cannons slowly got louder. I repeated my message.

Finally an answer came. "Halloo The Furies! I say, good to hear from you!"

Relief flooded my body. I'd really gotten to like those crazy Anglic women. "Yeah, me too. Listen, we have take out that Great White."

"Very astute, pet, did you just figure that out?"

"Not a good time for sarcasm, Gwen."

"Oh posh, every time's a good time for sarcasm."

"I have a plan, but we need a distraction. The Furies is grounded, so we'll be flying in on our Deathwing packs."

"I say!"

"Yeah," I said, then outlined my plan. Gwen answered with a string of curses like nothing I'd heard from her otherwise genteel mouth.

I grinned. "Exactly. Anyhow, you get everyone who's left to attack the starboard side, and we'll concentrate on the port. Alright?"

"Sunset, this is mad, you do know that?"

"We don't have a lot of choice, do we? It's either this or we cut and run and those Atlan bastards blow Libertia to bits. Besides, we have the advantage of them not expecting anything this desperate."

"Very well. Good luck, then. Good hunting."

"You too."

I raced back to the gun deck. My girls were waiting for me.

"Go time!" I yelled, grabbing a barrel of powder myself. It wasn't too heavy, but Inga had worked up some leather belts, which we used to strap the barrels to ourselves. It would make it easier to fly the Deathwing packs, which were pretty easy to use anyway, but whatever.

Inga strapped on a pack herself, carrying two of the bigger barrels. "You're not going without me."

I nodded, then led the way into the air.

"Spread out! Don't give them a target!" I yelled as we flew toward the bay and our prey.

Glancing this way and that as I flew in a zigzagging pattern to keep any riflemen or volley gunners with too much murderous motive on their minds from making me a messy mark on the street, I noticed the aerial battle had turned. Most of our ships were heading for the Great White. Gwen Tallyho must have gotten the word out, because they were all headed for the starboard side.

Unfortunately the port side faced out into the bay, which meant we'd have to fly all the way around the Great White to get to her port fin, or wing, or whatever. I'm sure by now you've figured out my plan. We'd fly to the port wing-fin-thing, blow it up with the barrels of gunpowder, unbalance the ship, and let the other pirates blow her out of the skies.

Naturally, it didn't work out that way. First of all, going around the ship would take too long. I know the way I've described the battle it sounds all exciting, swooping and banking and diving, with dramatic aerial battles and all that. But the thing was, the airships didn't really move that fast. For example, at full speed, it would take The Furies a full three minutes to make a right angle turn, in optimal weather conditions. Atlan Barracudas were a lot smaller and faster, and it still took them nearly two minutes to come about completely. There was a lot of waiting going on that I didn't describe all that much because, well, it's boring.

So going around the Great White would have taken like, a half an hour, and in all that time, they could fire on the town enough times to reduce the city to a smouldering heap of rubble. There was only one solution.

"Straight under!" I ordered, hoping my girls could hear me over the roar of gunfire overhead. I led the way, swooping, and in this case I do mean swooping. The Deathwings were much faster than any airship. Anyway, swooping down to the bay, only a few feet from the water.

Waves crashed beneath us, pounded by the explosive shockwaves from overhead. Spray filled the air, flying up to meet the rain that fell down. Lightning crashed. Thunder and cannonfire warred for auditory dominance. Honestly, my ears rang so hard and so loud it was a miracle I could hear anything at all, but when I heard a scream from behind me, I spun around. One of my girls had gone into the water. Jenny Squall,

I later found out. I saw someone hovering overhead, waiting to see if she'd come up. Finally a hand broke the surface, then a sputtering face. The hand waved the hovering one to go on without her, which she did. I turned and flew on, hoping Jenny would make it to shore.

We'd reached the point under the armada of pirate ships right about then, and the wreckage fell flaming to hiss itself silent in the sea below. We wound up keeping one eye high above and one eye ahead, to make sure nothing dropped on us. An ornithopter crashed into the ocean close enough to spray me with seawater.

Soon enough, though, the wreckage falling all around us changed to something else. Pieces that were identifiable as parts of ships (and, much worse, people) became just giant chunks of metal, huge splinters of wood. Once a cannon splashed down, right in front of me. Then the rain stopped, suddenly. I looked up. We were under the Great White.

It blotted out the rainy, cloud-filled sky. My plan suddenly seemed ridiculous. Our little barrels of gunpowder wouldn't do anything against something that enormous. I was about to order a retreat when Inga flew ahead of me, up, up, up.

There were gun turrets set in the Great White's belly, volley gunners who kept enemy ornithopters from getting too close. Inga timed her approach for when the gunner was changing his barrels, then flew in for the kill. One shot from the pistol in her hand, and he dropped into the ocean far below. Inga climbed into his turret, changed the barrels, and fired on her neighbouring gun turret, who was taken completely unawares. His turret exploded, and even from where I hovered, I could hear Inga laughing with bloodthirsty joy.

"Come on!" I said, recovering from my stunned amazement. "Let's do this!"

My girls roared their vicious approval and flew through the gap in the Great White's defences, heading for the fin.

Up close, the fin was bigger than I imagined. The sheer size of the Great White had made it seem small by comparison, but it was still at least the size of a basketball court. Its forward edge carried three propeller engines, and the wind from those nearly knocked us all off our feet, catching our wings and tugging at them, hard. It made for some very difficult landings, let me tell you. The girls with the equipment bags had an easier time than those of us who were carrying the barrels of gunpowder, but no one had it what you might call easy. I saw more than one girl go over the side, only to catch themselves mid-air and try again.

But finally, finally, we were all on the wing. Inga joined us and showed us the support structure, where we'd attach the barrels with rope and hooks. A couple of girls brought axes, and they made short work of the fin's outer skin. Gunpowder poured into the fin's interior would make for a much better explosion, Inga explained. "A contained blast will cause more destruction!" she grinned, in a way that made me very, very glad she was on our side.

"More destruction is why we're here!" I agreed, and ordered the remaining gunpowder poured into the fin's interior.

Inga set the fuses while I ordered the rest of my girls clear. I kept an increasingly nervous eye out for any sharp-eyed Atlan soldier or passing ornithopter pilot to notice us, but no one did. It was almost boring. Almost. No, it was nerve-racking. My nerves? Consider them really racked.

Inga lit the fuse and we took off, heading out to sea with the rest of my crew. Much safer than trying to fly back under a ship we were trying to blow up. The rains began to fall harder, and I hoped that they wouldn't put out the fuse, but Inga just laughed at the suggestion.

"Not my fuses!" she grinned.

When we'd flown a safe enough distance, we turned to watch the fireworks. It took longer than I expected.

"How long were those fuses?" I asked Inga, but she held up a finger, fierce fearsome fury on her face.

The thing I'd never considered was, those propeller engines? Had to have some kind of fuel tanks. They weren't steam driven, so it had to have been some kind of gasoline. Stored in the tanks that were inside the wing. The wing we watched completely, utterly disintegrate. A second later I heard the explosion, and a second after that the searing shockwave blew us out of the sky.

Ditching in the sea, I struggled out of my wings, then pulled hard for the surface. I sucked in huge lungfuls of air, then dove back under and helped as many of my girls as I could find.

In the sky, the Great White had already listed to starboard, away from us, and from what I could hear, the pirates were raining cannonfire on the command tower. The tower had its own guns, of course, and kept on firing despite their walls being turned into decks, and their decks turned into walls. Guess those gun turrets of theirs were really something.

Still, we'd made a real mess of her, and she was slowly but surely losing altitude. Not fast enough to stop them from firing on the town.

Until the dragon showed up.

No, seriously, a dragon. Out of the clouds.

At least, that's what it looked like, at first. Then I realized the dragon's head was just painted on the front of the balloon, and its 'wings' were actually ribbed stabilizers, huge horizontal sails to keep her even. It was long and lean, carrying a slender hull close up along the balloon, and painted in shades of red. A ship I'd never seen before.

Then its forward guns spat fire, catching the Great White's underbelly. The Atlan dreadnought caught fire immediately, yellow-green flames licking its bluish-white sides despite the rain falling. I saw shapes falling from the ship then, falling to splash into the ocean, and realized they were crewmen, abandoning ship.

We stopped watching and started swimming. The shore was a ways off, and the Great White exploded and crashed into the sea before we made it, but it was far enough that we didn't get hurt. Some small debris peppered us, but nothing serious.

We dragged ourselves to shore and lay there, breathing, thrilled just to be alive. I watched the few remaining Atlan forces try to escape, only to be hunted down by the last of our pirate armada.

It was over. We'd won.

Chapter Twenty Nine

Meetings and Partings

Six hours later, near sunset, I was sitting on a pile of rubble near the wreck of The Furies when the Tallyhos found me.

My crew and I were too tired, too beat and too sore to do much celebrating, even though all around us the town was going crazy, partying. Whatever Angel had given me for the pain had worn off by then, and my left arm wasn't singing an aria any more, oh no. It sang an entire opera of pain. The only thing that kept me from crying was exhaustion. I was too tired to care.

The Tallyhos sat by me, Gwen offering me a bottle of something alcoholic to drink. For once, I didn't care about any possible hangover, and poured myself a mouthful of something fruity. I swallowed and passed it to Guinny.

"How bad?" I asked, once I'd caught my breath. It hadn't been wine.

"Remy's missing," she answered, then drank to his memory. "Lawless' Highwayman went down, but he made it. Most of the ships went down, actually. What happened to The Furies?"

"Tyr Ebonfury's Relentless, that's what. Jumped us. I'm sure they got word to the Atlans somehow."

"Word? How? When?"

I shrugged. All I had was a firm suspicion and no evidence. "Does it matter? It's over now," I said, pointing down the street to where the wreck of the Relentless lay.

Molly had, of course, insisted we search the ship for Ebonfury and Enerva. I sent her with a few girls, mostly just to get her out of my hair. I'd had enough killing for a lifetime, all in one day, but Molly would never rest until Enerva's head was mounted on her cabin wall.

They hadn't found anything, though. If I hadn't been so tired, I might have worked up the energy to be worried that Ebonfury was still around somewhere, out for blood. As it was, all I'd done was nod, tiredly. Then

I told Molly to find some place to sleep and get some food.

Good advice, and I ought to have followed it myself. Still, if I had, the weirdest thing of all the weird things about that day might have not happened.

She was mostly naked, except for a few slender strips of strategic silk, and I would never have recognized her if it weren't for the mane of green dreadlocks hanging loosely down her back. Her features reminded me of native Hawaiians: slighted slanted eyes, button nose, wide mouth. It was hard to tell the natural colour of her skin, because she was tattooed head to toe in an glittering pattern of scales. When she smiled at me, walking barefoot through the rubble, I saw her teeth had been filed to sharp, even points.

She wore a triangular blade strapped to each wrist, about two feet long. The tip-most foot of each were caked in drying blood. If she had come looking for a fight, I was too exhausted to do anything but give her a target.

"You arre Ssunsset Val, yess?" she said, her Atlan heavily accented with clipped vowels, rolling arrs and long esses.

"Yes," I answered. "Captain Python?"

"I am sshe." She bowed, crossing her wrist-blades with a flourish. Behind her, her attendant came around the corner of a building, spotted her. A look of exasperated frustration flickered over the attendant's face, there and gone almost too quick to notice, and she hurried toward us.

"You arre sshe who made vulnerable the Atlan drreadnought, thiss isss sso?" Captain Python asked.

"Me and my crew, yes. We blew the fin off the Great White."

Her attendant had caught up to her and began unstrapping the wrist-blades from Captain Python's wrists. Captain Python let it happen without even noticing her attendant. "The firredrrake sship that finisshed the job, it wass ourss."

I'd seen her ship, before the attack. It was a beauty, painted in shades of green and gold, long and lean and built for speed.

"I'm sorry, Captain, it's been a long day. I'm not sure I understand."

"My Mistrresss wisshess to say that a Lemurrissian vesssel, the Drragon of Solar Triumph, wass rresponssible for the final blow," the attendant explained, holding out a robe for her captain.

"Thiss iss sso," Captain Python agreed.

"No offence, but why does it matter?"

"Salvage rights, love," Gwen explained, her eyes never leaving Captain Python's face. "Between the two of you go the spoils. Of course, several others will claim some measure of salvage. Us, for example."

"We all worked together to bring down the Great White," I said. "We should all get a fair share."

"Not many would see it that way," Guinny said. "You had the plan. You laid the bombs that took her out. We were just the distraction, you said so yourself. Then Captain Python's people swooped in and finished her off. No, the kill belongs to the two of you. Though we wouldn't say no to some small recompense to effect repairs on the Sisters, wot?"

"Capital idea, Guinny!"

"Why thank you, Gwen."

"No, no. Not at all."

Captain Python watched them talk like someone watching a tennis match and not quite following what was happening. She turned to me. "The enemy of my enemy iss my frriend," she said. "You arre welcome in Lemurrisss."

"Oh!" I answered, not really sure what else to say. "Um, thanks!"

Captain Python bowed again, and when she straightened, her attendant had her green and gold mask waiting for her to place over her face. Once her mask was in place, she bowed, turned, and left.

"So how, I wonder, did a Lemurisian firedrake ship know to come to Libertia, just in time for that battle?" Gwen asked.

"And who, I wonder, exactly is our Captain Python?" Guinny added.

"Well, the only thing I wonder is when I'm going to be able to get some sleep," I answered, hauling myself to my feet. I felt about eighty years old. Everything hurt. Just the act of walking took all of my concentration and energy. I made my way down the rubble and out into the rain, turning my face to the sky, letting the drops wash away the events of the day.

The owners of the house we'd totally taken over understandably wanted their house back, so we'd spent most of the afternoon getting everyone back on board The Furies, once Gigi and Moonchance had checked her out and made sure she was still airworthy. The ship had taken a hell of a beating, but she'd still fly. Slow and ugly and mostly in straight lines, but still, in the air. Not a lot of ships could say the same.

We hadn't flown her far, just far enough to let the home-owners in and out of their house easily. Basically we parked her in the middle of the street. Our three remaining ornies were parked around her, looking like chicks resting under their mama. The ruined house I'd found a dry place to rest in lay not half a block away from The Furies. Walking even that short distance seemed incredibly far.

The Tallyhos fell into step on either side of me, walking me all the way to our flight deck ramp.

"Cheerio, love," Gwen said, giving me a hug.

"Take care of that arm, wot?" Guinny added, taking her turn at hugging me.

"Will do," I answered. "See you in the morning."

I made my way through the ship, stopping only to count the dead bodies. Eight women, dead. Mostly new girls who hadn't seen any action before, ones I hadn't really had a chance to get to know. But there was Li, and next to her Padmini. There were others. It hurt too much to identify them all. I'd deal with it in the morning, when we found a new berth. We'd have to look for more crew, I supposed, but I didn't really want to think about it. I didn't really want to think at all.

On my way to my quarters I found Doc Regan, asleep in her chair, next to a sleeping, sweaty Restless. Doc held Restless' hand. I hoped she'd make it through the night. I hoped we all would.

My next stop was Serena's quarters, but she'd locked herself in after the Great White had crashed into the bay and we'd returned to the ship. I knocked, but she didn't answer.

Climbing the stairs to my quarters took more effort than I thought I had in me. Molly actually came up behind me and helped, as much as she could in a spiral staircase.

"Thanks," I said. My bed had never in my life looked so good. Although I could probably have slept on the cobblestone street outside.

Molly smiled and nodded, then left the way she'd come.

I sat down on the edge of the bed and it exploded.

Not an actual gunpowder and flames and killing splinters of wood explosion. It was more of a tearing sheets, feathers and hay everywhere explosion.

I don't know how it happened, but I was on the other side of the room in a heartbeat. I still don't remember moving. And I really had no idea how my sword wound up in my hand, but there it was.

And there stood my attacker, the patchwork assassin, kicking his way out of the wreckage of my bed. My bed. MY BED! All I'd wanted to do was go to bed, and he'd turned it into a pile of feathery kindling!

His knives slashed at me. All I could do to was counter his attacks, block his slashes and maybe try a riposte.

"Who are you? Who sent you?" I yelled, anger giving me the strength to fight him. My bed!

He didn't answer, of course. His focus frightened me. His every effort aimed at my end. A mistimed lunge brought his arm into my sword's slash, and I took it off at the elbow. No blood, of course, which made me completely grateful. I'd had enough blood for one day. Some of it had even been mine.

He grunted, his only admission of pain. Then he kicked me through the door, and I stumbled out into the rainy night.

You'd think with the balloon above us in a relatively light rain with almost no wind like we had that night, that the main deck would be mostly dry. Nope, guess again. Water dripped off the underside of the balloon in fat streams. We usually put out buckets and barrels to catch the rain, because for the most part our drinkable water was pretty hard to come by in the air, or over an ocean, or both.

Anyhow, Miss Merryweather really came through for me that night. At least a dozen girls were on the main deck, putting out buckets and barrels. After a day like we'd had, I didn't blame them all for being armed. And this part brought tears to my eyes – they all drew swords and pistols at the sight of me under attack.

The patchwork gave out a roar of fury and charged me. I didn't fight him. Instead, I ducked. The girls did the rest of the work. Bullets thudded into his flesh like hammers, opening bloodless wounds. Hilda and Inga jumped him, slashing at his remaining arm, Hilda with her kitchen knives, Inga with a hatchet. The arm fell to the ground, hacked to pieces. Then Tring got behind him and tripped him with a sweep of her leg. He went down like a tree felled by a lumberjack.

I jumped onto his chest to hold him down. Other girls jumped on his legs and the stumps of his arms. Someone grabbed the gizmo on his belt, the thing that supercharged him.

"Who are you?!" I screamed in his face. "Who sent you?!"

He laughed at me, then tried to headbutt me. Inga kicked him in the head, hard, twice. He laughed again, then tried to kick us off. At least, that's what I thought he was doing. Instead, what he really did was zap us all with electricity.

We all yelled and jumped off him, all but Inga, who kept her boot on his head, gritting her teeth against the spasming pain. When the arcs of electricity died down, I put my foot on his chest.

"Who sent you?" I asked again, leaning in.

He gargled something. A word. It sounded like, "Ca... lip... errrrrr..."

Then he died. As dead as patchworks ever get, anyway.

"What did he say?" Tring asked.

"Caliper," I answered. "Great. I'm only on this world for two months, and I have more enemies than a head cheerleader."

Tring looked at me oddly.

"Never mind," I said. "Get this lump of meat off my ship. Drop it in the bay, let the fish feed on him. I don't care."

I found an empty bunk and slept for nearly two days.

The celebration went on for a lot longer than that. Nearly a week, actually. Every single remaining pirate captain wanted to dine with me, or lunch with me, or even breakfast with me. I don't think I ate aboard The Furies once that week. Somehow, word had gotten out that I'd taken down the Great White, single-handed. People were calling me the "Hero of Libertia" and "Shark-Killer." Neither was true, but the first time I tried to deny it, or at least deflect it to me and my crew and the Lemurisian fire-drake – you know, the truth – people got angry at me.

"They need heroes," Serena explained it to me later. "By denying it, you deny them their chance to have a piece of your glory."

So I stopped denying it, even though the myths they were telling started getting outrageous. I heard one in a bar that had me facing off in single combat against the Great White's captain. I had no idea where that one came from.

We moved The Furies from the middle of the street to what was left of the Docking Tower, and Gigi and her girls got to work with the repairs. Actually, a complete overhaul is more accurate. "By the time we're done, with all this salvage, we'll have the finest, most dangerous ship in the sky," Gigi said, a worrying gleam in her eye.

I watched the repair crews working on my ship. The last of the sun's rays glimmered on the figurehead we'd had installed, miraculously untouched by the battle. The crew thought she was good luck. Not good enough luck, by my way of thinking. So many dead. Nearly everyone else wounded, some severely enough that Doc Regan didn't know if they'd survive.

We'd lost a lot of friends in the battle over Libertia, but it could have been much worse. Word came up the coast that the fleet that had attacked us had been just a part of a greater invasion, and that other Merinasy cities hadn't had the same luck we'd had. The battle continued all over the island. Lemurisian ships were stopping at Libertia, regrouping and refuelling, and then heading back out, hunting for Atlan Aerial ships. War had been declared.

We were out of the fight for the moment, but I had a feeling we'd be back in it, soon enough.

Keep reading for a sneak peak at the next Sunset Val novel,

Sunset Val's Hat Trick

Chapter One

A Horrifying Homecoming

The Starlight Dream had one hundred twenty passengers and twenty seven crew. Nearly four hundred feet long from stem to stern, she boasted a grand dining hall, a sun deck, and even an exercise room. Crystal chandeliers lit the dining hall with beautiful sparkling electric light. It was there that we'd assembled the passengers and crew. At gun and sword point, if need be.

The Starlight Dream was a luxury liner, filled with only the wealthiest Atlan citizens, people who profited from the misery their empire inflicted on the rest of the world. Against all reasonable advice, the owners had decided to continue using their flight routes, skirting the edges of the war zone, following their Neptopolis-Albion-Venecia-Kairo-Hindyastan route. Bad luck for them that their route brought them right into our patrol zone.

I'd come to this world, Ayrth, a helpless victim of a science experiment. I'd led a slave revolt, taken over the ship of my captors, forged frightened women into a crew, chased other slavers, been involved in the Battle Over Libertia and been called a hero for it. But in the six months I'd spent here, as captain of a pirate vessel, this just happened to be my first act of actual piracy.

"Ladies and gentlemen," I addressed the assembled Atlans. We'd attacked just after dinner; the men wore their tailcoat tuxedos or military uniforms, the women their finest gowns, sparkling with glittering jewels. "My name is Sunset Val. I am the captain of The Furies. You may have heard of us."

I know what you're thinking. How could they have heard of me? I was just a seventeen year old girl from another world. One pirate captain in a world of airship pirates. It stretched the limits of believability that the spoiled rich might have heard the stories about the Hero of Libertia.

Well, that may be, but it was true. Days after the Battle, really cheap books started being printed, telling all kinds of stories about me. My crew were the worst, buying every copy they could find, hoping for some mention of themselves in the penny dreadfuls. The so-called lucky ones read and re-read the tales of their exploits while the unmentioned majority had to suck it up. Personally if I ever found out who wrote those dreadfuls – and they really were dreadful, I mean, my 'bosom' does not 'heave like a ship at sea'. I barely have any 'bosom' anyway.

But that's not the point. The point was, The Furies had attracted a kind of notoriety, an infamy that we'd decided to capitalize on. If people expected us to be some kind of pirates amongst pirates, then that's what we'd be. We dressed the part, all ruffled shirts, knee-high leather boots, corsets, tricorn hats and bowlers and stovepipe hats, armed to the teeth with guns and knives and swords, showing off our scars and tattoos. I even padded myself, so that my 'bosom' would properly 'heave'.

In the dreadfuls, we were portrayed as vicious, merciless killers who took particular joy at meting out punishment against men. That wasn't true. But from the way the crew of the Starlight Dream had fought back, they'd believed it to be true. Doc Regan bandaged them up as I spoke.

"Some of you men may be thinking of fighting us," I said in Atlan. I couldn't get rid of my accent, so I hoped they could follow me. "Your days in the Atlan military might be fond memories. You may think your training will help you out." I paused and looked around at the assembled prisoners. "You'd be wrong. My women are bloodthirsty killers seeking revenge. Don't give them a reason to make an example of you."

I switched my epee to my off hand with a bit of unnecessary dramatic flourish, and pulled out my pistol. "Now then. Who's the captain of this vessel?"

A trim, middle-aged man with grey hair, a thick handlebar moustache, and a pristine white uniform stepped up. "I am. Now look here, you little –"

At which point I shot him.

I know, I know. Bear with me, okay? I was making a point, and I'd spent hours in training, aiming for the thigh, on the outside where it wouldn't hit anything fatal. Doc Regan herself had shown me where to aim for.

He stumbled and fell to the ground. Screams from some of the passengers hid his grunt of pain. I walked toward him, trying to look cold and calm, but my heart pounded. I focussed on breathing slowly.

The blood spread, staining his pristine white uniform a dramatic crimson. With one booted foot I shoved him over onto his back, then stepped on his wounded leg. He ground his teeth and took it, despite the obvious pain he felt. I had to hand it to him, he was tough.

I put the tip of my epee under his chin. "Who's the captain of this vessel?" I asked again.

Realization dawned in his eyes, followed immediately by a look of pure hate. "You are," he spat through gritted teeth.

"I'm not sure everyone heard you, sir," I said, quietly.

"You are," he repeated, louder. "The ship is yours, Captain Val." Then, quieter, so only I could hear, he added, "I hope you rot in Blackiron Prison."

I gave him a cold little smile I borrowed from Serena Heartlace, my vampyri first officer. No one does cold smiles like a vampyri. "Thank you, sir," I said for the benefit of our other captives, making a mental note to ask Serena about Blackiron Prison. I'd never heard of it before.

I turned to Doc Regan. "Doc?"

She was already on her way, carrying her medical kit, a sour look on her face. She hadn't liked this part of the plan at all, but set to bandaging the captain's wounded leg without a sarcastic comment, at least.

"Ladies and gentlemen," I said to our captives. "You will now notice my crew moving amongst you. You will give them your valuables. You will be searched. Even as I speak, your baggage and cargo are being transferred to our ship. Soon your cabins will be searched as well. I would not recommend resisting. If you do, there will be... trouble."

I turned to Miss Merryweather, my bosun. In a voice too quiet for the captives to hear, and in our own special multi-lingual shipspeak that we'd developed, I said, "Search the crew first, then separate them from the passengers. Come down hard on anyone who resists. We don't want to kill anyone we don't have to."

She nodded and started ordering the boarding party about. Boarding party, hah. Most of the crew were here. Since the Battle of Libertia we'd had so many applicants to join our crew that our ranks had swelled to nearly a hundred women and girls. Some of them had been pirates before they joined us, like Jenny Squall or our navigator, Violette Verdigris. Others had been seamstresses, or cooks, or knickerdancers, or pleasure girls, or nurses. Many had been mothers or daughters or sisters, orphaned or widowed by the war and desperate for a way to escape their shattered lives. In the end, we'd taken on as many as we could find bunks for. The youngest and oldest, we'd left aboard The Furies. All the others had come aboard the Starlight Dream, eager to see some action.

"Captain Val?" a girl called from forward. I spotted Svetlana standing at the doorway that led from the dining hall to the bridge. I went over to her. My bodyguards, Tring and Jenny, were not far behind.

"What is it?" I asked.

"Inga says the purser's safe is all set."

"Tell her I said, 'Go time'," I answered with a grin. The purser's safe would be where we'd find the best booty, and don't laugh when I use that word. That's what pirates call their loot, and I can't stop them. Anyway, whatever.

Svetlana answered me with a grin of her own, and a few seconds later an explosion shook the chandeliers. There were a few screams from the higher-strung passengers, and one of the crewmen stepped forward defiantly. Molly Wolfwood shoved him back hard, her mechanical arm more than strong enough to land him on his backside.

I turned to face the crowd. "Ladies and gentlemen, one last thing. You must understand that your belongings and valuables are all insured by the company that owns this beautiful vessel. Once you return to your homes, you'll be allowed to make whatever claims you care to make for the loss of your things, and the insurance company will reimburse you. I rather doubt that any of you made a perfectly accurate accounting or inventory of your valuables as you came aboard, so the company will have to take your word for it as to the exact amounts lost, stolen by infamous pirates. I say this because the loss of your valuables should really not be cause for any undue heroics."

Actually, I said it because I wanted them thinking about how much they could claim they lost, whether or not it was strictly accurate. If we stole five hundred sovereigns, the more unscrupulous and enterprising of them might claim they'd lost a thousand, and the insurance company would be forced to pay it. I could almost hear the gears turning in their heads, almost see the dollar signs in their eyes as realization hit them. After that, none of my girls had any problems taking wallets, purses, or jewellery from the cream of Atlan's wealthiest.

That little part of my speech had been Remy's idea. Remarkable Jones, who'd become kind of a leader among the leaderless pirate armada that trolled the seven skies, skirting the fringe of the Atlan empire, preying on the rich and fuelling the war effort. Remy knew the wealthy would fight hard to keep their wealth. At least, until we made it clear that they stood to profit from the initial loss. And crippling the Atlan insurance companies at the same time gave us even more reason to take all we could. The more these Atlan scumbags lost, the more they'd claim. The more they claimed, the more Atlan finances would suffer.

I made my way forward to the purser's office. Thick smoke and the noxious stink of one of Inga's home-brewed explosives filled the air. "Well?" I coughed, fanning the air in front of me to clear it.

The office was a shambles. Books and ledgers had been thrown everywhere, knocked off shelves. Papers lay piled in heaps, strewn about as chaotically as possible. Mrs. Shorty had a thick ledger in her arms, and she was thumbing through it as I entered. She looked up and nodded.

"It worked!" Inga grinned, staring at me with her one good eye. The other eye had been lost to an infected wound Doc Regan hadn't been able to heal, and replaced by a gleaming brass sphere.

It took me a while to figure out that the reason Inga spoke so loudly all the time was that all her explosions and cannoneering had left her hard of hearing.

When I answered her, I deliberately raised my voice and spoke as clearly as possible, knowing she'd have a tough time reading my lips in all this smoke. "Good job, Inga! Any damage?"

Even through the smoke I could see she looked a little insulted. "It worked, I said! No damage to anything but the safe door."

"Take it all, then." An unnecessary order, since a couple of Inga's girls were already emptying the safe. I turned to Mrs. Shorty and dropped my voice to a more normal volume. "You find what you needed?"

She nodded. "Aye Captain. This'll do nicely." A short, red-faced round woman with greying brown hair, she had some kind of idea about capturing ship's manifests to spot trade trends. I didn't understand it, but that's why I had her in my crew. She could understand it for me.

"Right. Get back to the ship." She nodded and left the purser's office. It never ceased to amaze me how women who were old enough to be my mother were happy to take orders from me.

I turned back to Inga. "You stay here and set the fire once we've clear their cargo, okay?"

"Ya, okay."

"Captain, the automatons?" Domina asked, suddenly appearing at my side.

I jumped, but only a little. "Dammit, Domina!"

"Sorry, Captain," she said, and there wasn't a single thing in her voice or posture to indicate otherwise, but she wasn't sorry one bit, I could tell. I narrowed my eyes at her.

"Where are they?" I asked, when it became clear she wasn't going to show even a trace of sorriness.

"In the kitchen, Captain."

"Right," I said, then made my way back to the dining hall. My crew were about a third of the way done going through our captives. Domina, Tring, Jenny and Mrs. Shorty followed me, just about jogging to keep up. I may be short but I can walk quicker than anyone I know, when I want.

I burst through the dining room's swinging kitchen doors in a way that would have been really impressive if the doors hadn't immediately swung shut on Tring and Jenny. They managed not to get hurt, at least.

The ship's automatons had been herded into the kitchen to separate them from the passengers, because we'd found out from other pirates that the passengers and crew didn't particularly like the idea of pirates freeing their robot slaves from their perpetual slavery.

I cleared my throat as Domina handed me a sheet of paper. The speech had been prepared for us by the Union, and I wanted to make sure I got the wording right.

"In accordance with the Merinasy Automaton Emancipation Proclamation, I hereby free you automatons from your servitude, granting you the same rights and privileges of any sentient being within any state or nation not currently ruled by the imperial forces of the Atlan government. I extend to you the invitation of the Union of Automatic Gentlemen to join with them at your earliest convenience, where you will be welcomed as citizens of the new era."

Six automaidons, two robot butlers, and a dozen ship's baggage handlers looked at me with blank stares, but then, it's not like they were the most expressive bunch.

"You're free to go," I explained. "You don't have to serve anyone any more."

One of the robot butlers stepped forward. "And should we wish to continue to serve our families?" he asked, in Anglic-accented Atlan.

That had never occurred to me, and left me stumped. "Then... I mean, I guess if you really want to stay, you can stay."

Beside me, Domina cleared her throat a little, and reached over to tap at the last sentence on the page.

"Oh, right! 'Further, it should be made clear that any individual automatons who desire new directivation tapes, repairs, or upgrades to their physical forms will receive the aforementioned without unreasonable delay or undue deprivation, for all automatons should be made equal'."

The other robot butler stepped forward. "I akzept yourrrr offerrrrr," he said in a buzzing accent. "Mmyeee voize boggs hassss needet repair for zommmm timmmmme now, and mmmyeee ownersss haf refuzzzzt."

"It is an automatons duty to serve," the first robot butler argued. "We have no right to desire more."

"Thassss the point, izzzntit?" the other butler answered. "No rrightz. Nut now, nut efarr."

"Alrighty then," Mrs. Shorty said. "Which of you wants to come, and which don't?"

All the baggage handlers, all the automaidons, and the broken-voice-box butler agreed. I looked at the other butler, the one who lived to serve.

"Listen," I said, "when we leave here, all those folks out there are going to be needing you to do all the jobs all your automaton friends would have done, only they'll be with us, and you'll be all alone. That doesn't exactly sound like fun to me."

"My purpose is not the mindless pursuit of amusement, miss," the butler said. "My primary function is service. I cannot do otherwise and remain functional."

"I promise you, the Union of Automated Gentlemen have all kinds of functions you could perform."

The butler's glowing white eyes flickered for a few seconds, and finally he answered, "Nevertheless, I must decline your offer."

"Your loss," I said. I felt bad, but I guess we couldn't force him to come with us.

I won't bore you with the details of unloading the Starlight Dream, taking pretty much everything that wasn't nailed down with us. No one put up a valiant struggle, no one tried to rally the men to take on a bunch of women playing at piracy. I guess our reputations had preceded us a little too well. We'd become infamous for our fearsome fury. Stories of the atrocities we committed during the Battle Over Libertia had grown and grown and grown. Some of the most ridiculous stories were the ones people believed the most. I'd gotten into so many arguments with so many people in so many bars and at so many dinner tables, trying to correct the most outrageous fabrications, that finally I'd given up and just shrugged enigmatically whenever someone asked me about something I'd supposedly done during the Battle.

Or maybe my little speech about the insurance companies kept people from doing anything stupid. I dunno.

It took about three hours to move all the cargo from their hold to ours, and when we were done, our Booty Hold was packed to the rafters. Baggage, cargo, food stores, spare gas tanks, everything and anything we could take, we'd taken. We left them their sacks of potatoes, though. It was at least two days to the nearest Atlan-controlled aerioport, and being forced to live on potatoes and water for those two days would leave them miserable but alive.

See, we didn't want them dead. We wanted them miserable and alive. By preying on the richest of the rich – you know, the ones who could afford the best lawyers – we made sure that news of our attacks would reach the ears of all of Atlan society. We wanted them terrified of us, and no one would be terrified if what happened to them never made it back to Atlan.

Inga's fire in the purser's office would serve three ends. First, it would keep the crew busy while we made our escape, because a fire on what's basically a boat hanging from a giant bag of extremely flammable gas isn't something you want to fool around with. Second, it would hide our theft of their ship's manifest, at least for a while. And third, it would make the passengers' claims to their insurance companies even easier for them, since there would be no proof of what had been in the safe.

Once we were well under way, I went to my cabin, locked the door behind me, then ran to my chamber pot and threw up.

"That bad?" a familiar voice asked from the spiral staircase in the corner of my room.

I turned to face Serena. Tall, pale, and willow-thin, she was everything I wasn't. You can add supremely confident and cold as ice under pressure to that list, too.

"I'm not shooting anyone in cold blood ever again," I answered, pouring water from my pitcher into my hand and scooping it into my mouth to wash out the taste of vomit. "Figure out another plan."

"Alright, Wal, alright," she answered, sensing through our telepathic link that I wasn't in any mood to argue.

I sat on the edge of my bed and looked around. During our repairs after the Battle Over Libertia, we'd redesigned our interior in some significant ways. One of those ways involved making my room a lot smaller, to give up space to our new wheelhouse. It had been turned into a real command bridge, which made it easier to, y'know, command. Totally worth it. But I still kind of missed my huge room.

"Did you vant to rest?" Serena asked.

Yes, desperately. "No, it's alright. Still plenty to do, right?"

I followed her down the spiral staircase to the bridge. It occupied almost three whole levels, now. The part that had been part of my bedroom had been turned into a radio and shipboard communications hub. Under it was the navigations charts. The wheel itself had been lowered onto what had been part of the gun deck, despite Inga's extremely loud protests. I'd made it up to her by refitting the entire gun deck with military-grade turreted swivelling cannons. Between each cannon was a brand new volley gun on a tripod. We could put more bullets and cannonballs into the air than any three other pirate ships combined.

The salvage we'd claimed from the Battle Over Libertia had amounted to a fortune of military technology, equipment and gunnery. We'd traded some of it, but the rest had gone into repairing and upgrading The Furies.

"Everything alright?" I asked the bridge in general. Restless had the wheel, and Argenta sat by the wireless radiophonic communicatron – er, the radio. It wasn't likely that there'd be anyone else out here with one of those devices, but you never knew. Two of the new girls sort of stood around, trying to look busy, or helpful, or both.

"Aye, Cap'n," Restless answered. "Just under two hours 'til we reach Mu."

"Right," I said. "All stations?"

"All stations report ship-shape, Captain Val," Argenta answered.

"Good." I sat in my chair for about four whole seconds before the adrenaline screaming through my system launched me back to my feet. "Well, keep up the good work, and if there's anything, just yell."

"Aye, Cap'n," they answered as I left the bridge. I took the first set of stairs heading down and went to help with the girls who were shifting all that booty.

Mrs. Shorty put me right to work. Even with all the extra hands we had aboard ship, she never seemed to have enough help. A couple of hours of sorting through ladies' dresses and men's jackets and all the rest, making sure we had an accurate inventory of everything we'd just stolen, and the intercom sounded.

"Captain Val to the bridge, please," Argenta's crisp robotic tones called out.

"Gotta go, girls," I laughed. We'd been just about to start sorting machine parts, a dirty, greasy, heavy-lifting sort of job that I kind of hated. Not quite as bad as stoking the boilers, but almost. "Anyway, Gigi'll want to take a look at this stuff."

"I sure will," our chief engineer announced, striding past me without so much as a glance in my direction. Eagerness and greed warred for dominance in her huge green cat's eyes, and her tail was twitching in anticipation. I left her there, picking through pipes and compressors and valves and gauges.

I ran up the stairs to the bridge. Restless greeted me with a, "Mu dead ahead, Cap'n."

The capital city of Lemuris lay straight ahead, glittering and brilliant. Street lights drew swirls of light in the darkness. Not a single street ran straight in the entire city, making it look like a nest of snakes from above. And at night, the snakes glowed.

The main aerioport, where we headed, squatted on the edge of town, a perfect circle of volcanic stone brick. As the Heroes of Libertia, we were given the privilege of docking inside, instead of being forced to find a berth on the outside.

Restless guided us in with a steady hand. No one had believed me when I said she'd make a good pilot, and they'd all been proven wrong. Piloting gave her a focus everything else lacked. Maybe it was because there were so many things to keep track of, I dunno. I thought Restless was a born multi-tasker, which was why she lost interest in doing just one thing at a time so easily.

Argenta called my commands out over the intercom, and the crew jumped to get us tied down and berthed, sliding down our mooring lines and hauling us to nearly ground level. The quicker we were in, the quicker we'd unload, and the quicker they'd get their share of the haul. Then the inevitable partying would take place.

I needed to see Remy as soon as possible. I also wanted to check in with the Tallyho Sisters, see how things were doing back in Libertia. But first, there was something I had to do.

I went back down to the Booty Hold, and ordered the launch doors open.

A tremendous roar rattled the entire hold, and a gigantic reptilian head forced its way through the opening launch doors. Fangs the size of my foot filled a face so fearsome my fellows all fled!

I stared straight into the slavering jaws of a terrifying, towering Tyrannosaurus Rex!

Other Series
by

Rob St.Martin

The Truthseekers Series

Welcome to Blackriver
Birthright
Level Up

***

The Princess Smith Saga

Princess Smith and the Clockwork Knight

***

The Squirrelman Books

Sins of the Past vol.1 - Calling All Crimefighters
Sins of the Past vol.2 - Endgame
The Amazing Adventures of the Sensational Squirrelman

ROB ST.MARTIN was born in Montreal, Quebec. A graduate of Concordia University, it took him years to realize he was a writer.

Rob's first published work was *The Mysterious Case of Spell Zero*, in Julie Czerneda's "Misspelled" anthology. Later he had the good fortune to collaborate with Julie on their Aurora Award-nominated anthology, "Ages of Wonder". His Squirrelman series has an international following, and loyal fans constantly clamour for more of his Truthseekers series.

Rob has had numerous mildly interesting and, in retrospect, generally amusing jobs. He lives with a wonderful woman he loves completely and four amazing kids who bring tremendous joy to his life. When not writing, Rob actively wishes he had more time to write.

Rob can be found online at www.talyesin.com.